THE REAPER

THE REAPER

SOLDIERS OF ANARCHY

NIKKI J SUMMERS

Copyright Material

This book is a work of fiction. Names, characters, businesses, places, events, and incidents are either the product of the author's imagination or used in a fictitious manner. Any resemblance to actual events or persons living or dead is purely coincidental.

Any trademarks, product names, or names featured are assumed to be the property of their respective owners and are used for reference only.

Copyright 2022 by Nikki J Summers.

All rights reserved. No part of this work may be reproduced, scanned, or distributed in any print or electronic form without the express, written consent of the author. A CIP record of this book is available from the British Library.

Cover Image: Michelle Lancaster

Cover Designer: Lori Jackson Design

Editing/Proofreading: Lindsey Powell at Liji Editing

Caroline Stainburn

Interior Designed and formatted by: Lou J Stock

THE REAPER

OTHER BOOKS BY NIKKI J SUMMERS

Soldiers of Anarchy Series
The Psycho
The Reaper

Rebels of Sandland Series
Renegade Hearts
Tortured Souls
Fractured Minds

Stand-Alone
Luca
This Cruel Love
Hurt to Love

Joe and Ella Duet
Obsessively Yours
Forever Mine

All available on Amazon Kindle Unlimited.
Only suitable for readers 18+ due to adult content.

THE REAPER

THE REAPER

PLAYLIST

Available to download on Spotify
https://spoti.fi/37BxuBm

The Reaper – NerdOut
Middle Finger – Bohnes
Sucker for Pain – Lil Wayne, Imagine Dragons, Logic, Wiz Khalifa, Ty Dolla $ign, X Ambassadors
Enemies – Shinedown
Crazy – Daniela Andrade
Nightmare – Halsey
Darkside – Grandson
Heathens – Koosen, Green Bull, Strange Fruits Music
Enjoy the Silence – Bodybangers Remix- Caleidescope, gxldjunge, Bodybangers
I'm a Slave 4 U – Jazmin Bean
Lost My Way – Plan B
Bring Me to Life – Evanescence
Creep – Daniela Andrade
Take Me to Church – Hozier
A Thousand Years – Christina Perri
Chasing Cars – Snow Patrol
Points of Authority – Linkin Park
Living Not Alive – The Veer Union
Die Trying – Art of Dying
All of Me – John Legend
A Song For You – Carpenters

TRIGGER WARNING
A message from the author

Welcome to *The Sanctuary*.
A place where the rules of our fucked-up society don't mean shit. We make the rules here and we take care of anybody who dares to break them.

Who are we?
We are the soldiers of anarchy, and we make no apology for the way we are.

If you're triggered by violence, scenes of a sexual nature, flashbacks of child neglect and abuse (physical not sexual), attempted sexual assault that leads to revenge torture scenes and murder, issues around mental health and suicide (attempted), then please proceed with caution.

If a morally grey hero with a thirst for vengeance and a penchant for weapons turns you off, then stop reading right here. If a heroine who is curious, persistent, and open to everything that comes her way scares you, then this book is not for you.

This is a slow-burn love story. A journey of self-discovery, and a tale to remind us that nothing is ever quite what it seems. If you're happy to join us, then strap yourself in.

I hope you enjoy the ride!

'You can be a king
or a street sweeper,
but everyone dances
with the Grim Reaper.'

ROBERT ALTON HARRIS

14 THE REAPER

PROLOGUE
The Birth of The Reaper

Fifteen years ago...

I always thought there was something truly hypnotic about fire. The way the flames danced around, seductively spreading and consuming everything in its path without a thought for the destruction it caused. How it crackled and spat like a beautiful, venomous demon—so pretty to look at, and yet, so deadly to touch. The ethereal, other-worldly smoke that whirled and curved in elegant waves, escaping up the chimney as if it'd already done its bidding and was off to find new adventures, new victims.

It was the perfect contradiction.

And right now, as I sat on the floor of my living room, chained to the radiator on the wall, I wished I could be like the fire I was staring at. I wanted to have the capacity to control my surroundings just like those flames. The ability to rise up and be free of this room and everything in it, like the smoke that billowed in plumes and danced away. To possess the ultimate power to destroy whatever came near me without thought, without care. People had a respectful fear of fire and all that it encompassed. I wanted them to feel the same way about me, and they would, eventually, when I was older. My day of reckoning would come.

But that day wasn't today.

It was always the same when my mum was working nights. The same battle to survive to see the morning, both physically and emotionally. She wasn't a bad mother, my mum. I never blamed her for one second for everything that had happened to me. I was eight years old, and she had to leave me with someone so she could go to work. I just wished it didn't have to be him and his fucked-up friends. I respected her though because she did everything she could to keep a roof over our heads and pay the bills, all while she was heavily pregnant. Her multiple jobs helped to put food in our mouths and clothes on our backs. But it also put beer in my stepfather's already bulging, sagging gut. Beer that gave him the fuel to carry out his sick and twisted games. God forbid he should get off his fat ass and earn an honest day's wage.

Why would he?

I once heard him say to one of his sick friends, "Why would I have a dog and bark myself?" That's how he saw my mother––a free ride, an easy option.

It'd always been my dream that one day we'd escape. I'd take care of my mum so much better than he ever had, and there'd be no fear, no reason to watch my back. I'd make sure of that. But now that my mum was having another baby, my dream was fading fast. She would never leave him, and he would never let her go. She was his golden ticket. The key to maintaining his lazy lifestyle. But on nights like tonight, he wasn't lazy, he was energised. He had purpose to his existence.

Tormenting me.

He'd used his old handcuffs to chain me to the pipe at the bottom of the radiator. I'd learnt early on that it was pointless to struggle against the restraints and try to break free. All it did was make my wrists hurt and give me welts that'd last for days, making it even more painful the next time he chained me up. So, instead, I curled into a ball, making myself as small as I possibly could. The more of my body I protected, the less likely I was to sustain an injury that'd make him bristle with pride. He wanted to hurt me as much as he could, but more than that, he wanted to live off the fear he created.

My fear.

That was something I'd never give him.

I'd never cry or scream no matter how much it hurt. I wouldn't beg or plead either. I'd take his abuse and file it away in my brain, ready to be recalled at a later date. Like a macabre catalogue for revenge, I'd never forget, and when I was ready, I'd use the memory of these nights to pay him and his friends back ten-fold for what they'd done to me.

I'd decided early on, when he started playing these games, that my purpose in life would be revenge. I would live to see death brought to fuckers like my stepfather and his vile, sadistic friends. I also wanted to protect my mum as best I could, and that's why I'd become a master at hiding the marks and scars. It would devastate her to know what was going on, and I didn't want her to feel any shame because of me. Better that he took his anger out on me than my mother, or God forbid, my baby sister that was growing in her tummy. I'd rather die than let him hurt them. Every time he rubbed my mum's bump and called them his girls, I seethed inside with anger. They weren't his, they were mine. Mine to protect from people like him.

Tonight, the game was darts. My stepfather, Vinnie, prided himself on the ideas he thought up each week. Last week, it'd been noughts and crosses. There were only Vinnie and Ray here that night. Ray had been crosses, and he'd grinned as he scratched his x's with his penknife into their chosen canvas—my thighs. The x's weren't the worst of it though. Vinnie was noughts, and he'd used his cigar to scorch my skin with the burning end, sizzling it deep into me as he chuckled and twisted the nub for full effect. I'd clenched my jaw and stiffened every muscle in my body with every burn, but I never made a sound. Even when the sweat trickled down my back at the searing hiss of pain that I'd had to endure over and over again, I never gave him the satisfaction that he craved.

He wanted to break me.

But how could you break something that didn't exist?

You see, in those moments, I was able to check myself out of this life. I wasn't Devon, the little shit, like he used to call me. I was just a vessel. A body of blood, bones, muscles, and nerves. I'd learnt to reinvent myself from the boy I'd been to a ghost, an echo of myself.

Empty.

No feeling, no fear.

I was devoid.

But my soul?

That was somewhere else, floating over the scene playing out below. Lying in wait until the time came to show everyone how tainted and twisted I truly was. How vengeful they'd made me. Once I had the power to back it up, of course. My soul was a darkness that I kept caged, but it fed off events like these. Vinnie's games only served to feed the demons inside of me. I would get my revenge.

I watched out of the corner of my eye as Nigel, one of Vinnie's mates, took a swig from his bottle of beer and then dropped it on the floor by his feet. I was glad they were drinking heavily tonight because it weakened their aim. Nigel ran the back of his hand over his mouth and then squinted at me as he aimed his dart.

"What's the score for getting his shrivelled little dick?" he asked, turning to look at Vinnie, who sat next to him on our threadbare sofa.

Vinnie shook his head and gave a grunt, rolling his eyes as if he was fed up already and wanted to up the stakes. The suffering and brutality obviously wasn't going fast enough for him tonight.

"Your aim is shit anyway, why do you wanna know?" Vinnie scowled in irritation, desperate for it to be his turn so he could inflict more pain on me.

"Jesus, Nige, you've got the memory of a fucking sieve," Ray piped up, taking a drag of his cigarette and blowing the smoke in my direction.

These men were devoid of any human decency. They were the worst that Brinton Manor had to offer, and I prayed that one day I'd be able to wipe our manor clean of filth like them. That would be the ultimate dream, turning their nightmares into a

THE REAPER

reality of my own making.

I didn't make eye contact. I just kept myself curled up, my knees tucked into my chest, my head down to protect my face, and my arms clutched tightly around my legs, braced and ready to handle the impending stabbing pain of their darts.

Vinnie gave a gurgled cough as he cleared his throat and stated, "It's ten for the body, fifteen for the legs, and twenty for his head. Get his dick and you get the bullseye."

They'd never get the bullseye. They'd have to hold me down for that. I wasn't stupid.

"And does it have to stick into his head, or can it bounce off and still count? I mean, that's a hard one to score with my shitty darts."

I peeked from the corner of my eye to see Nigel turn his dart to look at the arrowhead, tapping it with his finger and tutting to himself at the bluntness he felt.

"It's not my fault you didn't come prepared. You should've had them sharpened. I told you what we were playing tonight," Vinnie scolded, like it all meant nothing and the darts were being used on a regular dartboard, not me. The fucker had zero emotion.

"Oh, fuck it," Nigel snapped and lifted the dart in the air, narrowing his eyes and sticking his tongue out of the side of his mouth as he took his aim and flung it towards me with as much force as he could muster.

I braced myself and tried not to cower too much as it landed right in the middle of my thigh. The initial sting of it piercing through my skin made me freeze, then I wriggled my leg to try and make it fall free.

The darts weren't as bad as noughts and crosses, but I

dreaded to think what would happen next week. Vinnie had already said it was a toss-up between marbles and tug of war. I couldn't bear to think what that would entail. Both sounded sadistically painful.

Eventually, I felt the dart work itself free and clatter to the floor beside me. Nigel groaned and reluctantly pulled himself out of his chair to retrieve it.

"My turn." Vinnie cackled and lifted his dart, moving it back and forth as he closed one eye in concentration and glared at me.

He grunted from the effort of using such force as he jabbed his arm forward and threw the dart. I thought I'd done a good job hiding my face, but I hadn't been quick enough, and the dart landed in the side of my neck. It was embedded deep, and I held my breath as I scrunched my eyes shut and tried to stay as still as I could. This one hurt.

"Oh fuck, almost a twenty," Ray quipped, and instantly, I felt a shift in the air as tensions grew.

"It got his neck. That *is* a twenty," Vinnie argued back, and I could tell from his angry tone that his face was probably tinged red now, his eyes bulging as he dared his friend to argue with him.

"Fair's, fair, Vin, you didn't get his head," Nigel piped up using a sing-song voice that I knew would rile Vinnie even more.

"I got his neck, its close enough," Vinnie snapped, and I could hear the beer bottles that were discarded on the floor start to clatter around as someone, probably Vinnie, stood up. They were all drunk and they were starting to turn on each other.

"You got his body, that's ten. See? I can still remember the scores," Nigel called out, proud at his short-term memory recall, but I could tell their night was turning sour.

The stench of stale beer and body odour filled my nostrils as one of them knelt beside me, then I winced in pain as the dart was viciously yanked out of my neck.

"I won, fair and square," I heard Vinnie say close to my ear. "Now fuck off out of my house, both of you. I've had enough for one night."

I braced myself, waiting for the punch or kick that usually followed when he was this pissed off, but surprisingly, it never came. Instead, the door slammed shut and I flinched at the bang as it shook the whole house. Gently, I opened my eyes just a little to see if Nigel and Ray had gone too. They hadn't, but they were gathering their stuff together—their coats and wallets—and they were picking up any beer bottles that still had beer left in them to drain the dregs before they went home.

"Your stepfather is a sick fuck," Nigel sneered, but I stared straight ahead, shivering from the rush of adrenaline that coursed through me, and I willed myself not to acknowledge him. "If I were you, I'd get out of here as soon as you can. One day, he'll kill you, you know."

There was no doubt in my mind that what he said was true, apart from one tiny detail… they'd all underestimated my will to fight back. I would get out, and I'd take my mum and baby sister with me. But I'd kill him before he ever got the opportunity to kill me. I'd toy with him just like he'd done with me, but I wouldn't play stupid kids games like he did. My games would be better, more sophisticated, more twisted than anything he'd ever come up with. I'd be the master of my games. And my weapons? They'd be my trump card, my ace. I'd wield my weapons like tools that I was born to use. I'd respect them, revere them. I certainly wouldn't be sloppy and drunk like my fuck-up of a stepfather and his shitty friends.

"Come on," Ray called out to Nigel, pulling on his coat and striding towards the door. "Let's leave them to it. The Red Lion on the corner should still be open. No need to ruin a decent night of drinking because he's a fucking sore loser."

Ray breezed past without giving me a second glance, but Nigel bit his lip as I turned my head to look at him. He must've had a guilty conscience, because he walked over to where my stepfather had put his wallet, picked up the key to the handcuffs and rolled it between his fingers. Then he walked over to where I was chained up and knelt down. He glanced nervously at the door, then reached over to grab my hands, putting the key in the lock and turning it to release me.

I pulled away, freeing my wrists, and rubbed each one in turn to ease the dull ache. Even though I tried not to pull or yank the cuffs during these games, Vinnie always tied them too tightly, so they pinched no matter what.

Nigel lingered next to me, but I didn't bother saying thank you. I wasn't thankful. This man had played a part in Vinnie's game tonight, and he was as guilty as the rest of them, despite his rare moment of compassion.

Then when he leant down to my ear, I froze as he whispered, "Run. If you know what's good for you, you'll get the fuck out of here, kid. If you don't, he'll make it so they never find your body. And between you and me… you wouldn't be the first." And with that, he put his hands on his knees and lifted himself up, giving a heavy sigh from the effort it took, then he strolled out of the door without looking back.

I didn't have the energy to move, so I stayed sitting on the

THE REAPER

floor and stared into the fireplace that still burned and crackled.

Fire.

It grew from a spark, expanded at will. It was an element that no one could tame.

I had my spark, and it was growing. Death wouldn't come for me, not at the hands of my stepfather. I wouldn't, *couldn't* let that happen.

I wanted to be death.

I wanted to become that dark, silent visitor that everybody feared.

Vinnie Shaw would rue the day he'd ever wronged my mum or me. His cards were marked. Nigel had got one thing right tonight; they wouldn't find a body. I was smarter than that. When I took care of Vinnie, no one would ever know.

The reaper was going to enjoy taking his soul to hell.

CHAPTER ONE
Devon

Present Day

When we bought the old Sandland Asylum——a macabre, gothic, desolately eerie looking building that sat on the outskirts of Sandland and Brinton Manor—we decided that the name for our new business, our nightclub, was a no-brainer.

The Sanctuary.

None of us had ever had a stable home life growing up. Our childhoods had been marred by a concoction of abuse, neglect, and all-round general shitty parenting. Very few people really cared about us. It wasn't until our schools decided they couldn't cope with our deviant behaviour and sent us to the pupil referral unit that we'd found each other. There we found a home, a kindred spirit in each other. Boys that the system didn't want to waste time or energy on. Lads who were a stain on society. The Lost Boys but without all the Peter Pan, fairy-tale shit. We were always more Kiefer Sutherland and Jason Patric, anyway.

Our story was grim.

Our futures uncertain.

Until we decided to take matters into our own hands to make the kind of future we wanted.

One we could control.

A sanctuary was a place of refuge and safety from the world. Well, that's what a sanctuary was supposed to be, but to us it meant freedom. Our place, our rules, and we loved it.

Our sanctuary served as a home and a business. We all lived here on the top floor; Adam, Colton, Tyler, Will, and me. Oh, and Tyson, our rottweiler. It was big enough that we weren't in each other's pockets, but close enough that we could stand shoulder-to-shoulder at a moment's notice if we needed to. You see, soldiers, street soldiers like we were, we always worked as a unit. Hurt one, hurt all, that was our motto and we lived by it every single day.

As for the business side, we ran our club from the other two floors. The ground floor was for the mainstream partygoers. The vanilla crowd as Colton liked to call them. We had a resident D.J., a decent bar, and the vibe was always electric. But the second floor was where the real action happened. That was reserved for exclusive guests. Our themed rooms were the stuff of legends in Sandland and Brinton Manor. Legends we were quite happy to fuel and expand upon to keep the interest high. All publicity was good publicity, right?

Tonight, I was tasked with monitoring the ground floor.

Colton and Will were assigned to the second floor, and Tyler was taking the night off, although chances were he'd find his way into a room or some trouble at some point in the night. We had security in place, good security, but we didn't like to take a backseat when it came to our business. We wanted to be visible. Let the guests know that the soldiers were in attendance. That way, we could intercept any trouble at a moment's notice and make sure everyone knew we didn't take any shit. Not that they needed reminding on that score.

So, where was Adam, our self-proclaimed leader and resident psycho?

He'd announced that he was taking a few days off. He was going to spend some quality time with his girlfriend, Liv, after the shit they'd both been through recently. We didn't argue. We felt more than confident that we could hold down the fort for a few days while they were gone. Adam assured us they wouldn't be far away though, and if anything happened, we had to call him immediately. He hated being out of the loop. Adam was a control freak. We all were in our own way, but he always took it that little bit further.

I stood at the side of the bar, a perfect spot to observe the room, and I gestured to the barman, Joel, to get me another glass of coke. Colton and Will would probably be drinking beer or Jack Daniels as they manned the first floor, but I preferred to keep a clear head. I was never off duty, and I liked it that way.

I watched as the strobe lights darted across the dance floor, flickering and flashing over the heads of the crowds as they gyrated against each other, a mass of bodies all jumping to the beat. It made the hairs on the back of my neck stand on end, knowing that out of all the clubs around here, these people had

THE REAPER

chosen to spend their Saturday night with us. Our club was fucking killing it, and the feeling of pride that gave me made me stand taller as I sipped my drink and glanced around.

I took my phone out of my back pocket and placed it on the bar in front of me. No missed calls and no messages. That was a good sign. We had radios that the security team used to stay in touch with each other as the night wore on, but we preferred to use our phones; it was more private. Sometimes, we had shit to say that we didn't want anyone else to know about. As soldiers of Brinton Manor, we kept our cards close to our chests. It took a lot to earn our trust, and we trusted very few.

Despite the party atmosphere around me, I felt a nervous tension. I was on high alert, ready to attack at a moment's notice, and something about tonight felt off. My sixth sense was hinting at a shitstorm about to explode. Don't ask me how I knew; I just had a feeling about these things. Always had. And it was my job to deal with this shit. Keep it away from the customers so they'd leave our club buzzing and ready to tell everyone what a good night they'd had. Word of mouth was the best advertising you could get, after all.

I glanced around the room, blocking out the steady beat of the music so I could hone in on the conversations going on around me. It's amazing what you could pick up from idle conversation. When people had alcohol in their system they dropped their guard, and nine times out of ten, they spoke the truth. We'd found a lot of targets in our line of vigilante work through eavesdropping.

Despite the tension I felt, everything appeared to be running smoothly. I couldn't settle though, so I pocketed my phone and decided to check in with our head of security and wannabe soldier, Gaz, to see what was happening with the rest of the club. I pushed my way through the mass of bodies crowded around until I came to the staircase that led to the second floor. Casually, I nodded to Gaz and asked, "Is everything okay?"

"It was," he replied, glancing behind him and up towards the second floor. "But I've just seen Colton and Will run into one of the private rooms. I think some shit might be going down."

Right on cue, my phone vibrated in my pocket, and I pulled it out to see a message from Colton.

Colton: You're needed. Private room three. Now.

I didn't react. I kept my face expressionless as I closed the message and slid my phone back into my pocket to keep the details away from Gaz's prying eyes. He was a good security guard, an even better clean-up guy when we needed him, but he wasn't a soldier, he never would be, and from the prickle I felt on my skin in anticipation of what I'd find in that room, I knew this would be soldier business. Maybe I'd get to expend some of my pent-up aggression after all?

"Everything okay, mate?" Gaz asked, the desperation to be included burning in his eyes.

"It's fine." I patted him on the shoulder as I started to climb the stairs. "Just a bit of business I need to take care of. Nothing for you to worry about."

He frowned and turned as I made my ascent. His instinct to follow me was strong, and from the confusion on his face and the way his body suddenly became twitchy, I could tell he was about to climb the stairs after me. He was itching to be in on whatever was happening.

"Stay put," I stated, pre-empting his intentions and gesturing to the crowds below. "We need your eyes and ears here." He nodded, but he didn't look convinced; he looked defeated. "You're the best security we've got here," I added, feathering his ego. "If you're not out here keeping this place in check, it could all go to shit."

He smiled then and rolled back his shoulders to show how right he thought that statement was. That was why he'd never be a soldier. He was too easy to manipulate.

"You're right, Devon, mate. I'll stay here. Keep this club running for you. You can trust me." He folded his arms and gave me a confident nod and a grin. I didn't bother to respond. I'd done my job and I was all out of compliments. He was lucky he'd got one out of me at all.

I reached the second floor, where the corridor was quieter. Doors leading off the hallway led to experiences that were tailored to our more exclusive guests. A few people were milling about, making their way to whatever adventure the night held, but I kept my focus ahead, not making eye contact, and strode with purpose towards private room number three.

The private rooms were hired out by our guests, usually for couples or small groups. From memory, I could recall that three of the four rooms had been booked for tonight. One for a regular's twenty-first birthday party. One for a couple who came here every weekend and often used the communal room, but occasionally they liked to retire to a private room. And then there was the third booking. A new guest. A guy who came with impeccable references and one we'd checked out thoroughly, or so we thought. It looked like someone needed to be taught a lesson. A reminder that trying to pull the wool over our eyes only led to us gouging out theirs.

Before pushing the door open, I glanced over my shoulder to make sure no one was behind me. I didn't want anyone else witnessing what I was about to see in this room. Then, when I opened it, I stepped over the threshold and closed the door swiftly behind me.

Inside was a blonde girl who looked to be in her early twenties. She was sprawled on the bed and completely out of it. Her eyes were open, but she wasn't focusing on anything, her pupils were fixed and dilated, staring at a spot on the wall opposite. She was breathing in regular, shallow gasps, and her arms were limp, laid haphazardly next to her head. Her legs were closed, and the skirt of her dress pulled down, but from the look of what was happening across the room, and the pure venom on Colton and Will's faces, I guessed she hadn't been like that when they'd got here.

Colton had a man pinned to the floor. He was sitting on his back and had twisted his hands back to hold him steady. The guy lay with his face to the side, spitting out his raspy breaths and glaring at me. Will was kneeling beside them, probably giving his unique form of interrogation before I walked in. Both were fully charged and prepared to strike hard. It made me smile, knowing this guy had no fucking clue what he was about to endure. We were the hunters, the lions, and he'd just strayed into our den.

The door behind me opened, and Tyler slid through the gap, shutting it as quickly as I did so no one outside could get a glimpse into this room.

"So, is someone going to tell me what the fuck is going on?"

THE REAPER

Tyler hissed, coming to stand beside me and crossing his arms over his chest. I knew he felt the same way I did. He couldn't wait to show the prey how we ranked as predators in this jungle. He was waiting for the excuse to stir up hell in this room.

"We got a tip off from another guest," Colton said, baring his teeth as he stared down at the piece of shit underneath him. "Said they saw the girl slurring her words and falling all over the place. Apparently, Romeo here thought he'd make it look like he was doing the decent thing and bring her in here. But decency was the furthest thing from this fucker's mind, wasn't it, *mate*? You had some pretty fucked up plans for what you wanted to do, didn't you? And it doesn't take a genius to guess who fucking drugged her, either. Bastard."

Colton used one hand to hold the guy's wrists, and then with his other he grabbed a fistful of the guy's hair. He yanked his head up and then banged it back down hard on the wooden floor. I knew we should've put concrete down. Wood made him howl and curse, but concrete would've knocked the fucker out cold.

"He'll pay. Tonight, we'll make sure he gets what he deserves," I stated. I didn't need to know anymore. The fact that he'd come in here and shit all over our rules was reason enough to fuck him up. But hurt a woman? A guest of the sanctuary? That'd just got him an extra dose of payback, soldier style.

"We got here just in time, not that that changes anything," Will said, keeping his eyes fixed on the restrained guy. "She was lucky. Any later and he'd have raped her. Isn't that right, you dirty little shit?" Will leant near his face and then spat at him. The guy squeezed his eyes shut but didn't answer.

"You spiked her fucking drink, didn't you?" I snapped, feeling the demons inside me stir. I already knew what the answer was, but I carried on regardless. "You drugged her and brought her in here, thinking you could do whatever the fuck you wanted. Did you really think you could come into our club and piss all over our rules? Hurt a woman and get away with it?" I knelt next to Will and shook my head, tutting, but the guy didn't look at me. He obviously thought silence would benefit him in this situation, but his silence only pissed me off even more. "I suggest you speak, because right now, I'm making up all kinds of sick fucking scenarios in my head, and all of them involve ways in which I'm going to make you pay for what you've done. I bet you've done this before."

Colton flared his nostrils and took over the reins.

"Do you know who we are? Or do you have a fucking death wish?" Colton, our joker, wasn't a clown anymore. He was drowning in his dark side, vengeance oozing from his pores as he panted and gripped the guy like he was ready to tear him apart.

"I don't think he cares," Will piped up, stoking the fire. "I think he thinks he's untouchable. That's why he isn't talking, he's thinking of a way to get out of this."

Colton tutted in the guy's ear, and then he gave a sadistic chuckle as he twisted his wrists and made the guy whimper a stifled, painful moan.

"You should care," Colton whispered to him. "You should be fucking shitting yourself, because we're about to show you what we do to men who don't follow our rules. Men who think they can fuck us over. Men who hurt innocent people."

Tyler came over and Colton stood up. With Will's help, Colton grabbed the guy under his arms and yanked him off the floor to stand up. Then, Colton secured the guy's arms, grabbing

THE REAPER

his elbows and pulling them behind him, holding him in place. When he was fully restrained, Tyler reached into the guy's pockets and took out his wallet and keys, pocketing them before retrieving a mobile phone that he tapped to unlock and started to scroll through.

"Take him down to the chapel," I told them, knowing we needed to move this away from the business to a place where our revenge could be carried out exactly the way we wanted it to.

I stood up and then moved to the bed where the girl lay, totally oblivious to what was going on around her. Gently, I reached forward and brushed the long blonde hair out of her face. She'd had a lucky escape tonight, thank God. And I prayed she'd wake up with no memory of what'd happened here in this room, or what could've happened.

"Shall I get Gaz to move her out of here?" Will asked, but I shook my head.

"No. Tyler and Colton can take this piece of shit to the chapel and wait for us there. You can help me get her upstairs and settled into one of our rooms." I wasn't going to pass her off to just anyone. She was vulnerable, and it was our responsibility to see that she was safe now.

"We're going to need to call Adam and let him know what's going down," Tyler added, and we all nodded in agreement.

"I'll do that," I said, as I bent down to lift the girl into my arms.

"We need to get someone to watch her, you know, in case something happens," Will stated as he went to open the door for me.

"I'll ask Faye to come off the main desk. But no one else

can know about this. Not Gaz, or any of the other security staff. No one. We keep this between us." I turned with the girl in my arms to face Colton, Tyler, and the sick fuck who was hanging his head and cursing under his breath behind me. "Make sure no one sees him. Take the back stairs down to the chapel and use the rear entrance." I didn't want anyone to see what was happening, and luckily, we had hidden corridors that ran around the periphery of this building. Ideal for taking care of situations like this.

Will and I headed out of the room first, and I shielded the girl in my arms from the guests who were wandering around. Will called Faye, who manned the front desk for our more hardcore rooms, and asked her to meet us in our living quarters. I kept my head down and strode towards the stairs, then took each step carefully, holding the girl protectively. We'd had shit happen at the club before. We'd had even more fucked-up stuff happen to us outside on the streets. But no one had ever hurt a girl under our roof. We took that shit personally.

When we got to the main landing, I headed to my room, and Will opened the door for me so I could walk straight through. I laid the girl on my bed and arranged her arms and legs so she wouldn't get cramp. She'd wake up with enough pain and anguish, she didn't need anything else added to that.

Once I knew she was settled and safe, I took my phone out and called Adam.

"What's happened?" He answered on the first ring, already seemingly on edge.

"We just caught a guy in room three. He'd drugged a girl and was about to rape her—" I didn't get chance to finish, Adam cut me off.

THE REAPER

"Did he do it? Did he hurt her?" he hissed in desperation, and I could hear Liv in the background asking what the fuck was going on.

"No. We got there in time."

Adam exhaled down the phone then cursed, "Where the fuck is he now?"

"Colton and Tyler are taking him to the chapel."

"And the girl?"

"Me and Will brought her up to my room. She's still out of it. Faye's going to come and sit with her while we deal with him downstairs."

Adam took a second to answer and then he stated, "We're on our way. Tell Faye the girl drank too much. I don't want her knowing any more than that. Once we get there, Olivia will take over. And Devon?"

"Yeah?" I asked, just as Faye came through the door and pulled a chair to sit beside the bed.

"Give him hell. Don't wait for me to get there to do your job. You know what you're doing, and I trust you."

"No need to worry on that score," I stated and hung up the phone.

I nodded at Will. I didn't need to tell him what Adam had said, he knew him well enough to know the outcome. I turned to Faye and added, "She's had too much to drink. I recognised her from Brinton Manor and thought we should bring her up here to sleep it off. If she wakes up, ring me. Any problems and I want to know. Adam and Liv are on their way, so when they get here, you can go home. Thanks for this, Faye."

"It's all part of the job," Faye replied, giving the girl a pitiful stare before taking out her phone and tapping the screen like nothing was wrong.

"You don't tell anyone about this, do you hear?" I said, but Faye didn't look up from the screen. She just smiled and said, "I know how to do my job." Then she mimed zipping her mouth shut with her finger and locking it with an imaginary key.

The girl was safe. Now, it was on to our next job. Making the low-life fucker pay for bringing this to our door.

CHAPTER TWO
Devon

We entered the chapel, and the sound of the thumping bass from the music in the club became a distant thud as we closed the door behind us. The chapel was poorly lit, and the dust circling up from the floor—courtesy of the biting rough wind that blew through the cracks in the windows and decaying walls—made me cough and shudder. Despite the dim lighting, we could see the guy slumped in a chair in the far corner as Tyler and Colton stood over him. Tyler grimaced as he scrolled through the guy's phone. Colton had both hands fixed on the arm of the chair that the guy sat in, and he was glaring right into his face, giving him the psychotic grin he reserved for scum like him.

This was the asylum chapel. My chapel.

It was the reason I'd wanted us to take over the lease of this building months ago. Something about the crumbling old walls held an eerie, ethereal magic within them. A beautiful decaying monument that represented goodness, holiness, deception in its purest form. When we viewed this place, I took one look at this chapel and the stained-glass windows casting a kaleidoscope of colour onto the worn flagstone floor, and the desire to turn everything on its head overtook me. I wanted to destroy it, but at the same time, I wanted to reinvent it, just like I'd done with myself all those years ago. I liked twisting and moulding things to suit my purpose. Taking control and creating my own narrative after years of silent subservience. I wanted this to be my church. The reaper's den.

The crumbling stone walls were no longer adorned with crosses and religious symbolism. Instead, they held weapons that I'd collected from every corner of the globe. Weapons that I'd studied and practised using until I'd perfected my skills— skills that would rival any warrior. I had a collection of battle axes, stakes, and crossbows on one wall. Opposite that, I kept my swords, bats, sledgehammers, and my favourite of all, my katana sword. On the stone altar, I had scalpels, every brand of hunting knife you could think of, as well as meat cleavers and machetes. This was my church now, and these were my weapons of worship.

When we first got here, the other soldiers had thought it'd make a good private room, an exclusive experience for the second-floor crowd. But I didn't want that, and after the local church diocese kicked up a fuss about it being sacred ground and worked tirelessly to restrict our use of the chapel, I took it upon myself to claim it as my own. The church didn't need to know what I was using it for. As long as the general public weren't streaming in here every weekend to party or do anything else the diocese deemed inappropriate, it was fair game as far as I was concerned. What I used it for was none of their fucking business.

We made our way over to the guy sitting in the shadows, awaiting his fate. He was the damned, and like the reaper I was, I was creeping closer, bringing with me his impending doom.

"Adam said to start without him," I announced drily, eager to cut the crap and get to the good part. Tyler nodded grimly in understanding as he continued to scroll through the guy's phone.

Without looking up, he said, "I think the sooner we put this fucker down and the women he's tormented out of their misery, the better."

"Women?" Will asked. "Are we talking about a lot here?"

"Oh, yes." Tyler held the phone up, giving it a shake. "And it's all on here. Our guy's got form. A lot of form. From what I've seen on his photos and videos, this isn't the first time he's drugged an innocent girl. He's a fucking pro at it. Only difference is, he didn't get to finish it tonight, did you, you dirty fucking rapist cunt?" Tyler pocketed his phone and then smacked his fist into the side of the guy's face. "We're going to enjoy getting pay back tonight for each and every one of those women. You're scum," he sneered, and spat in his now bloody face.

The guy didn't speak, just wiped the blood from his nose on the back of his hand and glared at us. When Colton removed his hands from the chair, the guy darted up and ran for the door. I laughed.

Did he really think he could escape us?

Without missing a beat, I reached for my throwing knives; cold steel with long blades, no weak kunai shit that'd bounce off the target. I only had the best. Taking up my throwing stance, I aimed at his back. I threw one then the other, just like I'd done to Ray, my stepfather's friend, all those years ago. This fucker fell to the ground, folding like a pack of cards, and Colton marched over to where he was slumped forward, gasping on his knees. Colton pulled the knives out, twisting them as he did, then he wiped them on the guy's jacket, smearing his filthy blood onto his sleeve.

"Well, that was fun. Try running again, see what we use next time. I think Devon might have a flame thrower here somewhere." Colton leaned down near his ear and whisper-yelled, "Go on. I dare you."

The guy just hung his head, panting out his cowardly breaths.

Tyler, Will, and I stalked over to where he was, and I pulled him up to stand, throwing him against the solid stone walls. I put my hand around his throat, squeezing with everything I had, and I asked him, "Do you think we're fucking amateurs? That you can run from us?" I leant into him. "There's no running from the reaper. He'll find you no matter where you hide, because when your time is up, it's up. Game over."

"You don't scare me." The guy spoke quietly, trying to keep a defiant look in his eyes, but he wasn't fooling anyone.

"Oh, we do." I smiled back at him. "I can tell how fucking scared you are by the way your veins are pulsing, almost bursting through your neck. You're like an animal baring the whites of your eyes. I can see the fear. I can smell it too. You see, I do this for a living. We all do." I tilted my head to the side as I smiled and squeezed his throat even tighter. "We're just your friendly neighbourhood assassins, and you, my friend, have become our

THE REAPER 41

next hit."

"You're making… a big… mistake," he spluttered out as he clawed at my hands that constricted around his throat like a mother-fucking boa.

"I don't think so," Tyler spat, as he came to stand right next to me and shoved the phone into the guy's face. "There's a shit-load of evidence on here that you've raped a lot of girls. And I'm betting none of them have had the justice they deserved. They'll get it tonight though."

"They will," I nodded in agreement. "But I think we might do things a little different this time."

I took my hand off his throat, and like the weak fucker he was, he started coughing and spluttering. I wiped his grimy filth off me onto the legs of my jeans, then I took a throwing knife from Colton and held it against the guy's throat. If he thought he would get the easy option, he was wrong. Our night was only just beginning.

"See, we could torture you here. Have a little bit of fun making you feel some of the pain you put your victims through, and we will, don't get me wrong. But I'm thinking… does this fucker really deserve to die in the shadows? Disappear from sight, never to be seen again? I think not." I shook my head and sighed a disappointed sigh. "Those girls will never get the peace they deserve if we do that. They'll continue to live a life where they're always looking over their shoulder, wondering if you'll come back to haunt them again." I tutted and pressed the blade into his skin, and his blood trickled down his neck into the collar of his shirt. "They will always live with the fear. We might not be able to take the pain away, but that fear? The dread? That's something we can sort out."

"What's your plan?" Will asked, and I noticed he'd already chosen a knife from my altar. The same brand of skinning knife I used to scalp Nigel, another one of my stepfather's fucked-up friends.

I ran the blade of my knife down the guy's neck, watching the blood trickle and create a path for me to follow.

"We do what we do best," I announced. "We torture him, have our fun. But then we take him to Granges Park. I know the perfect tree for him to swing from. Once the police find his phone on his body, I'll make sure they call it in as a suicide. It'll be all over the papers in hours, how the dirty rapist hung himself. Those girls will get some justice, we get a kill, and him? He goes straight to hell to enjoy an eternity of living the nightmare he put all those women through. I think that sounds like a fair deal." I stopped my knife from making its trail further down his body, and I pushed the blade into his stomach, grinning as his eyes widened from the pain. "Welcome to justice, soldier style."

I pulled the knife out and stepped back. Tyler and Colton grabbed him under his arms and dragged him across the chapel to the chair he'd been sitting in before.

"Showtime!" Colton said with a wicked grin, and even though we didn't have speakers in here, he still had to take his phone out and choose a song from his killer playlist for us to work to. *Shinedown's 'Enemies'* echoed off the walls, letting him know that he was caught, stuck here with the worst fucking enemies he'd ever made, and there was no getting out.

The chapel might've housed my weapons store, but usually, we didn't use it for a hit. We preferred to keep our soldier business away from the club and do our kills in the warehouse we'd always used. But this was a special case. There wasn't

THE REAPER 43

time to mess about and move him to a place where he could be strapped in or strung up. Time was of the essence.

Will decided to commence proceedings as Colton stood behind the chair, restraining the guy and holding a knife to his throat so he wouldn't move. With steady precision, Will ran the skinning knife down the guy's left arm, slicing the flesh and exposing the red, bloody muscles beneath. The guy screamed a blood-curdling howl of a scream, but Will didn't flinch, he just moved to the other side and did the same to his right arm. Blood dripped onto the floor, making the grey flagstone turn crimson. The guy's face beaded with sweat, and as he panted and drifted into unconsciousness, Colton slapped his face to keep him with us. He would lose a lot of blood tonight, but not enough that he'd pass out and miss the grand finale. We'd make sure of that.

Tyler took over next, firing up a blow torch with gusto and waving it in the guy's face. The guy's eyes widened in horror as he mouthed no and vehemently shook his head. But his fear only spurred us on. Will stepped up to hold his wrists in place as Tyler angled the flames so he could scorch the exposed muscles on his arms. The guy writhed and thrashed in the chair, screeching in pain as we turned our noses up at the rancid smell of burnt flesh that filled the air. Colton laughed manically, running his knife over the guy's neck, making shallow slashes in his skin. Enough to cause pain, but not enough to put him out of his misery. Then Colton lifted the knife and slashed across his cheeks, the left side, then the right. Making him as ugly on the outside as he was on the inside. We were in our element. In the zone. This guy was getting the full soldier experience.

I was getting hungry for my turn. I glanced at the katana sword; the ultimate weapon that could slice through the body of a man like it was cutting through silk. But I decided it was too special to waste on this piece of shit. The katana was unique, revered, reserved only for our top kills. This kill was a dirty one. He was an animal, and I had enough hunting knives to serve this evil fucker the justice he deserved. I picked up my new Bowie hunting knife—the double-edged tip could pierce through anything. Then, I walked over to where he sat, his arms dripping filth onto my floor, his face slashed and hanging off his bones, and I leant close to him to whisper, "This is for all the girls. Every. Single. One." I plunged the knife into his groin, tearing through the material of his jeans and the muscles of his dick, severing his filthy appendage from the rest of him. Castration of the worst and best kind, because once I'd twisted and gouged, I pulled the knife out then stuck it back in again at a different angle.

The guy was shaking, convulsing in the chair, and when he eventually passed out, Tyler asked if I wanted to try and revive him. That's if he wasn't dead already.

"No. Leave him like that. We'll shove him in the back of the van and drive him to Granges Park. Once he's strung up, ready to be hung, we'll wake him up and then watch him die." I started to grab the things we'd need; rope, gaffer tape, and I turned to Tyler and added, "Don't forget the phone. We need to plant that on him so the police know why he's there. They need to know exactly what he's done."

Tyler held the phone up to show he'd got it, and Will asked, "What about the injuries? We need to put in a few phone calls to get that dealt with. We might be stringing him up to make it look like suicide, but no copper in their right mind is going to believe it when they see what we've done to him."

THE REAPER 45

"I've already thought of that," I told him. "I'm going to ring my contact on the force now. Let him know what he's got to deal with. When the Brinton police see the videos on the phone, they won't have a problem overlooking it. Evil is evil and we've taken care of it for them. Less paperwork for them to deal with makes it a win all round. They really won't care about proper policing once they know what he is."

What we did could be deemed sadistic to the outside world, but sometimes, the outside world was actually grimmer and more fucked-up than anything we doled out. Tonight, we'd rid the streets of Brinton of this guy's terror. Women were safer because of what we'd done.

"What's his name?" Colton asked, peering down at what was left of his face. "Is it Hugo? He looks like a Hugo. Or a Monty."

Tyler fished the guy's wallet from his back pocket and flipped it open. "Dale," he said, shrugging.

Colton winced and curled his upper lip in disgust. "That figures. He looks like a cunt, and he's got a cunt's name to go with it."

I couldn't give a fuck what he was called. His name meant nothing to me. The fact he'd soon be wiped out like the stain that he was on this world was all that mattered. I wanted to get this done and dusted.

***

We drove past the main car park for Granges Park and carried on, taking the van through the back alleys where it was more secluded. There was no CCTV in this part of the park, and no buildings overlooking it. When we eventually pulled up by the tree I had in mind for the last stage of Dale's final reckoning, we heard him start to groan and kick out in the back of the van. This fucker really was holding on until the bitter end, but I had to hand it to him, he had perfect timing.

I pulled up at a clearing and shut off the engine. As I jumped out of the van, I shivered from the icy cold wind that was whipping through the trees, making the branches bend and the leaves rustle to create an eerie soundtrack to the events that were about to unfold. There was a full moon tonight, and the shadows it cast through the trees created a hellish effect. Almost like shadowy, bony fingers from hell were creeping and dancing across the grass, desperate to get their next victim. To wrap their claws around his ankles and wrists and drag him down into the depths of despair to devour him in their flames.

I smiled at the sweet irony and pulled my jacket tighter around me. Full moons always brought out the best in all of us. Dale had chosen a good day to die. Not that he had a choice in the matter.

My footsteps crunched as I strode along the pebbled path, walking to the rear of the van. Will, Tyler, and Colton were waiting, and together, we opened the doors to get to our target. Dale had left a filthy mess of blood and shit all over the walls and floor. Colton reached forward to grab him by his ankles and yank him out of the van. Dale didn't put up much of a fight, and his head smacked off the bottom of the van as Colton managed to drag him out onto the path.

"I suggest you let us do our job," Colton said as he leered over him. "We've had about as much as we can take for one night from you, and I'm freezing my bollocks off. I don't want

THE REAPER 47

to be here any longer than I have to. Understand?"

Dale didn't respond; he just lay on the ground, limp and lifeless. If he had dared to speak, in the mood I was in, I'd have probably cut his tongue out.

Will grabbed Dale's other ankle, and the two of them began marching across the grass, dragging him towards the large oak tree in front of us. Tyler picked up the rope and gaffer tape, and I followed them all, tapping on my phone to set up the video. I knew Adam would want to see what we'd done when we got back. I propped my phone up against a rock on the ground, facing the main event, then I walked over to help Tyler secure the noose and thread the rope through the higher branches. Will and Colton took turns taunting Dale; their feet pressed hard on his chest to keep him on the cold, wet ground. Once we were ready, Colton pulled Dale's arm to force him into a sitting position. As he slumped his head forward, Will and Colton grabbed under his arms and lifted him to stand.

"He's like a fucking dead weight," Will complained.

"He fucking will be a dead weight in a few minutes," I replied.

Tyler put the noose over his head and pulled on the rope to secure it tighter around his neck. Then he took Dale's phone out, wiped it clean of any fingerprints, and slid it into Dale's jacket pocket. That last drop of fear must've entered Dale's system because he started to fight back, thrashing against Will and Colton's strong hold and grabbing for the rope in a feeble attempt to free himself. But it was no use. His fate was already sealed. The police had been tipped off, and when Tyler and I pulled on the rope to lift him into the air, his will to fight soon ebbed away.

Once it was clear he couldn't escape, Will and Colton let go of him and joined us in our efforts to pull the rope faster and make him swing from the branches. When his feet lifted from the floor and he started to twitch and convulse, Tyler let go of the rope and stood in front of him, watching as his face turned a deathly shade of blue. When he knew the time was right, he nodded at us, and we took the rope and tied it to the trunk, stepping back once it was secure so we too could see for ourselves that he was dead.

I stared into his pale, bloated face, his eyes bulging out of his head, and I didn't feel a thing other than pride. I'd learnt from my mistakes, and I was glad the girls would get some form of comfort, knowing he was dead. All those years ago, when I killed my stepfather, I hadn't left the body for anyone to find. And still, to this day, my mother was convinced that he would come back to her. I'd fucked up. I should've left his rotting corpse somewhere for them to see. That way, she'd have moved on. It would certainly have made my life a lot easier. As I said, I'd learned from my mistakes.

"Well, that's a wrap." Colton sighed. "Didn't see our night going quite like that, but I can't say it hasn't had its highlights."

"I'm fucking filthy," Will moaned. "I need a shower."

"We all need a shower," I stated, looking down at my own blood-stained clothes. "Ty, ring Gaz and get him to do a clean-up on the chapel. We'll stop by the warehouse on the way back to shower and change there." We always kept spare clothes at the warehouse for this exact reason. Death wasn't exactly a clean pastime. "I reckon Adam and Liv will be home once we get back, and I doubt Adam will want Liv seeing us like this," I added, gesturing to the splatters on my body.

THE REAPER 49

"Good call," Tyler said, and pulled his phone out to sort the necessary arrangements.

I picked my phone up from the floor and stopped the recording.

Just another chapter in the life of a soldier of our manor. Brinton's reaper was forever on-call.

CHAPTER THREE
Devon

Once we got back to The Sanctuary, I checked in with Gaz to make sure the clean-up was all taken care of, and then I headed upstairs to join the others. Adam had sent a message to say he was here, and he'd sent Faye home. Apparently, Liv was watching the girl, which left Adam, no doubt, pacing a hole into the floor, waiting for the low-down from us.

When I walked into our living room a moment later, I was proven right. Adam's arms were folded over his chest, and his face was twisted into a scowl as he marched up and down like the queen's guard. The other three were sitting forward on the sofa, still buzzing from the adrenaline rushing through their veins, but no one spoke. I guessed they were waiting for me before they started.

The minute Adam saw me, he barked, "Talk."

I sat down next to Colton and replayed the night's events with all the gory details that I knew Adam would want, seeing as he'd missed out. The others occasionally waded in with their comments, and Adam nodded. He knew we'd done the best job we could. Every loose end was tied up, every line of enquiry that the police could make wouldn't come back on us—I would stake my life on it. The only question we had now was what to do with the girl.

"You did a good job," Adam announced, furrowing his brow in frustration. "I only wish I could've been there to help reinforce the message that nobody fucks with us. Nobody." He pointed at Tyler and added, "Tomorrow, we go through every member application with a fine-tooth comb. Any discrepancies and they're out. This never happens again."

"Damn fucking right it won't," Colton replied, taking out a cigarette and sparking it up. He took a long drag and then blew out a cloud of smoke before asking, "What about the girl?"

"Olivia is with her now," Adam said, taking the seat opposite Colton. "I say we let her sleep it off, then get her home safe tomorrow."

"And if she wants to go to the police?" Tyler asked, looking around the circle at each one of us.

Adam just shrugged. "We cross that bridge when we come to it."

"Is Liv going stay with her all night?" I asked, hopeful that he'd say yes. I saw myself as an expert in combat and torture, but emotions and all that other shit didn't come naturally to me. I could do without facing that part of the job.

But Adam had it all figured out. "Yeah, we thought that'd be best. That way, if she wakes up, she won't freak out seeing one of our ugly mugs staring at her. Olivia will put her at ease and explain what's going on."

"Does Liv know what we've done tonight?" Will asked tentatively, and we all turned to look at Adam. No one else had ever been let into our unit quite like Liv had.

"She knows enough," he stated, not giving anything away.

"Don't take this the wrong way, boss. I know she's your girlfriend, but do you trust her to know about stuff like this? Our other business, I mean," Will ventured bravely. The adrenaline he had coursing through him had obviously given him bigger balls if he was questioning Adam over Liv and what he told her.

Adam's jaw tensed as he gritted his teeth and took a breath before he answered. "One, its none of your goddamn business, and two, yes, I do trust her. I trust her with my life. You should know that by now after what happened on the roof of the community centre, but that's beside the point. You shouldn't need to question me or my decisions. Oh… and three, she isn't my girlfriend. She's my wife."

We all froze, not quite believing what we were hearing.

"Are you fucking joking?" Colton spat, his eyes bugging out of his head.

"No. Why would I joke about that?" Adam narrowed his eyes and stared at Colton. He wasn't in the mood for him tonight, judging from his surly stare.

"When did this happen? And why didn't we know about it?" Tyler added.

"A few days ago." Adam sat back, a hint of a smile appeared on his face before he schooled his expression. "We did it at Sandland Registry Office, and no one knew, not even her friends. We wanted to keep it to ourselves."

"So romantic." Colton slapped his hand on his chest for effect.

"Fuck me. Does this mean you're moving out?" Will asked, cutting right to the chase. "Are you going to get a house with a white picket fence and start popping out kids?"

"It changes nothing," Adam fired back. "We're staying here. We have no plans to move out… yet. And as for kids, that's way off in the future."

Colton rubbed his chin and smiled. "Fuck me. Never thought I'd see the day when Adam Noble would be talking about having kids."

"I'm not. That's the whole fucking point. We're married and she's mine. End of."

We weren't going to argue with that. And in all honesty, I kind of liked it. I liked Liv. She fitted in.

"Well, now I just feel bad because I didn't get to buy you a gift or wear a tuxedo," Colton whined.

"I'm sure you'll survive," Adam responded without a hint of humour. "If it bothers you that much, check with Olivia tomorrow. I'm sure she'll have an idea of something you can buy her."

I could see Colton's mind going into overdrive, so I butted in and said, "Congratulations, mate."

I was pleased for Adam. We all were. At least one of us had a fighting chance at a normal life after everything we'd been through. A rare opportunity to escape the reality of this godforsaken world that, for the most part, had dragged us all down. We were infected by the virus of life, the dirty underbelly that others preferred to ignore. Sworn to do our duty to bring justice at any cost. There was chaos all around us, it consumed us, but we consumed the chaos. We lived for it. It was our purpose.

Settling down?

I doubted that'd ever happen for me. Besides, what would any sane girl see in a killer like me?

CHAPTER FOUR
Devon

I woke up on the sofa in our living room, feeling like my joints had been on a bloody torture rack for the night. My back was stiff, my arms and legs ached, and even before opening my eyes, I could feel the burn in them from lack of sleep. Across the room, I could hear the whistle of the kettle as it boiled and the gentle clatter as mugs were placed on the counter.

"Morning, sleepyhead," Liv sang as I rubbed my eyes and then peered at her busying herself making hot drinks. She was like an angel, cast aside, forever to live amongst the demons who'd fight to the death to protect her. Black and white, night and day, she was proof that miracles were possible. That someone like her could see the good amongst the evil that surrounded us.

The girl from the night before was standing next to her, looking sheepishly at the floor. Her cheeks were flushed red with embarrassment, but she had nothing to be embarrassed about. She'd done nothing wrong.

"Are you okay?" I spoke quietly, not wanting to freak her out any more than she already was. I didn't look her way though. Instead, I swung my legs to the floor so I could sit up on the sofa and I rubbed my hands over my face to help wake me up.

"I'm fine," she replied, and she sighed before adding, "I can't remember much about last night. The last thing I can recall was being at the bar and chatting to some guy. He bought me a vodka and coke, and then nothing… it's all a blank."

That's probably for the best.

"Liv has filled me in though, and I'm really grateful that you let me stay here, you know, after everything."

"No need to thank us. It's what any decent person would do."

I looked up, and Liv smiled a knowing smile over her shoulder at me. She got it. She understood that in our world, decent meant taking out the trash. We had our own code that we lived by, and we made no apologies for it. I stood up, stretching out my tired limbs before I announced, "I'm taking a shower, then I'll drop you off home."

"Oh no, it's fine." The girl waved her hands in protest. "I can get an Uber."

"I'm driving you home," I stated plainly. It wasn't up for debate. Even though I knew she'd be safe, I wasn't about to throw her out onto the street or leave her in a taxi with a stranger. I didn't work like that. "Give me ten minutes."

"Give her twenty," Liv said, chastising me with a stern glare as she put a steaming mug into the girl's hands. "At least let her enjoy her tea and toast. She feels like shit."

THE REAPER

"Fine. Twenty minutes." I didn't wait for a reply, I just walked away, and as I stalked down the corridor towards my room, I realised I hadn't even asked the girl what her name was.

***

Fifteen minutes later, I made my way back into the living room, ready to take her home. Colton was sitting with Liv and the girl, holding Liv's hand and twisting it so he could see the rings on her finger.

"Liv Noble," he exclaimed, testing the name out loud. "Does this mean I get to call you sis now?"

"It means I get to call you out on your bullshit," Liv replied, pulling her hand away.

"You do that anyway," he moaned then glanced to the side to where I was standing, loitering in the doorway. "You are allowed to come in." He raised his brow in question, but I stayed where I was and pulled the car keys from my pocket to give them all the hint that I had stuff to do. I didn't have time to waste today. I needed to check in with the police, for a start, and make sure Dale's case was being reported to the media exactly how I'd requested it. We couldn't afford to have any shit coming back on us. Tyler had already wiped the CCTV. Security had been briefed to deny any knowledge of that man ever stepping foot in here.

No stone unturned.

"I guess that's my cue to leave," the girl said and stood up.

Liv stood up too and hugged her, then added, "You've got my number. If you ever need anything, just call. It was lovely meeting you, Jodie."

Jodie.
So, that was her name.
Not that I'd remember after today.

***

Once we were in the car, I asked Jodie where she lived, so I could put it into the sat nav.

"I'd prefer not to go straight home," she replied, wringing her hands in her lap and staring out of the passenger window to avoid looking at me.

She probably didn't want me to know where she lived. Either that, or she didn't want her family to see her like she was this morning; haggard, tired, and no doubt emotional after what she'd woken up to. So, I sat silently and waited for her to tell me where she wanted me to take her. It didn't bother me either way, as long as she was somewhere safe.

"Can you drop me off at St Michaels vicarage?"

I tensed hearing her say the name of that place. St Michaels was Reverend Johnson's church. The same Reverend who'd tried to stir up trouble for us with the church diocese over the asylum chapel not so long ago. He'd since gone quiet. The fact that we weren't using it for anything involving the public seemed to placate him. But I didn't trust him, and I certainly didn't want to rock up at his door on a Sunday morning with this girl.

"It's my cousin's house," she elaborated. "It'll be easier for me to go there and sleep this off. The less my parents know, the better."

I shrugged. She didn't need to give me an explanation. I

THE REAPER

really didn't care. I wasn't about to stick around. I'd drop her off and be gone in less than a minute. But I had to ask, "Won't the vicar be there?" Curiosity had got the better of me.

"On a Sunday?" She laughed. "My uncle will be at the church giving his sermon. But Leah will be home, I've already text her to ask if I can crash for a few hours."

I started the car, not bothering to use the sat-nav. I knew where the vicarage was. I hadn't ever been in the church or the actual vicarage itself, but I knew it. Reverend Johnson had made a brief appearance on my shit list prior to me acquiring the asylum chapel for my own devices. Because of that, I'd done a few recon visits to the area. But in the end, I saw his meddling as a blessing in disguise. I got what I wanted. I guess, in a way, so did he. Although, I doubt he'd see it that way if he'd been in the chapel last night.

I drove in silence through the streets of Brinton Manor, heading towards St Michaels, but Jodie couldn't stay quiet for long.

"I'm not going to the police, by the way. I'd rather just forget it ever happened. Not that there's much to tell."

Only because we got there in time.

"I doubt he'll try anything else anyway after you all spoke to him."

You have no idea who we are, do you?

"Thanks for giving me a lift. And for letting me have your room for the night."

I sighed as we pulled onto the country lane where the vicarage was situated. The spire of St Michaels stood tall and proud, a short distance behind the old Victorian rectory. A beacon of false hope in the cloudless blue skies. The rectory was pretty non-descript. Hidden behind vines that twisted and clung to the brickwork, the house itself looked simple, basic. As if it was hiding from the world, unseen in the shadows of the grander, mightier church. But I liked it. The small wooden windows and black wooden door made it look like something from another world, another age even. A time when life was simpler, kinder. Maybe Reverend Johnson wasn't all bad?

I pulled up beside the stone wall that ran the length of the rectory, separating the narrow lane from the small garden at the front of the house, and I kept the engine running, waiting for Jodie to leave the car so I could be on my way.

"Well, thanks for everything," Jodie said, fiddling with the door handle to get out.

She stood up and closed the car door behind her, but when I saw her heel catch in the uneven pebbles of the country lane, making her stumble and fall to her knees, I turned the engine off and shot out of the car to run around and help her. Seems I'd be walking her to the door after all.

When I approached, she jumped up and announced, "I'm fine!" She kicked her shoes off and pushed herself up off the floor. "No need to panic."

"I'll walk you to the door," I stated plainly, but she didn't wait for me, just strode on ahead, opening the small wooden gate and shouting over her shoulder, "No need. I'm here now."

I followed her down the path anyway, and when the front door shot open, every nerve, every muscle in my body froze.

I stopped dead in my tracks. A peculiar paralysis flooded my system, and its unfamiliarity made my brain scream in protest. I had never felt nervous or unsure about anything in my life, not for a long time, so this new, strange wash of adrenaline that was drowning me felt alien, and I didn't like it.

I was stifled, constricted, like the breath in my lungs had become heavy rocks that pounded against my rib cage. I tried to stay focused and take deep breaths, but sparks of light started to dance in front of my eyes, and my head felt dizzy. If it wasn't for the fact that my legs had become lead weights anchoring me to the floor, I'd have probably passed out.

What the fuck was happening to me?
Was I ill?

Trying to refocus myself, I glanced up at the girl that stood in the doorway. She was dressed all in black, with onyx black hair tumbling in waves over her shoulders. Her skin was pale, but her cheeks were flushed red, and her mouth was open like she was in shock. She stared straight at me, with the widest, bluest eyes I'd ever seen, and for a split second, I saw a forlorn look of sadness. But she blinked, painted on a smile and stuck her arm out towards me to shake my hand.

"Hi. I'm Leah May," she said with too much enthusiasm considering the withered emotion I'd seen in her eyes just a moment ago. "It means God will judge you in Hebrew, but don't worry, there's no judgement here. I might live by a church but it's all forgiveness and love. I wouldn't ever judge anyone's choices, and…"

She carried on wittering mindlessly, but I paid no attention to what she was saying. All I could do was stare at her outstretched arm, wondering if I should shake it or not. I couldn't think straight. For some strange reason, this girl was fucking with my already frazzled brain. But before I could decide, Jodie reached out and pushed Leah May's arm down and out of the way, snapping, "For Christ's sake, Leah, did you really have to pull out the hellfire and brimstone shit?"

Anger surged through me. I didn't like the way she spoke to Leah May, but I tried not to react, not to show any weakness. I kept calm, measured, and as I looked up into her eyes, she swallowed nervously and listened tentatively as her cousin continued to chastise her. "I already told you, stop listening to what your dad said. We googled it, remember? Leah means pretty girl, or weary girl, but let's go with pretty."

I thought weary girl suited her better.

"I like weary girl," she said, mirroring my thoughts, and I tilted my head as I studied her closer.

Leah May's cheeks turned a darker shade of red under my gaze, and I could see her hands start to shake. Funny thing was, mine were shaking too, but I was better at hiding that fact. How was it that I could gut a man without breaking a sweat, but this girl was making me question my sanity? I didn't do nerves, or so I thought.

I didn't usually like looking into people's eyes either, or even their faces, not unless I was threatening them, but something about this girl made me want to stand and stare. She had delicate features, alabaster skin, and as I studied her, I realised what it was she reminded me of… a china doll. Only her eyes weren't lifeless glass beads; they shone with a desperation to be understood, a need to be accepted. Her eyes told me everything I needed to know about her. This girl was a caged animal, and she wanted to be set free.

She swallowed again, and I moved my gaze from her eyes to her slim neck as the muscles in her throat contracted. The urge to touch her, bite her and mark her flawless skin crept over me like the vines that clung to her house, and I clenched my

THE REAPER

fists, trying to contain the beast inside me that this girl seemed to call to.

"Is this your new… boyfriend?" Her voice cracked as she spoke. Was she disappointed?

But when Jodie replied, "God, no. He just brought me home," Leah May let out a huge breath, and her shoulders dipped in relief.

"Well, in that case, thank you so much for bringing Jodie here. Did you know, in the bible, Jodie means praised? You're the one we need to praise though." Jodie groaned, but Leah May kept her fake smile in place and added, "You're welcome to come in. I've just made a pot of tea…" She started rambling nervously again about the merits of drinking tea and how it boosted your immune system and helped ward off cancer and heart disease. Jodie huffed impatiently and stepped forward, pushing her way past Leah May to get into the hallway.

"He's a busy man, Leah, no time for tea and chats. And tea's tea. Nobody cares about your public health announcements. Just let him be on his way." Jodie was condescending, and part of me wanted to go in and drink the tea just to piss her off, but I didn't.

"Nice to meet you, Leah May," I said and turned to walk away, but not before I heard the slight gasp that she gave. A gasp that seemed to drift through the air, penetrating right through me and placing a sting on my heart.

That was new.

But I couldn't read into it.

She was the vicar's daughter.

From what I'd seen in the two minutes since I'd been on her doorstep, I could tell she was awkward and clumsy with her words. She had an inane desperation to please others, especially her cousin, and a goodness that made her vulnerable, an easy target for manipulation. But she was also the most intriguing, puzzling, beautiful girl I'd ever seen.

But none of that mattered.

I was a killer.

She was as far away from my world as a fish was to a bird. Our lives were at opposite ends of the scale. And with that thought, I got into the car and drove off without looking back.

CHAPTER FIVE
Leah May

He didn't look back.

I stood on the doorstep, waiting, hoping he would, but he never did.

For fuck's sake, Leah, you've made yourself look like a prize dick. Your one chance, and you blew it.

"Close the door, Leah, you're letting all the hot air out," Jodie shouted from the kitchen, and I huffed as I shut the door, feeling like I was closing it on a chapter of my life. Dramatic, I know, but I couldn't help it. It felt painful closing that door, like my heart was splintering in my chest.

Moments ago, I'd heard the car engine as they pulled up outside, and I'd run to the window in excitement, desperate to see Jodie with her latest hook-up. What would this one be like? Tall, dark, and handsome, unlike the last one? But when *he* got out of the car to walk her down the path, Jodie swinging her shoes in her hands and him looking like he wanted to be anywhere but here, my heart dropped out of my chest onto the cold, hard floor.

Not him.

Anyone but him.

In the beginning, I'd tried to keep my head, play it cool as I fought hard to block out the images that were flickering through my brain of what might've happened last night between the two of them. Images that made me want to double over and wretch onto the soil. I cringed, remembering how I'd rambled on about names and their meanings. It was all my brain could come up with in the moment. A rabbit caught in the headlights had nothing on me.

I heard Jodie groaning in the kitchen, and I dragged my feet forward, even though I didn't want to go in there. I didn't want to know what she was about to tell me. Sometimes, it was hard to play all the different roles I had to play. Most of the time, it was hard to fake your real feelings and emotions. This morning, I had lied to my cousin and pretended I was as clueless as she thought I was. But I wasn't stupid. I knew more than I'd ever let on.

When I saw her lying on the sofa in our kitchen, I went over to her and stroked her hair. She liked it when I pandered to her.

"I'm sorry I was snippy with you earlier," she whined. "I just wanted him gone and to come inside and be with you. I've had the worst night ever."

I decided to abandon the tea, and I slid onto the end of the sofa, lifting her legs to rest on my lap.

"What happened?" I asked, dreading the answer. Part of me couldn't wait a moment longer, and the other half didn't want to know what role he'd played in her night. Ignorance was bliss sometimes.

She rolled onto her back but covered her eyes with her arm and groaned. She looked like death, smelled like it too, but I'd never tell her that.

"I went to The Sanctuary last night," she announced. "And before you start, yes, I was with friends, and no, I didn't make a show of myself, at least, I don't think I did."

Despite her reassurance, I could tell from the way she sighed and took her time that I wouldn't like what she was going to say.

"I met this guy at the bar."

My stomach rolled over.

"He seemed nice."

And?

"He bought me a drink; vodka and coke. But after drinking it, I must've passed out, and when I woke up this morning in Devon Brady's bed, I knew I'd fucked up."

I was going to throw up all over my dad's new Persian rug.

"You slept with him? You slept with that Devon guy, after he bought you drinks?" I almost couldn't say the words. My tongue was like a dried-up lump of muscle, totally useless. It didn't want to work because I didn't want to know the answer.

"No!" She flung her arm to the side to look at me. "I had my drink spiked. For fuck's sake, Leah, keep up. Dale spiked my drink. Devon's friends saved me, and I crashed in Devon's bed. He slept on the sofa in another room. There was no bed sharing. What the hell do you take me for? Do you think I'd actually go near one of those soldiers?"

My heart, which had splintered in pain, suddenly flickered with hope.

"I just thought—"

"I know what you thought." She sat up and shuffled backwards, bringing her knees to rest under her chin and wrapped her arms around her legs. "Leah, I know your dad has sheltered you a lot over the years, and that's a good thing... most of the time. But there are bad people out there, and the soldiers of Brinton Manor aren't the best guys for any of us to be associated with. I mean, don't get me wrong, I was grateful for their help, and Devon seemed like one of the nicer ones, despite what I've heard, but you can't let anyone know he brought me here, do you understand? I don't want my name associated with them."

I nodded, pretending I didn't know who they were.

I did.

I also held my tongue, even though I wanted to ask her, 'If they were so awful, why did you go to their club?' But if I'd said that, she'd know I knew more than I let on, and what I knew about the soldiers, I was keeping close to my chest.

"That guy... Devon, was it?" I was putting on an Oscar-worthy performance here. "He didn't look that bad. He had kind eyes. You can tell a lot by a person's eyes."

"Kind eyes?" She was mocking me again. "He was dead behind the eyes."

Maybe when he looked at you.

"They weren't dead. There was a real kindness there. A warmth." I recognised it. I always had. "Anyway, he can't be all bad. He made sure you got home safely. He even walked you to the door."

"Because I tripped on my bloody heels."

"See? Only a gentleman would care."

THE REAPER 69

He wasn't like the others.

He wasn't like any guy I'd ever met in my life.

"Seriously, Leah, you need to get out more if you think Devon Brady is a gentleman. He's two letters away from being the devil himself. Devon… devil. Pretty close, wouldn't you say?"

"No, I wouldn't say. Are you going to tell Helen down the road that she's two letters away from hell? That's just rude."

"Whatever." Jodie sighed and stood up. "It's not like the soldiers of Brinton Manor have actual feelings."

I bit my lip, keeping my opinions locked up deep inside me, and I watched as she sauntered to the door.

"Can I sleep in your spare room for a few hours?" she asked, standing in the doorway and glancing back at me. I don't know why she asked; she was heading that way anyway. "When Uncle Nathan gets home, tell him I came over for coffee and started feeling ill, so I went for a lie down. Please don't tell him about last night. Don't tell anyone."

"Who would I tell?" I replied, because it was true. I preferred to keep myself to myself. I also knew that the minute she woke up, she'd be spilling it all to my dad over a cuppa. She might leave out the date drug thing, but she always told us everything. That's what Jodie was like, an open book.

"I know. I trust you." She smiled and walked away, closing the door behind her.

I waited until I heard her footsteps on the stairs, then I slumped down on the sofa and took deep, ragged breaths, trying to calm my racing heart.

My cousin thought I had no idea who the soldiers of Brinton Manor were, because I played the part of the dutiful daughter to a T. I didn't stay out late or run with the wrong crowd. I was well-versed in keeping my father happy.

She thought I didn't know who Devon Brady was because the only boys I'd ever socialised with were the ones in the church youth group that my dad ran. But I wasn't an idiot.

I knew exactly who Devon Brady was.

The Reaper.

A vigilante.

A man who would do anything for his friends and everything for his beloved town.

I'd watched him for a long time. Always in the shadows and always from afar. But today was the first time I'd ever stood in front of him, and right now, I had mixed feelings about it because it'd been the best and worst experience of my life. Best, because I'd got to talk to him. Look into his eyes. Be near him. But worst, because he'd walked away. He probably wouldn't even remember my name. But I'd remember his. I always would. His name was engraved on my heart, scorched into my soul. Devon meant defender. It suited him perfectly. In the bible, Devon appears in Revelations 4:4 and means judgement. No better name for a reaper like him.

Some might call what I felt an infatuation. An obsession even. But I knew what it was. I loved Devon Brady. I could never admit to it out loud, but I did. I had felt this way for a long time. And that was a secret I couldn't tell anyone. Ever.

Mine was a love born in the shadows.

Even he didn't know about it, but it still existed.

As real as the air that I breathed, the water that quenched my thirst, the food that kept me alive, he was like a life force to me. Hidden, yet all around me. Everywhere. Secret, and yet, it made me want to scream. A wonderland in my mind that made living my real life feel like I was forever in a daze.

Until today, I was content with keeping things as they were. I was happy to preserve the status quo. But now, I felt all out of sorts. After standing so close to him, breathing him in, would watching him from afar ever be enough?

I had a feeling it wouldn't.

I had a feeling that this was the start of a whole new chapter.

CHAPTER SIX
Leah May

I went up to my bedroom, grabbed my guitar, and sat on the floor with my legs crossed, ready to play. Of all the instruments I played, the guitar was the one that seemed to work best at quietening the voices in my head. But as I strummed the chords for the version of *Crazy* that I'd been composing, I could still hear them.

Why do you let her speak to you like that?

You need to show her you're not the doormat she thinks you are.

And him? You should've made him stay.

He needs to know who you are, know that you won't be ignored anymore. Make him notice you.

I hummed along with the tune I was playing, trying to drown it all out.

THE REAPER

Kindness is weakness.
They think you're a pushover.
You need to show them who you really are.
Why do you always act like a weak little girl?
If you want him, show him you're his equal.

Round and round the voices went, arguing, belittling me, making me want to grab my head in my hands and scream for them to shut the hell up. I knew what I was doing. I was doing things my way. The gentle approach. Subtle. Hell, did I really know what I was doing?

Your subtlety has got you nowhere.
He's stronger than that.
Do you think he wants a shrinking violet who acts like she wouldn't say boo to a goose?

I knew I wasn't perfect, but I was doing things my way. Maybe I hadn't gotten the results I'd wanted so far, but I was in control.

You have about as much control as limp lettuce on a plate of steak.

I frowned. What did that even mean? It made no fucking sense.

Neither does your weak-ass approach.
Take the bull by the horns.

Own your future.

I did own my future. I owned it by not fucking bulldozing through my hopes and dreams like a bull in a china shop and fucking it all up. Some things needed more care with how you approached them and dealt with them.

I stood up, throwing my guitar onto the bed in frustration, and I went to stand in front of the mirror on my wall. I stared deep into my eyes to remind myself that I would take charge. I wouldn't ever give up. Those feelings I had downstairs when I closed the door as he left, those feelings of defeat and despair, I wouldn't let them take hold. I would dictate what happened next.

And what is that, exactly?
More brooding on street corners while you watch him with his friends?
He doesn't even know you exist.

"Shut the fuck up!" I screamed and punched my fist into the mirror. It didn't shatter, and the pain in my fist made me want to punch myself in anger at my stupidity for reacting the way I had. I'd just used my right hand, my playing hand, to smack a fucking mirror on the wall. What use would I be now if I couldn't play my instruments because I'd caused myself damage? I had a gig soon. I couldn't let people down.

I used my other hand to rub the pain away, and that's when I noticed it on my pillow. A raven. An origami raven, folded from black card and sitting right there, waiting for me to find it. When my mum was alive, she'd always called me her little raven because of my dark hair. She liked to tell me I was a good omen, and that her greatest wish was for me to fly high. Be free. Live my life always soaring to catch my dreams. She'd often leave origami ravens on my pillow for me to find at the end of the day. It was her way of giving me an omen of my own, her special way of showing me she cared.

I'd bought a black ornate birdcage to keep them in, and I still had every single one she'd ever made. Some were placed on the bottom of the cage, some on the perch, and some I attached to strings and suspended them from the top, making it look like they were flying.

When she died, I thought the origami gifts would stop. Dad was never able to make them even when she was alive; he was hopeless at it. But Mum must've had a supply she'd made that my dad kept hidden somewhere because every now and then, a bird would appear out of nowhere, perched on my pillow. I guess it was my dad's way of keeping her spirit alive, letting me know she was always here. I didn't realise I needed to see one of her ravens as much as I did right now, and I picked it up like it was made of glass, carried it to my birdcage and then opened the clasp on the door and placed the bird on the floor of the cage.

"Thanks, Mum," I whispered into the air, thankful that the voices had gone quiet, and I felt more grounded.

When I heard the sound of our front door closing, I closed the cage and headed downstairs. Dad would want a heads-up that Jodie was here, and I needed to find something I could strap my hand up with.

"I killed it this morning. Even Mrs Danvers on the back row didn't fall asleep," my dad said as I entered the kitchen.

"You kill it every week. I don't know what you're worried

about," I answered, giving him a meek smile. I opened the cupboard under the sink and started to root around, trying to find the first aid kit. "Before I forget, Jodie is upstairs asleep in the spare room."

"Another rough night on the tiles?" he asked with a smirk. He wasn't stupid, he knew Jodie was a party girl, and that didn't matter. She was his niece, not his daughter.

"Let's just say, we should keep our noise to a minimum. I don't think her delicate head would appreciate anything else."

It wouldn't be hard to stay quiet. Since my mum had passed away ten years ago, there'd always been a sombre blanket of silence over our lives. Noisy in my head, but quiet in the house.

Finally, I located the first aid bag and put it on the counter, unzipping it and pulling out a bandage.

"Are you okay? Did you hurt yourself?" My dad came over to me, peering down to where I was nursing my hand in the other, and he reached forward to take my right hand in his. Delicately, he brushed his fingers over my knuckles and said, "It looks like you need some ice on this. What happened?"

"It was nothing," I replied, playing it down. "I dropped a paperweight and…" I screwed my face up, hoping I didn't have to explain the rest. A paperweight? It was a shit explanation, but it was all I could think of in the moment.

"Ah!" My dad nodded like dropping paperweights on your knuckles was an everyday occurrence. Maybe he just didn't want to admit that it wasn't true because that would mean facing the fact that I'd lied, which would be worse than any injury. "Let's sort the bruising first, then we can strap it up properly."

He opened the freezer and took out a packet of peas, wrapping them in a tea towel before placing the homemade ice

THE REAPER

pack carefully on my hand. "You need to be more careful, Leah May. I know accidents happen, but this is your playing hand." I stared at the floor, not wanting him to see the guilt in my eyes, but he leant down to look at me and smiled. "You'll be fine. My clumsy little angel." And he kissed the top of my head.

I'd always been my dad's little angel.

Clumsy angel.

Forgetful angel.

The quiet little angel who always did as she was told.

I didn't mind being that for my dad, but deep down, I was no angel. I'd never let him know, but I preferred the shadows, and not because I could hide, although that was a bonus. The shadows were where *he* played, and where he was, I wanted to be.

I liked the dark.

I liked danger.

And he was danger.

He was the silent breeze that blew through the night, sending shivers down my spine and igniting my soul.

Darkness and fire.

Death that made me feel alive.

From the moment I'd laid eyes on Devon Brady all those years ago, I was drawn to him. The proverbial moth to the flame, and I couldn't get him out of my head, even now, while I was standing in the kitchen with my dad, nursing a bruised fist, he was there, right at the forefront of my mind.

Was he a virus infecting my soul? Or the blooms of life being injected into my veins? I didn't know, and I didn't care. But I knew one thing, he made me want to live the life I'd always dreamed of. He made me want to break free. He made me want things I'd never even whisper to myself in the darkness of my room.

He made me want, and I wanted him.

"Shall we take our tea into the living room and watch a few episodes of *Friends* before I put the dinner on?" my dad asked, pulling me out of my reverie.

"Yeah, sure." I painted on the smile I used just for my dad and followed him as he carried our mugs through to the lounge.

I lived a life of contradiction and little white lies. I had to. But I couldn't go on like this. Something had to change, or else I was going to lose my mind.

CHAPTER SEVEN
Leah May

Jodie pulled herself out of her pit when she smelled Dad's Sunday roast wafting through the house, and she came down to eat with us. She looked a shade less green and sickly than she had done earlier, so Dad's suspicions of her night being anything other than a booze-filled overindulgence were put to rest. We ate, Jodie filled Dad in on some of her less salacious escapades that made him laugh and roll his eyes, and I tried to stop my mind from wandering into the dark avenues that it seemed to want to go down. I couldn't settle though, no matter how hard I tried to tune into their conversation and act normal.

After dessert, Jodie announced that she was going to walk home. She didn't live too far away, and she told us the fresh air would do her good; help to blow out the cobwebs from the night before. I thought she'd need more than the wintery breeze outside to do that, but what did I know?

I didn't want to stay cooped up in the house with nothing but the riotous voices in my head to keep me company, so I offered to walk with her. That way, Dad could work on his sermons and other church stuff without any distractions, and I could avoid playing the role of his devoted flock, listening to every word. I don't know why he asked for my critique anyway; he never changed anything.

Jodie didn't have a decent coat with her, so I lent her one of mine.

"Thanks for dinner, Uncle Nathan," Jodie called out to my dad in his study. "Same time next week?" She laughed.

I heard Dad chuckle and call back, "Sure. But try not to have a hangover next time."

He pretended like he was okay with it, or that it was only mildly irritating, but I knew when I got home, he'd be cursing her out for bringing shame to her family. Those immortal words, 'She could do with taking a leaf out of your book,' would probably feature too. Dad thought I was the epitome of graciousness and excellence. Good job he couldn't see into my brain; I don't think he'd like what he found there.

We took a slow walk through the country lanes that led from my house to Jodie's. The conversation stayed shallow and inconsequential. But when we eventually arrived at her front door, she hugged me and whispered in my ear, "Thanks again for this morning. And thanks for staying quiet too. I owe you."

I pulled away, and I could see something like shame shine in her eyes.

"You don't owe me anything. And remember, you did nothing wrong last night." She gave a sad nod and then turned to unlock the door.

"Doubt I'll be going to The Sanctuary again," she said in a grave voice. I didn't respond, just watched the door close quietly behind her.

I was glad she was home and safe. Despite everything, she was my best friend. But my reason for leaving the house today hadn't been all selfless. I knew that I had to pass Jodie's house to get to my real destination. I had no intention of turning around and going home. My subconscious wouldn't let me. No. I wanted to go to the old Sandland asylum, the building he used as *his* sanctuary. There was a wall on the street corner opposite that I'd often sit on, waiting and watching. He'd never spotted me there, no one had. It was my special place. A place I often went to if I needed to think, or just to see what he was up to, if I was lucky enough to catch him coming out.

I wrapped my coat tighter around me and pulled the hood up to stay warm. The streets were practically empty, and I liked it that way. A quiet Sunday afternoon. Nothing to see here. As I approached my corner and took my place on the uneven stone wall, I glanced over at the asylum. The gothic, menacingly dark, yet intriguing building was like a beacon of all things forbidden, calling out to me, pulling me in.

I rubbed my hands together to warm them up, cursing myself that I'd forgotten to bring my gloves, and I blew into my cupped hands to help bring some life back into my fingers. But when I saw movement at the side of the building, I froze from something other than the cold air. I froze in anticipation.

Their dog came bounding out of the side door first, swirls of grey air circling as he panted out his breath.

Then I saw him.

Dark clothes, a hoody pulled up over his head, but I'd recognise it was him in any crowd.

Devon Brady.

He picked up a stick from the floor and threw it for the dog to catch. Then he cupped his own hands and blew into them just like I had. I sat on the wall, watching him play with the dog, and I started to daydream about the first time I ever saw him… ten years ago, at a community centre drop-in that my mum had organised through the church.

"The turnout is way better than I thought it would be." My mum beamed as she looked out across the hall of Brinton Manor community centre at all the people who had come today for her cupcakes and coffee morning. The bunting she'd sewn herself was strung up around the room and it gave the place a homely, welcoming feel. "I was worried they wouldn't bother on a Saturday. Plus, the whole church thing sometimes puts people off."

"It's free cake and coffee, what's not to like?" I joked, putting a plate of fresh strawberry and vanilla cupcakes onto the china stand my mum had brought from home to display her homemade delicacies. My mum had made all the cupcakes for today. Biscuits too, but that's what she lived for, making others happy.

There were a lot of families from the manor, sitting around, chatting as they devoured the free cake. Kids ran between the tables chasing each other, and their parents occasionally shot out an arm as they raced past to grab them and slow them down. They'd wipe off a few crumbs and smeared frosting from their children's faces and curse them out with a smile.

These people weren't as lucky as we were, but for the most part, they were happy. You could tell from their shabby clothes and worn-out shoes that they appreciated what my mum had done today. They had a warm place to meet friends, somewhere for their kids to let off steam, and my mum always made of point of mingling, listening to their stories, offering a friendly, non-judgmental ear. My mum and dad were like yin and yang. Where he preached, she provided, listened, accepted, and the women of Brinton loved her for it.

"Let's put some of these on the tables," Mum said, gesturing to the cake filled plates, and she picked up one in each hand and then she turned and leant into me and in a low voice she whispered, "I might stop to have a chat with Kay Brady over there. She's had a terrible time of it since her husband left her. Two kids as well. She's really struggling with the oldest."

I had no idea who Kay Brady was, but I didn't pay much attention to the gossip my mum told my dad every night over the dinner table. My mum's idea of good gossip was different to mine.

We circulated through the tables, placing our plates down as we went, and avoiding the raucous kids. Eventually, we were left with one plate—a plate destined for Kay Brady's table. She was sitting on her own with a little girl about four years old snuggled in her lap. My mum put the plate down, then took a chocolate chip muffin and placed it in front of Kay.

"Your favourite." My mum smiled, and Kay sighed and reached forward to take the cake. I knelt down next to them and said hello to the little girl, but she just curled her face into her mum and hid from me. She didn't want to play; she was quite happy sitting with her mum and cuddling.

"Leah, why don't you head out to the gardens at the back? A few of the older kids are out there, and Kay's son, Devon, might be out there too."

Mum looked hopeful, but Kay blurted out, "He won't talk to you. He won't talk to anyone. He doesn't like making friends. He's a loner, my boy."

Nothing would deter my mum though, and she ushered me away from the table so she could have a chat with Kay.

I did as I was told, even though I had no idea who this Devon kid was. If my mum wanted me to make an effort, I would.

So, I wandered to the back of the hall, where the double doors led onto a small garden area. There were a few kids around my age outside. Some of the lads were kicking a can around like a football. The goalposts were marked by two jumpers on the grass. Close by were two girls sitting on the floor, giggling and watching the boys, and then I noticed a boy on his own. A boy who looked a little dirty and unkempt. He wore jeans that didn't cover his ankles. His jacket looked worn, and his face was ruddy, with specks of mud on his cheeks. But as I crept closer and watched him from behind the fir trees that lined the garden, I could see the determination in his eyes as he stood huddled over, crafting something in his hands. The way he gritted his teeth in concentration was mesmerising. I couldn't help but watch him. I felt drawn to him.

I took another step closer to get a better look, and I noticed that he had a small knife in his grubby hands. A Stanley knife, I think it was called, and he was using it to sharpen the end of a stick he'd found on the floor. I should've been wary of him bringing a knife here today, but I wasn't. He was using it to create something, and the focus he was giving his task was *inspiring. He didn't see me, and nothing seemed to pull him from his world, not even when a group of three boys came over to him and started to taunt him.*

"Oi, Brady. I'm surprised you've got the nerve to show your face around here after what you did at school yesterday," one of the boys said, and when Devon ignored them, he kicked out at him to get his attention.

It didn't work.

"I heard Simcox's parents are going to sue yours for damages," the boy stated, curling his lip in disgust.

"Good luck with that, we've got fuck all." It was the first words I'd heard Devon speak, and I held my breath.

He really didn't care about these boys; he didn't even look at them as they started to circle him threateningly.

I didn't know whether to go back inside and get my mum. I glanced around, hoping someone else was watching too, but the rest of the kids out here were all lost in their bubbles, oblivious to everything. I didn't want any trouble at my mum's event, but despite that, I couldn't seem to move. My legs were stuck firmly in place, fascinated by how this would unfold. Even though things were taking a sinister turn, judging from the way the boys stood with their arms folded, Devon wasn't fazed. He just kept on sharpening his stick and whistling to himself.

"You do know you almost broke his jaw?" one of the boys piped up. "You're a fucking psycho."

"He's a bully," Devon spat back. "Maybe I should've tried harder and actually broken it. He needed shutting up." There was no emotion behind his words. He cared more about the stick than what these boys were saying.

I gasped as one of them lashed out to hit Devon, but he

had reflexes like a cat, and he slashed the boy on the hand with the Stanley knife. The boy hissed and pulled away, cursing and swearing. Another boy tried his luck, but Devon turned on him, using the sharpened stick and jabbing it into the boy's side. It was like watching a Marvel movie; only the hero didn't look like your regular hero. He was dark, mysterious, a dangerous opponent with deadly weapons he'd crafted himself.

Two of the boys were cowering and panting, and I heard Devon turn to the third and say, "Do you want to try your luck?"

He shook his head and backed away, but still tried to get a verbal punch in. "You're a weirdo. No one likes you. The sooner you get expelled from our school, the better."

Devon just ignored them, no recognition of their existence flickered on his face, all of his focus remained on the arrow stick he was carefully whittling.

The three boys skulked away to lick their wounds, but I stood still, watching in fascination. Devon never saw me, and I was glad, because I'd seen him, and that was enough. I'd got to see him in all his unedited, raw honesty.

Devon didn't need a friend. He didn't need me disturbing his peace. He wanted to be alone. But something still drew me to him. I liked looking at him, studying him. He wasn't like anyone I'd ever met before. He was real. Unapologetically so.

I must've gone into a trance, watching Devon in his world, because when my mum came up behind me and put her hand on my shoulder, I jumped out of my skin. She smiled down at me, but I looked over to where Devon stood, praying he hadn't been disturbed. He hadn't, but he was walking away towards the bottom of the garden, leaving me behind. It made me feel a sense of sadness and longing.

"He's a troubled soul, that one." Mum sighed as she put her arms around me to hug me from behind. "He could do with a friend. Someone to watch over him. Kay said he's been getting into a lot of trouble at school. Maybe you could talk to him?"

"He doesn't go to my school, Mum," I said, wishing that he did.

"I know that, but there's always weekends and events like this. Brinton Manor is a small place." She let me go and came to stand in front of me. "You could invite him to your church club."

"I don't think he's the church club kind." I knew he wasn't, and I wasn't about to embarrass myself by suggesting something like that to a boy like him.

"Okay, well, what about your guitar lessons? Or violin? Maybe he'd like to learn to play an instrument?" Again, she was barking up the wrong tree, but she had good intentions, so I nodded in agreement.

"Maybe."

"Thank you." Mum gave me one last hug. "Kay worries about him, and I worry about them both. If I know someone's looking out for him, it'll make me feel a little better."

That someone being me.

I took one last look at the boy who seemed to live like a ghost. He appeared to like it that way too. I never thought I'd see him again. I didn't realise the impact that first encounter would have on my life. But two days later, my mum was knocked down at a zebra crossing by a drunk driver. She was killed on impact as he ploughed her into a wall. At her funeral, I saw Kay Brady. I didn't see her kids, but I remembered what my mum had said.

He needed a friend.

She'd feel better knowing someone was watching out for him.

And so, I made a pledge to my mum that day, under the drizzly, grey skies of Brinton Manor. Right in front of her coffin at the altar of my dad's church, I vowed I'd do what my mum had asked of me.

I'd be a good person, just like her.

I'd watch him like she'd wanted me to.

My mum wanted Devon Brady to have a friend.

Devon Brady didn't want to make any friends.

So, I'd be his shadow friend. A secret friend that even he didn't know about. A friend in the dark.

One day, I'd do more to help him, but I was only twelve, and there wasn't a lot I could do right now. One day, I'd find a way to be what he needed me to be, even though he didn't know I existed. Even though he never even knew my name.

Back then, I'd wanted to be a friend.

A guardian angel.

Some years, I only checked in on what was happening in his life sporadically. I knew he'd been permanently excluded from school. I watched as he made new friends with boys that were like him. Boys that understood him, like I did.

But as the years went on, my interest in him changed. I thought about him way more than I should have. I fantasised about him too.

I became obsessed.

Some might say, how could someone like him be followed and watched for so long without knowing? A man that made it

THE REAPER 89

his business to know what was happening in his town. To know everything of importance.

But that was the point.

I wasn't important.

I was a nobody.

A faceless, nameless whisper in the shadows that didn't warrant a second thought.

Most of the people in my day-to-day life found me inconsequential. Why would Devon Brady be any different? And maybe, once upon a time, he had noticed me watching. But if he or any of the other soldiers had seen me, they'd never let on. One quick check into my background would tell them all they needed to know. I was a vicar's daughter, who worked hard at school and got good grades. A loner who played various instruments but never seemed to get anywhere with it. Honest, responsible, reliable, boring.

With credentials like those, who would bat an eyelid?

No. Devon Brady had never known who I was, but I felt like I knew him better than anyone.

He was mine.

A sacred, dark secret that I kept locked in my dark heart. That was until today. Today, two worlds collided when I found him at my door. And I was tired. Tired of living in both of those worlds. I couldn't pretend any longer. I had loved watching from the shadows, but now, I needed more. Now that he finally knew I existed, I wanted to go that little bit further. Like my spirit animal, the raven, I wanted to spread my wings and fight for what I believed in.

With renewed vigour, I stood up, surprising myself at my intention to go over there, but when I saw another figure exit the building, I stayed still. Adam Noble emerged, carrying a dog lead in his hands as he strolled over to Devon. I watched as he spoke a few words to him, then whistled for the dog's attention. When the dog bounded up to him, he bent down and scratched his head, then attached the lead to his collar. Adam strolled away to take the dog for a walk, and Devon took a few steps back, ready to go inside. But I didn't move. My raven had perched itself back on my shoulder and was keeping me in place. So much for flying free.

As he turned to go inside, he lifted his head, and that's when he saw me. For a split second, he stopped dead in his tracks and just stared. Then, as if it was nothing, he disappeared into the asylum. Even standing across the road from him, he'd seen right through me, like I was a ghost from another world.

I took a few deep breaths to calm my nerves, then I shoved my hands into my pockets and kept my head down, marching to the end of the street to go home. I didn't pay attention to anything around me, I just stared blankly at the pavement beneath my feet and tried to block out the voices in my head telling me I needed to get a fucking life.

As I turned the corner and strode forward, I stumbled, almost crashing into a body coming from the opposite direction. Feeling irritated that I'd been disrupted, I looked up with a scowl into the face of the person who'd disturbed my thoughts, a face hidden inside a black hoody that was pulled low over their face. A face, that once I peered closer, made the hairs on the back of my neck stand to attention. Suddenly, everything went from dull black and white to a screeching technicolour that my brain couldn't handle. In front of me, frowning like I was a puzzle he'd never work out, stood Devon. Beautiful, complicated Devon.

Being so close to him again, it was like time stood still. I couldn't stop myself from gazing into his dark green eyes—eyes that seemed as though they could pierce right through my soul. The way his eyebrows arched made it look like he had a permanent stare of wicked intent, and my skin prickled with goosebumps as I shivered, thinking about what that intent could be. His hair was as dark as his stare, and when I glanced at his full lips twisted into a disapproving glower, I knew I had to steel myself for what was about to come. He wasn't here to play nice. He was pissed.

If I'd thought Devon Brady hadn't noticed me before, he certainly had now.

CHAPTER EIGHT
Devon

I thought my mind was playing tricks on me when I saw her in the distance. That sensation that someone was watching had plagued me as I stood with Tyson, waiting for Adam to come down and take him for his walk. I didn't mention anything to Adam, I didn't want to spook him. Plus, it wasn't unusual for me to feel like eyes were on me. It was a hazard of the job, and if I was honest, I'd felt it ever since my stepfather had been taken care of all those years ago. But when I looked up, I never in a million years expected to see her.

Leah May.

Dark hair, pale skin, and eyes that shone with something I wasn't used to seeing in my line of work.

Hope.

That was until she realised I'd seen her, and then I noticed

THE REAPER

something else in her demeanour, not so much fear, more apprehension. Nerves. Embarrassment.

What was she doing here?

I had every intention of letting it go, going inside and carrying on with my day, but she was like poison infecting my mind. Creeping into my brain and squeezing tightly, begging for my attention. Out of nowhere, this girl seemed to have a hold on me, a pull that I couldn't explain. I couldn't let her go without knowing what was going on.

Why had she come here today?

And what the fuck was going on with my reaction to her?

I stormed right through The Sanctuary and out the other end, hoping to catch her in the street. When I saw her, eyes glued to the floor and hands stuffed into her pockets, I felt a burning inside my chest.

Did she need my help?

Was that why she was here?

Was that why I was feeling this way? Because she had a vulnerability that called out to me?

I stood in the middle of the pavement, but she didn't see me, not until it was too late and she was about to bump right into me. I held out my arm to stop her, get her attention, and she jumped back, a grimace marring her delicate features.

Ethereal beauty. That's how I'd describe her. Beauty that was rare, breath-taking, unique, and for me, nothing but heartbreak. I didn't have time for the feelings and emotions stirring inside of me. I wasn't ready to face up to what they meant for a man like me. I wasn't like Adam. There was no room in my life for anyone else. Only the soldiers, the club, my family, and all in that order. It didn't matter that she made the breath catch in my throat or my chest constrict with something I couldn't explain. She was a distraction I couldn't entertain. A force I had to repel.

She stared at me for a moment, her eyes softening as she steadied herself. I kept my body tense, my arms folded over my chest, and my eyes narrowed on her with a stern, fierce glare. I had to appear as if I had my guard up even though my mind was whirling with self-doubt.

"What are you doing here? Did something happen with your cousin?" I asked, my jaw twitching as I waited for her response.

My eyes drifted down to her neck, just like when I'd seen her earlier. I liked how the delicate muscles of her throat contracted as she swallowed nervously. That small action made the beast inside me rear his ugly head. Smooth skin, soft, flawless, so tempting. In another life or another time, I'd have devoured her. Made her mine. Buried myself inside of her and claimed every inch as my own, but that wasn't an option. Not for me. A man like me would destroy a girl like her without even realising. A girl like her needed protecting not possessing.

"No, everything's fine. I... I was just out for a walk," she stammered. I didn't believe her. Not for a second.

"Did you follow me?" I tilted my head, trying to catch a telltale sign in her reaction to confirm that she was lying.

"I didn't follow you." She scoffed, looking hurt and frowning at me. "Why would I do that?"

She wasn't lying. But why was she here?

"Why would you be on the corner of our street watching me? That's a pretty big coincidence after what happened this morning." I noticed the hesitation in her response. She was hiding something.

Did she come to find me because she was in trouble?

THE REAPER

She quickly righted herself and lifted her chin in defiance. Then she gave me a wide, wicked smile and said, "And yet, here I am. Maybe I like watching."

I huffed out a laugh and shook my head. I liked that answer. It showed she had some backbone. She wasn't afraid to stand her ground, stand up to me and challenge me. I still felt pissed that she hadn't given me a proper answer though. If she needed help, I wanted to know.

"You shouldn't be here." I gestured around me to the derelict buildings close by. It wasn't the most scenic route for a Sunday afternoon stroll. Broken bottles, litter, shit all over the street. Even I wouldn't choose to walk here.

"Why not?" She challenged me. "You're here."

"I live here. This is my home, but you don't belong in a place like this."

"Brinton is my home too." She was so naïve. Her version of Brinton was rose-tinted, protected, a far cry from the one we all knew.

"The vicarage is your home. The safe little rectory with its—"

"You don't know anything about me," she spat back defiantly.

I didn't, but something deep inside told me I wanted to. And yet, I felt as if knowing more about her would be like Icarus flying too close to the sun. I wouldn't survive.

"You need to leave," I told her.

"What do you think I was just doing? Practising for the speed walking championships? I *was* on my way home until you stopped me with your giant body taking up the whole pavement."

I had to laugh at her attempt at being angry with me. She was too cute.

"Don't give me stupid answers," I chastised, fighting back a grin.

"Then don't ask stupid questions."

This girl was the definition of a conundrum. I don't think even she could work out what she felt in this moment, and I didn't know whether to laugh or wring her neck.

I leaned towards her to make sure that I made my point clear. Stern, but not nasty. I didn't want to scare her completely. I had to give her a warning. Let her know she needed to be more careful and look after herself.

"Don't come here again. This part of Brinton isn't safe for a girl like you, *Leah May*."

The way her eyes widened as I said her name made my heart beat a little faster.

"And you don't know what a girl like me is capable of, *Devon Brady*."

Fuck me.

Hearing her say my name like that made my dick twitch. I needed her gone. She needed to leave so I could go back to my carefully orchestrated life of self-made mayhem. I didn't do well with chaos I couldn't control. Chaos that came with yearning blue eyes and a full, pouting, smart mouth.

"I'm driving you home," I stated, but she smirked and held her hand up, waving over my shoulder. I turned to see what she was waving at and saw a taxi crawling to a stop beside us.

"No need," she sang, mocking me. "A *girl like me* is capable of finding her own way home."

She bristled with pride at her little victory as she opened

THE REAPER

the car door and jumped into the back seat. Every instinct that I possessed told me she needed protecting, no matter what kind of show she put on to try and fool me into thinking otherwise. My heart screamed at me to get into that taxi and see her safely home. So, I yanked the back door open, climbed in next to her and then shut it behind me. Her head spun around, and she glared across at me and huffed, pretending to be pissed. When she reached over my body, trying to open the door so she could force me to leave, I laughed and batted her away.

"I don't need a chaperone," she hissed. "I'm quite capable…" But her voice became white noise as something caught my eye. There was bruising on her right hand. Fresh bruising.

Without a second thought, I took her injured hand in mine. A spark of electricity jolted through me, but it was nothing compared to the anger I felt at the thought that someone had hurt her.

"What's this? Who did this to you?" I asked, rubbing my thumb gently over her knuckles.

She didn't pull away from me at first, just looked down at our joined hands, then slowly, she slipped her hand out of mine and placed it gently in her lap.

"I caught it in a door. It's nothing."

It wasn't nothing, and the way she looked at me with a sad longing in her eyes told me she wanted me to drop it, but I couldn't. It wasn't in my nature to back down. Just the thought of someone hurting her made me want to rain down hell. If I found out it was actually true, I wouldn't ever be able to hold back.

"You don't get bruises like that from a door. You've hurt your knuckles, not your fingers. Did you have to hit out at someone or something? Were you protecting yourself? If you're in trouble, I can help you."

The cab driver turned around, looking at us with annoyance, and asked, "I haven't got all day. Where to?"

"I'm going to St Michaels vicarage, and he's getting out," Leah May replied sharply, clearly hoping I'd drop it. I wouldn't.

"I'm not leaving this cab, so if you want to get paid, I suggest you drive and pay no fucking attention to anything that's going on back here, am I clear?" The taxi driver shrugged at me and then turned around and pulled away from the kerb. Leah May did a cute impression of a girl trying to look annoyed and tutted under her breath as she turned to look out of the window.

"Fine," she whispered to herself. "If you want to waste your day making pointless journeys to the vicarage, go right ahead."

I ignored her fake snippy response and reiterated, "If I find out someone hurt you, I will be making it my business, you know?"

She didn't look at me, just responded with, "I'll bear that in mind. Thanks for caring."

"It's my job," I snapped back, and suddenly, a stab of guilt hit me at the realisation that I might've made her feel like it was nothing, just business. "I don't like to see women hurt," I added, but it felt like pointless words falling into the air between us.

We travelled in silence for a few minutes, and I saw her, from the corner of my eye, turn and open her mouth to say something. Then she shut it and stared out of the window again, thinking better of it. When I heard her muttering something about ravens, I moved to face her and asked, "What did you just say?"

"Nothing. I didn't say anything."

Her body language indicated that she was feeling defensive.

THE REAPER

I could tell from the hunch of her shoulders, the fact that she wouldn't look at me, and the way her arms were crossed over her chest like she was holding herself back. But then she shifted slightly and turned her head, blushing and widening her eyes at me.

"You did," I carried on, pushing her to respond. "You mentioned ravens."

She opened her mouth again, closed it, and I was about to argue when she bowed her head and whispered, "Did you know the raven is my spirit animal?"

"Why would I know that?" I frowned at her, but she didn't listen, just carried on regardless as she stared absent-mindedly out of the window.

"The raven is a symbol of death. A bad omen. That's according to my research, anyway. But in our country, they say if the ravens ever leave the Tower of London, it'll bring about the downfall of our kingdom. Not such a bad omen for us then, hey?"

"I think we're safe," I replied with a hint of sarcasm, but she continued to ignore me. She clearly wanted to get this off her chest.

"Charles the second instigated a law that six ravens should be kept at the Tower at all times to avoid a disaster. There's seven there now, six and a spare." She gave an ironic little huff then added, "But in Greek mythology, ravens are the bearers of bad news. They're God's messengers in the mortal world, just flying on in to let you know your days are numbered. I don't think the Greeks would want to hang out at the Tower, do you?"

I had no idea what was going on in this girl's mind. I don't think she could keep up either. I'd heard people ramble nervously before, but she was taking it to a whole new level.

"In the bible, Noah released a raven from the ark to see if the floods had stopped. He trusted a raven, but you know what? I googled it and found out that some people believe the raven never returned to the ark, because it was too busy feasting on the corpses of all those that had drowned."

"I thought I was morbid," I joked, and she turned to look right at me, defiance shining in her eyes.

"Odin was the Norse God of wisdom, poetry, and death. If you search his name online, you'll see that he's always pictured with two ravens; one for his eyes and the other for his ears."

I couldn't stop myself from smirking. "You've really done your homework."

I had no idea why she was telling me all this, but then she said the words that made my heart still in my chest.

"The reaper and the raven. One can see death, and the other deals with it. They're a perfect pair."

I didn't know what to say to that. I was speechless.

"You should google it," she said, her eyes penetrating right through me. "There's plenty of paintings of the reaper and the raven. Some people even get tattoos of them both. Where one exists, the other will follow. The scythe and the shadow. A dual reminder that nothing lasts forever."

We pulled up in front of her home, and she turned to me one last time and said, "There's a lot of ways you can interpret things if you look hard enough, but my favourite is to see ravens as symbols of transformation. Freedom. Dark passengers setting people on the correct path from one world to another. A bit like the reaper. He gets a bad rap, but he's only there to make sure you leave this world and arrive safely in the next. He doesn't visit people unless he really has to. He's not so scary."

And with that, she opened the car door and left, walking away and leaving me feeling like I'd just been shot in the chest with an arrow. An arrow that could've come from cupid or the fiercest hunter. Either way, it churned me up inside.

What the hell had just happened?

I heard the driver clear his throat, and then with a mocking, derisive chuckle, he said, "Looks like you dodged a bullet there, mate. She sounded like a right weirdo. Less raven more cuckoo if you ask me."

Fury hit me like wildfire, burning with a hatred from within. Instantly, I lurched forward, grabbing the tie he was wearing and yanking him back in his seat. I pulled tighter to constrict his airways and he started to gasp and gurgle. In a feeble attempt to save himself, he clawed and scraped at the skin around his neck where the tie was choking him, but it was pointless. I had him right where I wanted him, and he knew it.

I wouldn't let up, and leaning forward in my seat I growled in his ear.

"I didn't ask you. And if I ever hear you or anyone else talk shit about her again, I'll string you up with this tie. Do you understand?" He nodded frantically. "You need to learn some fucking manners," I snapped, and let the tie go.

He slumped forward, grabbing the steering wheel like his life depended on it, but I didn't stick around. I pulled a few crumpled notes out of my pocket and threw them down on the passenger seat next to him.

"Keep the change," I sneered, opening the door. "I'd rather walk through fucking hell fire than stay in here with you." And I slammed his door and laughed as he raced off, his tires screeching from the effort he'd put in to his escape.

I stood on the cobbled street outside her home, feeling like my emotions had been stripped back. I was raw, naked and exposed. She spoke like she knew who I was, and she saw me, really saw me.

Where did all that come from, the reaper and the raven?

Who was this girl who'd crashed into my life this morning, talking about symbols and imagery like she was reading a script torn from my very soul?

Was she the universe's way of fucking with me?

A dark angel sent to test my resolve, my patience, and morality?

I took one last glance at her house and then turned to make my way home. I needed the walk to clear my head because right now, I didn't know which way was up and which was down. I was a reaper who worked alone. I didn't need a dark passenger to guide me, or whatever the hell she thought the raven was.

A shadow?

I had enough of those lurking around every corner. Phantoms from a past I tried to keep buried, but they were always ready to strike. In my life, shadows were always bad news, a darkness to steer clear of. I knew enough to know that anything in the shadows was full of evil intent, and that included me.

CHAPTER NINE
Devon

Throughout the week, despite my inner turmoil, I found my mind wandering back to the girl with the raven black hair. The girl who seemed to see straight through me and still smile like she'd witnessed a daydream and not a nightmare.

Why was she always there, dancing through my subconscious?

Did she think about me too when she was alone in her room?

The thought that she might made me grow even more irritable. How could one person have such an effect on me in such a short space of time? It didn't make sense.

By the time the weekend came around, I felt a little reluctant to pay my weekly visit to my mother. I didn't mind popping in to check on her, but she always insisted on a Saturday afternoon family lunch together, and knowing she didn't have much going on in her life, I always felt compelled to show up. I couldn't let her down, no matter how I felt about it. In my life, I did what I wanted, I answered to no one. But when it came to my mother, I had to make allowances. Plus, I got to see my sister, Brooke, so it wasn't all bad.

In all honesty, I didn't mind taking time out to be with them both; it was the other guest that I wanted to avoid. The one who made me want to cut my own ears off so that I didn't have to listen to her.

Stella Shaw.

Vinnie's mother.

My mum always insisted that she came around. She was part of the family, Brooke's grandma, and at times when we were all together, Mum would try to pass her off as mine too. She'd even try to get me to refer to her as gran, but she was no relative of mine. And she hated me as much as I hated her.

As I walked through the door of the home that held memories I didn't want to remember, I could smell my mum's home-cooked roast dinner. Brooke came bounding down the stairs like a Labrador, golden hair flying everywhere and a smile as wide as the Thames to greet me.

"Dev!" she sang, jumping at me and giving me a bear hug.

I loved my little sister. She might have Shaw blood running through her veins, but her heart was all Brady. I'd done a good job at protecting her. He never got a chance to taint her with his darkness. I made damn sure of that.

I pretended to squirm out of her hold, but I couldn't stop myself from placing a kiss on the top of her head. I reached into my jacket pocket and took out the little black box I'd bought for

THE REAPER 105

her and held it in the palm of my hand. She picked it up with a wicked grin on her face and opened it. The way her eyes shone made it worth every penny.

"You got me the firefly this week." She gasped. "It's even better than the moon and stars one you bought last week."

Brooke was collecting charms for her bracelet, and every week I got her a new one to add to her collection.

"You'll need a new bracelet soon for all these charms you're getting," my mum added, coming up behind her. "Hello, love. Have you had a good week?" She kissed me on the cheek, and I hugged her.

"I'm good, Mum. Work's been busy. Can't complain."

As I handed my mum the envelope of cash I always gave her, I heard the familiar sound of scoffing coming from the living room, and I grinned to myself. She could sit there and scowl all she wanted; I'd gotten the last laugh. I was still here.

Mum took the envelope, gave me a knowing smile and patted me on the back as we sauntered into the lounge to join Stella.

"You're a good boy," Mum said, and Stella rolled her eyes. If she saw it, my mum never let on.

"Stella." I said her name in greeting, and an icy smile was thrown back in response.

"Devon." She threw my name out with as much enthusiasm as she felt, which was none. "Where's *my* gift?" she asked, knowing full well there wasn't one. She didn't expect one either, but she liked fucking with me in front of my family.

"I left it back at home. I couldn't fit a ducking stool in the back of my car."

She laughed, but she understood the veiled insult behind

my comment. Well, maybe not so veiled if you knew what I was referring to, which she did. This was how we tolerated each other; innuendo, sarcasm, and when my mum and Brooke weren't around, pure unadulterated hatred.

"Why did you buy Gran a stool?" Brooke asked, wrinkling her nose. "You're weird sometimes."

"He hasn't," Stella replied, sitting up tall in her armchair, ready to deliver another blow. "He just called me a witch."

Brooke covered her mouth as she stifled a laugh, and my mum groaned and slapped me on the arm, then tried to make Stella feel better by adding, "No, he didn't. It was just a joke. You know what Devon's like."

"Yes, I do." Stella narrowed her eyes at me. "He's a regular Tommy Cooper, that one."

"Who's Tommy Cooper?" Brooke asked, frowning.

"A comedian from the eighties. Died on stage," Mum said, fussing around collecting empty mugs ready to make us all a cuppa.

"Sounds about right," Stella added, lifting her nose in the air. "Bet you'd die on stage too. That's if anyone actually bothered to show up."

"Will you two stop?" Mum snapped, standing in the middle of the living room and blowing a stray hair out of her eyes as she huffed at us. "This is family time. Let's enjoy it. Please? We know more than most how important it is to cherish the ones still here." The shine of unshed tears flickered in her eyes. "And that reminds me, I need to tell you something." Mum hesitated and bit her lip as if she was unsure whether to tell me or not. "I saw him again."

I sighed and sat down heavily in the armchair opposite

THE REAPER

Stella.

"Not this again. Mum, I've told you, it's not him. He's not coming back."

This wasn't the first time she thought she'd seen Vinnie. The last time was at the outdoor market across town. I'd sat through hours of CCTV footage that Tyler had downloaded, and it turned out to be some random guy with the same scruffy baseball cap Vinnie sometimes used to wear. The guy didn't even look remotely like him. She was clutching at straws.

But, as ever, my mum wouldn't listen, and Stella just glared at me as Mum carried on regardless.

"It was different this time. Two nights ago, when I was upstairs closing the bedroom curtains for the night, I saw him. He was standing at the end of the road under the lamppost. He had his big black overcoat on, but I could see it was him, clear as day. I'd know him anywhere."

"It wasn't him, Mum." I groaned and rubbed my hands over my face as I felt the daggers Stella was throwing my way.

"It was," she stated firmly. "It was my Vinnie. You think he's still out there too, don't you, Stella?" Mum turned to ask her with hope gleaming in her eyes.

Stella shrugged nonchalantly, failing to show her true feelings, but kept her beady eyes on me.

Mum added, "I don't know what's stopping him from walking back into this house. Maybe he had money troubles, or someone was after him? I don't know because he never told me. But I do know one thing. He's out there somewhere, I can feel it in my bones. One day, you'll walk in here and he'll be sat where you are, as large as life. You mark my words. Vinnie might've gone away for a while, but he's still watching us. And one day soon, this will all be over."

I knew it was bullshit, but I couldn't tell her. My mother lived in eternal hope that Vinnie would come back to her. But I knew better. I dealt in facts. And either my mum had started seeing ghosts, or she was letting her mind play tricks on her again. Either way, it was all complete bollocks, because the place where I'd sent Vinnie to, there was no coming back.

"You keep the dream alive, love," Stella added, standing slowly from the armchair and hobbling over to the dining table in the corner like she was a sweet, frail old lady. I knew better. "That's what he'd want. Never give up." She plonked herself down at the head of the table and glared at me, daring me to challenge her. She knew her words meant nothing, but she'd never let on, not to Mum or Brooke. If anything, she liked our game of cat and mouse; she liked taunting me.

Brooke and I followed her to the table and took our seats.

"Does anyone want a cuppa with dinner, or shall I make a brew after?" Mum asked, like nothing had happened.

"Let's eat first. Tea later." Stella grinned, steepling her fingers in front of her and resting her chin on them as she stared across the table at me.

Mum disappeared into the kitchen, and I got up to follow her and help carry the food to the table.

"It was him," she whispered to me quietly so that Brooke and Stella couldn't hear. "Before he walked away, he did that salute to me that Vinnie always used to do. Why would a stranger standing in our road do that?" She swallowed nervously, then added, "Don't tell Stella about that part. I think she feels jealous that he's never visited her."

I nodded but didn't say a word. The fact that whoever that

was had done that salute made the hairs on the back of my neck stand on end. There was no way it could be Vinnie, but maybe someone was messing with us? Someone who wanted us to think Vinnie was back.

I glanced at the cabinet under the sink, the same one that housed the sedatives I'd used to knock him out that night. Then I looked up at the knife block with half the knives missing. Knives my mum had broken because they were cheap or just getting old, but one had gotten lost for another reason. I'd used it to throw at him when he was slumped on the living room floor, unconscious, just like the darts he threw at me during the sick games he always played. I'll admit that as throwing knives go, it was shit, but it did the job at the time. It let me take my anger out on him. I'd picked up that knife and flung it at his paralysed, drugged-out body so many times the handle had eventually broken with the force of each throw.

I stayed silent, my mind wandering back to that time as I placed the food dishes on the table and took my seat. I picked up my knife and fork, twisting the knife in my hand as I looked at it, and remembered the skinning knife I'd stolen from the hardware store in town. The knife I'd used to cut, gouge, and scalp as best I could. I felt Stella's eyes on me, but I didn't look up. I let my mum fuss about, filling up my plate with food as I sat there in a trance.

It wasn't Mum's knife that killed him, or the skinning knife. I took inspiration from the worst game he'd ever played with me when I took my final stab of revenge.

Tug of war.

When he played tug of war with me, he'd used rope tied to various parts of my body and pulled. They all pulled. I was dragged around by my legs, chained to the radiator as they used force to create their own version of the rack. Then they'd unchained me and strapped my arms up, hanging me from the beams in our living room until it felt like my arms would pop out of their sockets. But it was when they put the rope around my neck that I lost it. They laughed as they pulled the rope and hung me from the wooden beams, only releasing me just in time, just before I lost all consciousness. And then, once I'd coughed and gasped, and managed to gain some form of composure, they did it all again. I thought I was going to die that night. It was only by pure luck that I didn't, because they didn't care.

I hadn't used rope to tug on Vinnie's neck as I squeezed the last ounce of breath from him. I used his belt and threaded it around his neck, then I put my feet on his back, and I pulled with everything I had to tighten the leather around him. I cut off his air supply until he was gone. Taken out of this world like the piece of crap he was. It wasn't easy after that, to roll his body onto the tarpaulin that I'd found in the garage and drag him down the garden. It made my arms burn and almost give way as I pulled his weight into the alley at the back of our house, and across the short distance to the canal. But if anyone wanted to know exactly where Vinnie Shaw was, it wasn't lurking on street corners throwing out hand gestures to my mum. He was at the bottom of Brinton canal, along with some bricks I'd placed on top of the plastic covers to weigh him down. He'd never been found. Never washed up anywhere. But I knew he was where he belonged, swimming with the filth at the bottom of the water. Only me and four other people knew what'd happened that night.

Me and my best friends. My soldiers.

It was one of the many secrets I'd shared with them, just like they'd shared secrets with me. We knew we'd take those secrets to the grave.

I buried the memories and the sour taste they left behind and ate my lunch, listening to Mum tell us all the pointless gossip from her workplace that week. Brooke shared a few stories from school. But Stella and I stayed quiet.

When the meal was over, Brooke helped Mum clear the plates from the table, and when it was just Stella and I sitting together, she hissed in a low voice so only I could hear, "I know all about you."

I sat back in my chair, and with my hands stretched out in front of me, palms down on the table, I cocked my head and replied, "Oh yeah? What? What do *you* know?"

"You're the reason he's gone."

I smirked and shook my head at her feeble attempt to unnerve me by insinuating that she knew something she didn't.

"You're getting old, Stella. Losing your marbles." I leaned forward in my chair, pinning my stare on her to make sure she knew I meant business. To show her she didn't affect me. "I've done nothing."

She huffed sarcastically. "We both know that's rubbish." She moved forward herself and hissed, "You're an evil little shit, and he always hated you. I've been to the police, you know. I've told them all about what kind of a boy you are, you and those degenerates who call themselves soldiers that you run around with. One day, they'll throw you in jail where you belong. I'll go to my death bed happy, knowing you're all rotting away."

"You're a crazy woman." I shook my head then lowered my gaze, giving her a warning glare. "But if I were you, I'd be careful what you're saying and to who. I wouldn't want you heading to that death bed before your time."

"Are you threatening me?"

"Of course not. I don't hurt women." I smiled and sat back again, giving her an air of confidence that I knew would piss her off.

"One of these days, I'll wipe that smug smile off your face, *Devon*."

Just then, my mum and Brooke walked into the room, and I gave a low, patronising chuckle.

"I'll look forward to it, *Gran*."

CHAPTER TEN
Devon

I stalked back into the sanctuary a few hours later, still feeling pissed about my face-off with Stella. I slammed the door behind me, keeping my head down and heading for the stairs. I needed to go and work off some of my tension. But when I got to the first step, I stopped and backtracked. Some random guy I'd never seen before was handcuffed to the banister. Life was never dull when you lived here.

"I see you've met our new friend, Ross." Colton's voice echoed through the empty building as he strolled down the stairs.

"Who the fuck is this?" I gestured to him with my hand, and Colton laughed.

"It's Ross. I just told you."

"And why is he tied to our staircase?"

"Because this little fucker needs to be taught a lesson, don't you, mate?"

Colton came to stand next to me, and he stared down at Ross sitting on the bottom step.

"I caught him trying to steal tools off the back of a builder's van this afternoon. This cheeky fucker thinks it's okay to steal from honest, hard-working men. But I don't."

Colton stepped forward then kicked the guy hard in the shin. Ross flinched but he didn't retaliate or try to fight back, just cursed quietly under his breath.

"You thought taking someone's livelihood, the tools that help him put food on his family's table, was okay, didn't you? Thought you wouldn't get caught?" Colton knelt to look straight into Ross's eyes, even though Ross was hanging his head in shame. "But it's not all right, is it? It's not okay to take from a man and sell his shit at the local pub for fuck all, so you can get your next fix."

I had intended to get a quick shower in before I gave the security briefing tonight and did all my checks for the club, but it looked like Colton had other ideas. I had to admit, with the tension I had bubbling under the surface after my encounter with Stella earlier, I was fully on board.

"We need to move him to the chapel or the warehouse. I don't want to get blood on the floor in here," I said, and Ross gasped.

I don't know why he was surprised. He'd been asking for trouble coming around here and taking what didn't belong to him. So, the fact he'd found trouble with us was all his own fault. Trouble was what we lived for.

"We'll move him. All in good time." Colton smiled as he

stood up and placed himself right in front of Ross. "Me, Adam, and Will are going to sort this. You and Tyler can get started on the checks for tonight." With a patronising grin, he slapped Ross on the cheek and added, "It's nothing that a little rap on the knuckles with a hammer won't cure."

"I don't think so," I argued through gritted teeth, but at that moment, Adam appeared behind me.

"You won't miss anything," Adam stated. "And you're the best one at briefing the staff. You've got a good rapport with them."

He spoke sense; I knew that, but I still didn't like it.

"If someone is getting taught a lesson, I want in." I wasn't ready to back down.

"And if it was any other time, I'd say have at it, but he's a ball ache we don't need right now." Adam gestured to Ross, who sat cowering on the step. "He won't be getting our full experience, just a clear reminder of what the rules are around here." He turned to face me and added, "And after what happened last week, with the girl in the private room, we need to stay on top of things here. I don't want a single thing going wrong tonight. Don't see it as missing out on a hit. He's not a mark—"

"He's a shit stain," Colton added, and Adam rolled his eyes.

"As I said, he's not a mark, just a fucking inconvenience. This is me delegating and making sure we're all playing to our strengths. Your strength is this place. Focus on that."

I wasn't happy, but I accepted Adam's reasoning. I *was* the best at running this place. I took pride in it. In a matter of hours, we'd be opening those doors to the public, and business needed taking care of. Will, Adam, and Colton were more than capable of teaching some low-life street rat a lesson without me.

"Fine," I said, making my way slowly up the stairs. "Call me if you need me. Oh, and Colton? Maybe try a sledgehammer instead of a standard hammer. The long handle will give you more momentum for a better, harder swing, and the larger, metal head will create more damage. It's the wider surface area, you see. Less cracking, more smashing."

And with that, I made my way back to my room, smiling as I heard Colton say to Ross, "Seeing as you like tools so much, I can't wait to show you the ones Devon has collected in his battle store."

A battle store.

I liked that description, and in many ways, we were fighting a war, but in others we weren't because wars end, and what we were faced with day-in-day-out was never going to end. Human nature would always harbour this curse, the virus in society. All we could do was hold back the flood. Do whatever we could for the common man. Give people hope in a world where hope didn't exist, not really. Not for us, anyway.

Once I was inside my room, I closed the door behind me. Feeling the weight of my mother's guilt, I sat down on my bed, gazing out of the window. There was a flutter against the glass as a blackbird landed on my windowsill, stared at me for a moment, then flew off into the dusky evening sky. Instantly, it made me think about her, the little raven who seemed to be flitting around my mind, pecking away at my subconscious.

The raven and the reaper.

Even though there were a million and one things I should be doing, things that needed my attention, I pulled my phone out and opened Google. I typed 'the reaper and the raven' into the search bar, just like she'd suggested, and clicked on the images.

THE REAPER

Paintings, cartoons, graphics of a dark, shadowed reaper flanked by a raven flooded my phone screen. I scrolled, fascinated by the imagery, the idea that the dark visitor had a dark passenger, a shadowed friend.

It felt like fate was tapping me on the shoulder with her bony finger. Pointing things out to me that I wasn't ready to acknowledge. My life already had a shitload of chaos piped through it like fucking Blackpool rock. I didn't need a girl thrown into the mix to add to that. And yet, I couldn't get her out of my head. She'd set up home there. Taken roost like the bird she seemed to love so much.

I threw my phone down onto the bed and headed into the shower. I needed to clear my head and get ready for what the night had in store for us. No distractions, no complications. That would be my motto.

I didn't need a raven to be the best reaper I could.

CHAPTER ELEVEN
Devon

A few hours later, after giving the staff the lowdown on how things were going to run tonight, I strolled into our living room to find a three-tier wedding cake sitting on the kitchen counter. On the top were two figures; one a bride dressed in white, the other was Shrek.

"That's Colton's idea of a joke," Liv announced, walking in behind me. "And if you think that's bad, you should've been here when Adam saw the box of sex toys he bought us as a wedding present." She huffed out a smile and added, "His face when Colton told him toys weren't his competition, and to see them as his tag team. Priceless."

"I'm not sure I want to know if he came around to the idea." And from the way she smirked, I didn't need to ask; I could tell what the answer was.

"He was just pissed that another guy had bought them. You know Adam. He likes control."

Liv came to stand next to me and started pulling open drawers, taking out a butter knife, and then rooting through the fridge.

"Adam's working the ground floor with you tonight," she told me as she grabbed the bread from the side and placed two slices on the counter.

I stole a slice of ham from the pack she'd taken out ready to use and said, "If it's the same as most Saturday nights, we shouldn't have a problem. I'll send him back to you and cover it all with the main security. It'll be fine."

She smiled and picked up a hastily thrown together ham sandwich, thrusting it in my direction before getting busy making another.

"Eat. You don't look after yourself. And don't take on too much, Devon. You're not superman. I think I can survive a few hours without Adam stalking me. Who knows? I might even get to shower on my own."

At that moment, Adam strode in and stated gruffly, "Where's the fun in that?"

He picked up a sandwich from the counter and started eating, winking at Liv as he did. I wanted to ask him about the lesson he'd just taught the guy downstairs, but I thought better of it. I doubted he'd want to discuss it that freely in front of Liv, despite his insistence that she was kept in the loop.

They started bantering with each other, and I heard Adam mention some guy called Ronnie. I really didn't want to know, I was too busy running through the security checks in my head, focusing on the night to come. So, I left Adam, Liv, and her giggles about Ronnie behind and headed to the ground floor.

***

Once the night was underway and the clubbers were flooding through our doors, the others took their places on duty. According to Colton, Ross—the thief that wouldn't be so handy from now on—had been taken care of and sent on his way. He was a nobody. Not worth the distraction. All that mattered now was making sure everything ran smoothly at The Sanctuary. Our reputation in this business meant as much to me as our reputation as soldiers. I prided myself on doing a good job, keeping the floor running like clockwork.

It was another busy night, and the dance floor was already heaving. The DJ was playing *Heathens, 'The Koosen Remix'*, and I was just thinking how apt the lyrics were and that he'd probably chosen it for us, when the hairs on the back of my neck started to prickle. I always felt like I had a sixth sense for bullshit, and I listened to my gut when I needed to. Something, or rather somebody, was about to test my patience. I turned, bracing myself for what I might find behind me, and when I saw her, I stopped dead in my tracks.

Leah May.

My little raven.

What the hell was she doing here?

Judging from the way she was glancing around nervously and sipping on the straw in her drink, she was on her own. That fact alone made me want to react, and not in a good way.

Did she have no concept of self-preservation?

In the short time that I'd gotten to know her, I could tell she

THE REAPER

was too trusting, too open. The perfect target for some of the vultures that circled around Brinton.

She was wearing a tight black dress, cut way too short for my liking, and I clenched my jaw. No man had the right to expect any woman to dress a certain way, so why was it bothering me that her skirt was short and showing off her legs? Since when did I turn into that asshole? If I carried on thinking this way, I'd have to kick my own ass.

Her black hair hung in waves down her back, and I tried to steady my breath as I thought about wrapping that hair around my fist, pulling her head back, seeing her neck twisted as she gazed up at me.

No.

Thoughts like that about a girl like her had no place haunting my mind. She was a fucking vicar's daughter, for Christ's sake. And yet, she looked anything but holy tonight. The taste of sin and corruption was all too tempting. *She* was all too tempting, and I felt all kinds of wrong for wanting to explore what could never be.

I watched her for a moment, lost in her world, oblivious to the stares she was getting from men around her. Stares that made me want to tear someone's eyeballs out. When a guy close by decided to tap her on the shoulder and try to talk to her, I couldn't stand it anymore, and without thinking about the consequences, I stalked right over there.

Once I was behind her, I glared over her shoulder at the guy trying to chat her up. His cocky face glared right back at me, so I made sure he got the message crystal clear.

"Fuck off. She's with me."

Leah May turned around when she heard my growling,

snarly voice, and her eyes widened.

"We were having a conversation," cocky guy spat back, and it took every ounce of restraint I had not to punch him for daring to answer me back. Who the fuck did he think he was?

I squared my shoulders, folded my arms over my chest and stated plainly, "Conversation's over. Like I said, she's with me."

I could feel the thump of my heartbeat banging against my chest, adrenaline racing through my veins in anticipation of a battle that he wouldn't win, and I would revel in. The music in the club was doing an excellent job at drowning out the screech of white noise in my ears. I didn't like being challenged, and certainly not in front of her. This man was pushing his luck and shredding the last nerve I was holding on to. When I looked down at Leah May, I expected to see something akin to fear or defiance, but all I saw was a strange look of awe sparkling in her eyes.

Did she like that I'd developed a possessiveness over her tonight?

"Whatever." The guy shrugged like it meant nothing and hid the fact that he probably felt like a prize dick for being shot down, and he turned back around to talk to his friends.

I took a few breaths to steady myself, but as I leaned down to whisper in her ear over the noise of the music, I couldn't stop myself from putting an arm around her waist and pulling her closer to me. Seems it wasn't enough to look at her, talk to her, or have her close. No, I needed to touch her too. Judging from the burning sensation that I felt in my gut, I liked it. She must've too, because she didn't pull away, only melted further into me.

"You never learn, do you?" I whispered, closing my eyes and inhaling the sweet smell of her hair and perfume. "I thought

THE REAPER 123

I told you to stay away."

She tilted her head up slightly and replied, "And I thought you'd learned that I don't like being told what to do."

I kept my arm around her, holding her tightly. She fitted against me perfectly, and when she rested her hand on my chest and looked up into my eyes, I felt as if the rest of the world had fallen away. Birds weren't meant to be caged, but this little raven seemed to like being caught by me. I liked it too.

I picked up her hand to inspect the bruising on her knuckles. In this light, it didn't look that bad, but I still asked, "Are you still hurting?"

"Not from the bruises on my hand," she said, and when I frowned at that response, she added, "I'm fine. It's faded and all I have left is a bruised ego. I need to remember paperweights are deadly weapons too sometimes."

My stomach twisted with the realisation that she wasn't telling me the truth. I didn't like being lied to.

"I thought you said you trapped your hand in a door?"

Her eyes went wide, but not in awe this time. She knew she'd been caught out.

"I did. I'm just talking rubbish. Ignore me."

I wasn't about to ignore her. She might talk in rhymes and weird cryptic shit sometimes, but I could tell when someone was lying to me, and she was lying.

"What's going on, Leah May? Why are you here?" I needed her to tell me the truth. I also needed her to ease the ache that was piercing my heart and my stomach. Holding her was helping somewhat, but I had to have more.

"I came to enjoy myself. That's allowed, isn't it?"

Her eyes told me what her words couldn't; she wanted to

see me, that's why she was here. Her rapid breaths told me even more; she liked being in my arms.

"Is Jodie here? Did you come with her?" I asked, but what I really wanted to say was, if you're lonely or you need my help, just ask. I need words. I'm not the best mind reader.

"No. Jodie doesn't know I'm here."

I sighed, toying with my inner demons that screamed at me, telling me she wasn't mine. I had no right to tell her what to do. If she wanted to have a night out, it was none of my fucking business. And yet, I was still pissed because I wanted her to listen and do as she was told. I wanted to know what was going on in her head. I wanted to know everything.

"Look, this place is as safe as we make it, but I can't protect you. Not all the time. Especially when you pull shit like this."

"Like what?" she challenged, her chin lifting defiantly.

"Coming out on your own."

She huffed and shook her head, looking around the crowded room and biting her lip, and then she glared back at me.

"Who said I'm on my own? Look at all these people around me."

Strangers, not people. She didn't know them, and I knew enough about human nature to know you can't trust people.

"You didn't come here with anyone, did you? Don't bullshit me, Leah. We run a tight ship here but look at what almost happened to Jodie. If you want to go clubbing, go with friends. Don't do it on your own." It was on the tip of my tongue to add, 'or call me,' but I didn't.

I felt her tense in my arms and she reared backwards, but I couldn't let her go. Not yet.

"That's a pretty sexist statement you just made," she said

angrily. "Why can't a girl be on her own? Why is it her fault if something goes wrong and not the person who chooses to be a dick that night and hurt her?"

She was right, of course. But life didn't always work out the way you wanted it to. It's why our vigilante skills were so in demand. Life was unfair and true justice was rarely served, legally anyway. I didn't want Leah May to become a statistic or a victim who needed our services. I'd rather die than let that happen.

"I didn't say it would be your fault. I just… worry—" I cut myself off. I didn't want to come across as a misogynist shithead, but after holding her in my arms, it made me feel a level of protection I'd never felt before. It made me feel possessive. Men were noticing her, and that didn't sit well with me. In reality, I'd known this girl for five minutes, I'd had barely any interaction with her, and yet, something about her just called out to me, affected me. It felt as though she was mine to protect.

"How is Jodie?" I asked, trying to change the subject and steer away from the male chauvinism I seemed to have developed.

"She's fine," she snapped. She was still a little pissed at me, but then she softened again, and staring at the floor, she added, "I don't think it's actually sunk in what could've happened to her that night if you hadn't shown up."

"It could've been a lot worse."

She lifted her chin up to stare straight at me, strength oozing from her as she did.

"Yes. It could've. But thank God it wasn't, and we have you to thank for that."

She looked at me then like the fucking sun shone out of my

ass, and I don't know why, but I couldn't handle it. I wasn't a fucking hero, far from it. I'd never want her to know exactly how fucking far though. That was shit that could break a girl like her. Antiheroes at their finest, that was what we were. Evil wrapped in good intentions.

She pulled away from me, and letting go of her felt wrong, but I let my arms fall to the side anyway and ignored the ache in my chest.

"Dance with me?" she asked suddenly, her eyes shining with a glint of hope. The thought of letting her down made the words in my throat feel like they'd travelled through razor blades to get out.

"I'm working."

She frowned and put her hands on her hips.

"You can't take five minutes off to dance with me?"

I never took time off, but with her standing in front of me, looking at me like she was, I wanted to fight my own instincts and say yes.

"No, I can't. And anyway, I don't dance."

"Everyone dances." She gave a gentle laugh. She wasn't mocking me, she was trying to put me at ease, but normal people danced. I wasn't normal.

"I don't."

She sighed and opened her mouth to say something, then thought better of it and took a few steps away from me before shrugging. "Okay." And then she walked off towards the dance floor.

Holding her in my arms had felt like everything, and now I was letting her go like a fucking loser. I hated my emotionally stunted self sometimes. This was why I didn't get attached; I didn't do relationships. I was shit at it. So why even try? Why make the effort if you're only setting yourself up to fail?

But you can't win if you don't play the game.

I ignored the whisper in my head giving me false hope, but I couldn't seem to engage my brain and walk away. My feet were planted firmly in place, watching her every move.

For a girl that seemed so meek and mild, she had no fear when it came to finding a space on the dance floor and letting the music take her away. Her hips swayed in time to the beat, her eyes drifting closed as she mouthed along to the words of the song, and when the DJ started to play the *Jazmin Bean* remix of *'I'm a Slave 4 U'*, I felt myself morph into some kind of fucking caveman. The urge to stalk over to her and throw her over my shoulder was like nothing I'd ever felt before. Raw, animalistic, natural, that's what it felt like.

But then it happened.

That gut-wrenching moment that I knew in my bones would come.

The guy from earlier appeared behind her, put his arms around her and pulled her back to his front, grinding against her.

He could've charged through this club wielding a machete and I wouldn't have felt any less violent than I did right now. It didn't matter that she was pushing him away, showing him she wasn't interested. He'd put his hands on her, and that was enough for me.

I flew across the dance floor, not caring who I knocked out of the way, and the instant I got to where they were, I clenched my fist and smacked him as hard as I could in the jaw.

One punch and he went down like a sack of potatoes. I wasn't finished with him though. All I could see in my mind was his sweaty hands all over her, his face next to hers, pouring God knows what kind of filth in her ear. His body close to her, grinding on her. I leant over and grabbed the front of his shirt, pulling him up off the floor so I could get another punch in. As I did, I felt hands pulling me back, arms stopping me from lurching forward again to get to him, and then Adam's voice in my ear.

"Not here. We've got you, mate. But let's take this outside."

At that exact moment, one of the guy's friends came over and put his hand on Adam's arm to talk to him, but Adam shrugged him off and glared at him like he was about to knock him out too.

"There's no need to take anything outside," the guy pleaded, holding his hands up. "He's drunk and he didn't know what he was doing. We should've stopped him from going near her, but I swear to you, he means no harm. We don't want any trouble. He's an annoying twat when he's had a drink, but he's harmless. Honestly."

"It's not up to you whether there's trouble or not," Adam hissed, getting right into his face.

There was tension in the air that was growing by the second, and we were ready to fight when Liv suddenly appeared and stood in-between Adam and the guy. She grabbed Adam's face in her hands, and staring right into his eyes she said, "Stop. It's not worth it. Go outside and calm down. Calm Devon down. Gav is sorting this guy out. He'll make sure he's barred and never steps foot in here again. I'll look after the girl. That's all that matters. Nothing else. Go and get your shit together."

If anyone else had done what she did, they wouldn't be left standing. But Adam took a few deep breaths, nodded reluctantly, then bent down to kiss her. Once he'd quietened his demons, he turned to face me.

"Outside. Now," he barked. He knew that right now, my demons would take a lot longer to conquer than his.

I watched Gaz, and a few of the other security men pull the guy away, ready to throw him out. I didn't like that it felt as though I was standing down—soldiers never stood down, it was our motto, but when I saw Liv put her arms around Leah May and lead her to the foyer at the front of the club where it was quieter, I knew I had to sort my fucking head out. I didn't know what'd gotten into me—well, I did, but I didn't want to admit it, even to myself. I was fucking losing it.

Reluctantly, I headed out of the club through the fire exit, and when I got outside, I saw Adam, Colton, Tyler, and Will all staring at me.

"So, are you going to tell us what the fuck all that was all about?" Adam asked.

"Someone danced with his girl. He got pissed. End of," Colton answered, shrugging and sparking up a cigarette.

"She's not my girl," I spat back, and Colton smirked.

"Yeah, because you always go around punching random guys on a Saturday night for no fucking reason. Adam's the psycho who acts before he engages his brain. You're the one who thinks first, remember? We know you." Colton glanced across to where Adam was throwing him daggers. "Sorry, mate. But you know I'm right. Before Liv, you were a bit of a loose cannon."

"I still am a loose cannon if I need to be," Adam growled, lifting his chin in challenge and stepping towards Colton.

"Just for one minute, can we focus on what we came out

here for?" Tyler intercepted. "Everyone needs to calm the fuck down. Colton, stop being an asshole. We don't need your smart-ass comments, not tonight. Devon, mate, I've no idea what's going on, but if that was your girl in there, tell us. Take a night off. Do whatever the fuck you need to do. We're all entitled to have a meltdown every now and again. Look at Adam when he was chasing Liv. A fucking disaster zone."

"Fuck you," Adam spat back, but even he knew there was some truth in what Tyler was saying.

"See?" Tyler stated. "That's my point right there. We're a team, but sometimes, Ad, you give the impression it's you against the world. It's not. Never will be. And Will?" He turned to look at Will, who was standing with us with a look of bewildered amusement on his face. "I have no fucking clue what to say to you, but I didn't want to leave you out."

"I appreciate the sentiment," Will replied with a smirk.

Tyler took a deep breath and looked at us each in turn, then added, "I think you should talk to Adam. He's been through this; he knows what you're going through. He went through it with Liv."

I shook my head in protest. "It's not the same. She's not my—"

"Don't bullshit us. We saw what happened. I saw the look on your face when that guy went near her. I saw the way you held her too. You might not be ready to admit it, but that girl in there? She means something to you. Don't fuck it up, she looks like a good girl. Another Liv, maybe, if you're lucky. She could be the best thing that ever happens to you."

I didn't do wishful thinking. I did reality, truths, and bare facts.

"She isn't mine. She's just a girl that needs protecting. And anyway, she's Father Johnson's daughter. Why would I go there?"

"Why the fuck not?" Colton gave one of his evil cackles. "Repressed church girl? Daddy's little princess? Just think of all the fun you could have smashing those… barriers down."

He winked, and I lurched forward, but Adam held me back and said, "It doesn't matter whose daughter she is. This is obviously fucking with his head. You making jokes and innuendos isn't helping, Colton." He took his phone out of his pocket and swiped the screen to life. "Olivia is taking her home. So, that's one problem taken care of."

The caveman that'd set up home in my brain suddenly reared back to life.

"What do you mean she's taking her home? I haven't fucking spoken to her yet."

"I thought you didn't care?" Colton smirked. "She isn't yours."

Usually, I could take Colton's crap, but not today. "Say one more fucking word…"

"Do not go chasing after her," Adam spoke up, pre-empting my own thoughts and actions.

"Says the guy who spent months stalking a girl into becoming his wife," Colton joked, but he was treading a very thin line.

Adam ignored him and stood in front of me, and in a firm voice he said, "Go upstairs. Take a fucking minute and try to remember the advice you gave me a few months ago. She's probably scared right now. Vulnerable maybe. Olivia will talk to her on the drive home, it's what she does. She'll make sure she's okay. Then tomorrow, or the next day, you sort it out. Whatever the fuck *it* is."

Adam was right, and if I was giving myself advice, that's exactly what I would say. When I was sane, in my right mind, and thinking straight.

I needed to give myself space too, not just her.

The reactions I was having weren't normal for me, especially since I'd only just met this girl. Nothing made sense anymore. My brain felt like it'd been rewired and didn't work properly. It was misfiring all over the damn place. I needed to get a grip, get myself back on track and start behaving like the leader I knew I was. A soldier dedicated to the cause. Not a weak ass who acted out at the slightest thing.

Those blinkers and my walls needed reinforcing, and quickly. The little raven needed to be set free, and so did I. She was too fragile for my world, and I was too brutal for hers.

CHAPTER TWELVE
Leah May

'There is freedom waiting for you, on the breezes of the sky. And you ask, "What if I fall?" Oh, but my darling, "What if you fly"

Erin Hanson

Earlier today, I'd sat on my bed staring at the poster that was stuck to my wall with that quote on it. A poster that hung above the ornate birdcage that housed all my origami ravens. The same poster my mum gave me when I was twelve years old to remind me not to overthink so much, to try and be brave. My mum was the only person I'd ever really spoken to about the self-doubt that plagued me. She knew about the damning voices in my head, and before she died, they'd gotten better, less invasive. But now, I'd just learned to live with them.

But more recently, I'd noticed they didn't sound so loud when he was around. Sitting in a taxi with him, standing in the street, even on my doorstep, the voices had quietened. Probably because they were drowned out by every other sense that was on high alert when I was near him, but it was a win. I'd take it. Previously, I'd used my instruments to give me peace. But I liked that I got actual silent, solitary serenity from Devon. That's what spurred me on to take another leap of faith.

I'd always wondered what The Sanctuary would be like inside. Always felt tempted to take a step into the unknown, but something had always held me back. Probably the thought of all the people in there, crowds surrounding him, wanting his attention. I didn't really like crowds. I preferred to watch from afar, when he was alone or with others that he could be himself around. This Saturday had been different. After our last few interactions, I found myself wanting to know more about him. I wanted to know everything. I craved it.

So, I'd ignored the voices that told me,

It isn't the place for you.
You'll make yourself look like a fool.
What makes you think he'll even notice you in a room full of beautiful people.

And I put on my favourite little black dress, curled my hair and applied light makeup. Soon enough, I'd managed to turn the voices to,

You look so different.
I like this look on you.

THE REAPER

You need to get out more, girl. Take that bull by the horns.

I took one last glance in the mirror, loving what I saw reflecting back at me, and I smiled, clenching the fist that a week ago I'd used to slam into this damn mirror.

Walking into The Sanctuary, I held my head high. I had as much right to be there as everyone else, and I wanted to live a little. I'd scanned the room a few times, it was so busy that it was hard to see amongst the crowds and the dimmed lighting, but I couldn't see him. Maybe he wasn't working tonight? That'd be just my luck. Come all this way, all dressed up, and never get a chance to actually see him.

I'd bought myself a drink and noticed a few men looking my way as I walked away from the bar. I had intended to head to a quiet corner for the night and wait to see what would happen, but a guy had stood in my way and started to talk to me. I didn't want to be rude, so I let him get all his ridiculous chat-up lines out, but I was ready to let him know I wasn't looking for anything and I was here for the music, that's all.

But I didn't need to.

The prickle of goosebumps that'd spread over my whole body when I heard his deep, gruff voice over my shoulder, telling the guy to, "Fuck off. She's with me," had made me tingle. My head swam in reaction to the nerves that had hit my stomach and charged through my body like that bull I was supposed to be taking by the horns.

She's with me.

I loved how that sounded. Like I was his. Like he didn't want anyone else near me, and I turned to look up into his eyes. I thought I saw a hint of possessiveness, jealousy even. But then, when the guy walked away, it was replaced by something else.

Was he annoyed with me?

The Devon that stood in front of me tonight was a far cry from the surly enigma that I was used to seeing stalking around in the shadows of Brinton Manor. Instead of his trademark dark hoody and jeans, he wore a black suit, white shirt, and black tie. Vigilante gangster chic looked good on him, and it smelt good too. I inhaled slowly, trying not to show that I was breathing him in as he leered over me. But my hazy sunshine was soon eclipsed by dark clouds.

"You never learn, do you?" he questioned angrily. "I told you to stay away."

His words would've cut deeper had it not been for the protective arm he put around me, pulling me closer to him, letting me feel the warmth of his body. A solid, strong body that made me want to melt right there on the spot. The feel of his breath on my cheek, against my neck... damn, I felt him everywhere. I couldn't think straight, so I stood my ground and argued back. I fought for what I wanted.

Him.

When he lifted my hand and asked me how I was feeling, I damn near lost my mind—I definitely lost my train of thought, and I started wittering on about paperweights, totally forgetting that I'd given him a different story to the one I'd told my dad. I couldn't ever think straight around him.

But then things took a turn. He started to say that he couldn't protect me and argued about the fact that I was out, alone. I didn't want him to see me as some weak female. I wasn't weak. I had weaknesses, but didn't everyone? And I wasn't some foolish little girl he had to take care of. I didn't want to be seen as a burden. My mind spiralled, veering from defending myself to trying to see things from his point of view. And then he hit me with the killer line, "I worry."

Inside, my heart screamed, *'He does think about you. He worries. He cares.'* And so, I squared my shoulders, cleared my mind of any doubts and asked him to dance with me. I wanted to entice him, draw him out, make him see me as something more than Jodie's cousin. A little bit quirky and a whole lot awkward, with a side helping of paranoia and insecurity. I wanted to be his equal. I *was* his equal. He just couldn't see it yet.

I took to the dance floor, and closed my eyes, dancing like only he was watching. But my doubts didn't stay hidden for long. When I felt arms wrap around me, I knew instinctively they weren't his. Then, in a flurry of chaos, Devon flew across the dance floor and punched the guy who'd grabbed me. The same guy that'd tried to chat me up earlier. The fury that radiated from him was palpable. The anger in his eyes was terrifying. And I couldn't shake the guilt that I'd brought this on myself. It was all my fault. Why did that guy have to dance up to me? Why couldn't I dance on my own without being touched? Why the fuck had I thought it'd be a good idea to come here tonight?

Adam and a few of the others stormed the dance floor, and when Adam said, "Not here. Take this outside," my guilt intensified.

I'd watched Devon for long enough to know he didn't like to lose control in front of others. He always held his restraint in public. In private, it was another matter, but in public, he was the master of self-restraint, self-discipline, and quiet control. This was the worst time and place for that to be compromised. This was his business, his livelihood. I felt ashamed. Angry that the guy had put me in that position, but ashamed all the same.

The other soldiers steered Devon away, and some girl came up to me, flanked by a security guy. If my shame wasn't written all over my face before, it was now.

"Hey," the girl said, pulling me gently from the dance floor towards the foyer at the front of the building. "I'm Liv. Are you okay? Do you want to come upstairs and have a drink to calm your nerves?"

I shook my head. I didn't want to be here anymore. I needed to leave.

"I'm just going to go," I said, turning and heading for the door, but Liv held out her hand to stop me.

"You don't have to go," she said with a look of concern etched into her brow, but I wasn't staying. I'd made up my mind. The damage had been done, and I needed to go away to lick my wounds.

***

Liv drove me home that night, all the time trying to get me to open up about how I knew Devon and whether something was going on. I gave her vague, evasive responses, instead steering the conversation towards subjects I felt comfortable sharing, like my dad's latest church group, my music, or just plain silence. When she eventually pulled up in front of my house, I thanked her for her kindness and got out, not once looking back as I ran inside and locked the door.

And so, here I was, sitting and staring at the poster on the wall, wondering why I hadn't flown high like it'd promised. I prayed that when I next saw Devon, he'd let me down gently.

THE REAPER

Because despite the way he'd held me in the club, I knew he didn't feel the same way I did. And knowing that hurt more than any fist on a mirror.

You always thought you knew him better than anyone, but you don't.
If you really knew him, the night would've worked out differently.
Maybe it's time to give up.
Throw in the towel.
He won't ever be yours, you're kidding yourself if you think otherwise.

There went the voices again, always challenging me, always thinking they knew better, but I knew one thing for sure. This obsession with Devon Brady would either make or break me, probably the latter, but I needed to find out one way or another. I had to see this through to the end, whatever end that may be. I would go down fighting. I was no weak woman, and even if I walked away, never to see him again, I had to prove that.

I had to keep my dignity.

CHAPTER THIRTEEN
Leah May

I took out my new notebook from the drawer at the side of my bed and opened it up. At the top of the first page, I wrote the title, 'Operation find your backbone', and started to list some of the things that I could do to get a bloody grip on my life. Mum always said it was easier to think when you wrote things down. The ideas wouldn't get stuck in your head and cloud your judgement. If you put them down on paper, you might start seeing the wood for the trees—at least that's what she used to tell me. I hated that saying. When I looked at trees, I didn't even see wood, only nature.

Thinking about nature made my mind wander to other things, and I began daydreaming about one of my favourite memories of watching Devon.

On the last Friday of every month, Devon would call on

his neighbour, an old man who looked about eighty years old. The man wore brown knitted cardigans every day of the week, no matter what the weather was like, and used a stick to get around, even if it was just three steps from his back door to the chairs in his back yard. Devon always offered to mow his lawn, do a bit of weeding, just basic gardening jobs that the man couldn't manage to do on his own. And on the last Friday of every month, I'd make up an excuse that I couldn't attend the church youth group that my dad ran, and I'd sneak off to go and watch him.

Devon would work hard, pushing the man's manual mower across the grass. He obviously couldn't afford an electric one, but Devon didn't complain. Sometimes, he'd take his top off, often using it to wipe the sweat off his face and chest before stuffing it into his back pocket. As a very naïve and innocent fifteen-year-old, I didn't fully understand why that made me feel sweaty too. Waves of guilt would wash over me when that happened, but it didn't stop me watching from behind the wall that I used to sit up against.

After an hour or so of hard labour, the old man always came out with a glass of what looked like lager for the two of them, and he'd call Devon over to have a rest. The two of them would sit together and Devon would listen as the old man talked.

I guessed the man didn't get many visitors, and from the way he lit up when he spoke to Devon, it was clear that he adored him. He lived for these visits. But that wasn't what made my heart hurt. It was the fact that I knew every conversation word for word because the old man told the same stories repeatedly. It was the same every week, yet Devon never let on.

The old man would start talking about how much he loved

his job at the football club, and how he used to go drinking with Peter Astley and Len Fellows after a match. They were players that I'd never heard of, and Devon was probably none the wiser either, but he'd never say anything. Instead, he'd widen his eyes as if he'd just been told the most exciting thing ever. Five minutes later, the man would repeat the story with the exact same words, and Devon would smile and react as if it was his first time hearing it.

That would happen at least five or six times more during their chat, and it'd be the same the week after too. But Devon treated this man like he was gifting him the most precious stories anyone had ever been told. It made my heart swell, and it made my stomach burn. I loved watching them together, and I often thought that Devon was like the grandson this man had never had, and he was the grandfather Devon deserved.

I knew what this town thought of the Bradys and Devon in particular. I'd heard the kids at school call him the reaper, saying he'd done some horrific things. I couldn't lie, I'd watched him do some of those things too, but to me, they were never bad. Necessary, yes. But bad? Not always.

If God did exist, like my father preached, then so did the devil. Only, it wasn't the devil's work that Devon and his friends carried out. It was righting the devil's wrongs.

They say the devil makes work for idle hands, but their hands were never idle. Bloodstained sometimes, bruised and battered most definitely, but never idle.

My father spoke about good against evil, God versus the devil. But no one liked to talk about the grey area in-between, not in my life anyway, and that's where Devon lived, in the darker, greyer shadows of life. Because not everything in life is clear

THE REAPER 143

cut. Evil deeds can be done for a good cause, and good people do bad things all the time. What matters is what we do with our lives, what's in our hearts, and from what I could see, Devon's heart was pure. As pure as my father's, despite the disparity in the way they lived their lives. One preached about peace for all men, the other made it his mission to make that a reality for a lot of the people of Brinton Manor.

They called him the reaper because they thought he didn't have a soul, that he only took other peoples. But I knew it wasn't like that. I knew the truth. He did have a soul, as well as a heart, and a spirit that shone brightly from the shadows where he hid. He put others before himself. He made the world a better place just by being in it. So, when the kids at school would talk trash about him, I'd never listened. There was nothing they could say, nothing I could see that would ever stop me loving Devon Brady.

CHAPTER FOURTEEN
Devon

I took a few days out, tried to talk myself around and gain some semblance of rationality in my mind. I even succeeded in convincing myself that I was in control. But I wasn't. Maybe the fact that I was fighting my own thoughts and feelings wasn't helping, but I didn't know how to be any other way. My life had always been about me, my family and my friends. Throwing someone into the mix that could potentially mean more to me than all of that had my systems shutting down in self-defence.

In my life, preservation had always been key—Vinnie taught me that lesson early on—so opening up, being vulnerable, it didn't come naturally. Killing did, and I'd always thought I had compassion too, but maybe I'd mistaken that for some kind of instinctive preservation. Protecting and safeguarding was one thing, but letting my emotions rule my head? It scared me. I didn't like being powerless and at the mercy of another. To me, it was like handing someone the key to destroy your soul—that was how I saw love. With family, you had no choice; you were born that way, but in relationships, you did, or at least I used to think I did. Now, I wasn't so sure.

When Liv returned from taking Leah May home that night, she'd come to my room to talk to me. If I were going to open up to anybody, Liv would've been the perfect choice. I liked her. She made me feel comfortable. But even she couldn't break through my walls. She'd tried, but I'd made them impenetrable.

"I've never seen you react like that before. You really like her, don't you?" Liv had asked, but I couldn't admit anything. I just wanted to be left alone.

"Was she okay when you dropped her off?" I'd asked.

Liv had smiled sadly and taken a few seconds to think before she replied. I guessed she was debating whether to call bullshit on the fact that I'd sidestepped the question about liking her, but she didn't.

Instead, she said, "She was quiet. She didn't say much. I talked to her, asked her how she was, but she didn't really want to chat, just told me she was okay. She must be a quiet one, like you."

Hearing that had set the wheels in my brain in motion. Leah May wasn't quiet, not when I'd seen her. That wasn't who she was.

Maybe she was frightened.

Maybe I'd scared her off.

Maybe all the procrastinating I was doing about my problem was all for nothing because my little raven had seen my claws, and she'd flown away. Better it happened now than later down the line, because if she thought the claws that I'd shown on that night were bad, she'd have lost it when my real ones made an appearance.

My conversation with Liv hadn't lasted long. I was evasive and abrupt when she questioned me, and she had nothing to tell me about Leah May, other than she'd dropped her off home safely. And so, I buried myself in work and anything else that I could to distract myself. I bought a new crossbow and spent time outside familiarising myself with the mechanisms, learning to handle it and fire it with precision. Mastering a new weapon was one way of focusing my mind, but even that had been a struggle.

I stood in the field at the back of the asylum, ignoring the bitter wind as I took a few more practise shots with the bow. But eventually, I grew tired and wandered back inside and up the stairs to the living room to get myself a hot drink. Tyson was padding down the corridor from Adam's room to join me, and when I went in, everyone was sitting around having a lazy afternoon. Silently stuck in my own head, I made myself a coffee and then sat next to Liv and Adam on the sofa. The newspaper lay on the table, and on the front page was the headline, 'Rapist found hanged in local beauty spot'. I picked it up to read the article, feeling satisfied the police had done their job and the death was reported as suicide. Just as I was folding the newspaper to put it back on the table, Tyler leant forward with a bunch of letters in his hand and threw them onto my lap.

"These are yours," he said, sitting back and turning his attention to Will and Colton, who were playing on the Xbox in the corner.

I flicked through the letters and one with no address or stamp on it caught my attention. I held it up and asked, "Is the postman delivering letters for free now?"

Colton stopped staring at the game for a second to tell me, "That was hand delivered, mate. I found it on the floor of the foyer about an hour ago."

I didn't think any more of it and ripped the envelope open. When I read what was written on the paper inside, my whole body suddenly felt like it'd been submerged under icy cold water, only to be yanked back out again.

> Devon,
> I'm watching you. I'm getting closer. And when we play the next game, I promise you, it'll be your last. You need to remember that I always win, and you will always lose. You'll never get rid of me. I can't be beaten.
> See you soon, son.
> Vinnie.

What the fuck was this bullshit? I was shaking, rage vibrating through me as I tried to take it all in. My breathing became ragged, and stars began to dance in front of my eyes as I panted out my breaths.

Liv shuffled closer to me and whispered, "Are you okay, lovely?"

I couldn't lie, I was far from okay. I shook my head and then leaned across her to pass the letter to Adam, my hands quivering as I did.

"Someone's fucking playing with me," I hissed, pissed that even more crap was coming my way. "And whoever it is, they're going to wish they'd never been born when I get a hold of them. I'm no one's fucking plaything."

Adam read the note, then with a look of thunder on his face, he reached over and grabbed the TV remote, turning it off. Will and Colton groaned in annoyance.

"Who posted this?" he snapped, holding the letter up. "Did you see anyone?"

"I didn't see shit." Colton shrugged, snatching the letter out of Adam's hand. He read it, then passed it over to Will, his face going from mildly annoyed to fuming after he'd seen what was written. "Check the CCTV," he said to Tyler, all joking forgotten. "Whoever posted it will be on there."

Tyler had his laptop on the table, and he started tapping away, trying to find the footage to see who had delivered the letter. When he twisted it around moments later to show us the screen, we all leaned forward, but it was pointless. The video was paused on a dark figure that could have been anyone; black overcoat, baseball cap pulled low, there was no fucking way we could identify who it was, not from this. Tyler replayed the footage, but it was useless. It looked like a man, but even that was debatable.

"Could it be him? Vinnie?" Will asked, as they all stared at me.

"No, it fucking couldn't," I shot back, trembling with fury. "I do know how to kill someone. He's dead. No need for you to fucking question it. He's at the bottom of Brinton canal with the rest of the shit from this town."

"But are you sure?" Colton added, testing my patience.

"What do you fucking mean, am I sure? I just told you, didn't I?"

"You were a kid. Maybe he wasn't dead? Maybe he was

THE REAPER

unconscious, and he managed to swim to safety?" I knew Colton liked his jokes, but this was taking the fucking piss.

"And hide away for the best part of ten years? There's no fucking way. It's not him. Someone thinks they can have a joke at my fucking expense, mess around, but it's not happening. I'll find out who did this, and when I do, they'll know that they fucked with the wrong guy."

"Didn't you say your mum sees him?" Will added, making the blood in my veins boil that little bit hotter.

"She sees a lot of things, but dead stepfathers isn't one of them." I went silent, remembering when my mum had told me she'd seen him at the end of her road.

"What? You've remembered something. What is it?" Adam asked, noticing the change in my demeanour.

"She might've mentioned seeing him again when I saw her a week ago, but it's not true. It's all bullshit…" I faltered, thinking about the details she'd gone into this time. "She did say—"

"What?" Adam pressed.

I screwed my eyes shut, fed up of dragging up the same old nightmares from my past. Why couldn't he stay buried at the bottom of the canal? Was he intent on haunting me for the rest of my life?

"She said he was standing on the corner of her road, and when he saw her in her window, he did this salute that he always used to do before he walked away. She's convinced it was him. But it can't be. I know he's dead. He was fucking gone when I dropped him in the water. I'd swear my life on it. I know how to do my job properly."

I did know how to do my job. I was the best at it. At least, I always thought I was, but it was beginning to make me angry that I was starting to doubt myself. Not that I'd ever tell anyone.

"We have to look at all the options here. He might not be dead," Tyler said, stoking the flames.

"Or you might've killed the wrong guy. Let's face it, we've fucked up like that before," Colton piped up, adding extra fuel to the fire.

I went to argue but Adam held his hand up, and with exasperation in his voice said, "There's also the possibility that when we did our little clean-up project after you killed him that we missed someone out. Someone who knew about what went on with you and your stepfather."

Back when we were kids at the pupil referral unit, I'd opened up and told them all about the games my stepfather used to play. I told them what I'd done to get my revenge too, and that day, we sat down and made a plan of attack, focusing on every one of Vinnie's sick friends. Vinnie might've gotten his justice, but the others hadn't, and so our game of consequences was born that day. Our first ever players were the friends Vinnie had invited to my house to torture me. One by one, we tortured them right back, only our games were slower, more sadistic, perfect for evil fuckers like them because in the end, we won. They didn't survive to see the light of day.

I frowned and recalled every name in my mind; every face that had been involved. It wasn't hard. Those men were eternally scarred into my brain. But there was no one else. We hadn't slipped up and left anyone out. We were thorough.

"There is no one. They're all gone," I stated, knowing what I said was true.

"Okay, so someone who knew about it but didn't take part?" Tyler asked, and I shook my head. My stepfather shared this secret with very few. Only the people involved knew what really went on. He knew how to cover his tracks and he was careful to protect himself from any accusations. He was a fucker, but he was a smart fucker.

"Why now?" I asked. "Why come forward now?" That was the part that didn't make any sense to me. We were in the best position we'd ever been in. If someone from my past was out to get me, why not do it back when I'd killed Vinnie, when I was younger and weaker? Because at this very moment, I might only stand with four other soldiers, but together, we were a fucking formidable army.

"Maybe it isn't just now," Tyler added. "Maybe this is their next step. A new angle. Didn't you say Stella was still harping on about going to the police again to report you?"

Stella.

Fucking Stella.

Was she behind this?

I wouldn't put it past her.

That woman was the bane of my life. I sometimes wished I could go against my own fucking rules and deal with her. Get her out of our lives for good.

"Yep. Could be Stella flexing her muscles, keeping you on your toes." Colton raised an eyebrow, and I gritted my teeth. He could be right, but in my gut, I wasn't convinced. She was a fucking nuisance, but death threats? Would she really go that far?

"We will get to the bottom of this," Adam announced as he stood from the sofa and held his hand out for Liv to take. "But in the meantime, I have something back at the warehouse that might help to take your mind off this. There's nothing we can do now, so let's do what we do best. Let's cause a bit of mayhem. Devon, go and load up the van, choose something good from your store in the chapel, because I think you're going to like what I've got planned."

CHAPTER FIFTEEN
Devon

It felt good to be working as a team again, doing what we did best. I'd filled the van with various weapons and tools we could use. I liked to take a selection and give them all the choice. I left the crossbow in the chapel though. I needed a few more weeks of practise before I felt comfortable using it for a hit. I didn't like to bring a weapon into play unless I knew my potential to cause maximum impact with it. For now, the crossbow was on the subs bench.

Tyler, Will, and I took the van. Adam and Colton rode behind us in the car. But we put Adam on speakerphone, so he could fill us in on the mark that was waiting for us as we drove over to the warehouse.

"He's a sick fucker. Burgled a few houses, but the last one he did was the home of an elderly couple. He tied them up, ransacked the house. The old guy struggled to escape so he could help his wife and ended up having a heart attack. This guy walked in, saw he was dying and fucking laughed in the wife's face. Then he left them. He fucking left them like that. The husband died right in front of his wife and there wasn't a damn thing she could do to help him because she was tied up. The son found them two days later. His dad dead and his mum just… broken. This fucker deserves everything he's got coming to him. I swear, I'm going to enjoy breaking this one."

Adam was right. What sort of sick fucker put money over people's lives? He could've phoned an ambulance or done something, but he was heartless. Only out for himself. Those kinds of marks were my favourites though. I lived to see them suffer; sending them straight to hell with the terror their victim's felt etched into their brain.

We hung up the phone, adrenaline coursing through our veins, ready to take out some of our pent-up aggression on a worthy target.

Once we got to the old warehouse in Brinton, we parked around the back of the building. There was no CCTV here. We'd taken care of that a long time ago, but it wasn't clever to park and unload the weapons in full view of the estate, no matter how run-down, desolate, and deserted it looked. And boy did it look shitty.

The warehouse was on an old industrial estate that years ago would've been thriving with the sounds of factories working at full steam. Workers busy earning their wages, shouting across to their mates over a noisy workshop. Machines banging and grinding away to keep the economy and livelihood of Brinton Manor going. But that community had been bled dry, much like the buildings that surrounded us. Windows were broken,

THE REAPER

walls were crumbling, and weeds grew everywhere, replacing prosperity with drudgery.

It was pretty much the same wherever you went around here. Brinton Manor had lost its way a long time ago. But it was still our home, and we served these streets as if they were paved with gold. One day, we hoped they would be. The place itself might be in decay, but the spirit of the people hadn't died, for the majority that is. The fucker we had in our warehouse waiting on us was a different matter.

Tyler, Will, and I started to unload the van, and Adam unlocked the doors to the warehouse, so we could set up. The old doors creaked open, rusty metal strained at the hinges as Adam prised them open and used a large rock nearby to wedge them in place. We pulled on our balaclavas, not that we cared about the mark seeing us, but because it made us feel powerful. Also, it looked fucking awesome on the videos we made when we were at work. The masks added that extra touch, an artistic edge, I liked to think.

We carried the weapons through into the warehouse, and a few stray birds flapped overhead, flying towards the rafters to hide, furious at our disturbance. The air stank of shit, piss, and sheer desperation. I heard a muffled cry and saw the guy we were here to take care of strapped into the chair that we'd bolted to the floor. There was a gag around his mouth, and when he saw us, he started to thrash in the seat.

"He fucking stinks," Colton moaned as he put the weapons he'd carried onto the table at the side of the room.

Adam walked over to the corner where there was a hose, turned on the tap that it was attached to and said, "He's been here all night. I'll wash him down, not that he deserves any humanity from me." And he pointed the hose at the guy, drenching him like he was hosing down a car.

The guy shook his head as the water dripped from his hair into his eyes, coughing and choking as it soaked his gag and made it harder for him to breathe.

Adam gave him a minute or two before he turned off the tap and asked Colton, "Is that better?"

"Your humanity towards my sense of smell is very much appreciated." Colton grinned and picked up an ice pick, twisting it in his hand and turning towards me to ask, "If I stick this in his ear, will it pierce his brain?"

Adam huffed out a smile and shook his head. I got busy giving Colton a brief lesson on anatomy while Tyler and Adam set up the video, and then Adam crouched down to give the guy a speech about why he was here and how we were going to annihilate him for every sin he'd ever committed.

Adam liked to play the role of the enforcer. He delivered the verdict and then took pleasure in carrying out his part to bring about justice. I watched as he took his phone out of his pocket and lifted it to show the guy his screen. There was probably a photo of the couple or the old man on there. Adam liked to smack them in the face with the reason why they'd landed on the soldiers' radar. A final reminder of who deserved revenge. Almost like he was reading them their last rites.

Tyler strolled over and picked up the meat cleaver from the table, and Will chose the Damascus steel hunting knife; he liked the effect etched into the metal of the blade, he said. Meanwhile, Adam sauntered over and took the baseball bat, walking right back to stand in front of the guy and stare down at him as he swung it in the air.

And me?

I chose the scalpel. It wouldn't be the only weapon I'd use today, but it was a good start.

"Can we do without the music today?" Adam asked, turning to look at Colton. "I've got a splitting headache." He lifted the bat up, swung, and whacked the guy over the head hard. "I think our guest might have a headache too."

Colton laughed, and holding up the ice pick he replied, "I don't think we need any music. I've got another way to make his ears ring."

I stepped back and watched Colton get to work, testing out his theory from earlier as the guy's muffled screams grew louder. Adam smirked, holding back for a moment, then he stepped up, swinging the bat hard and smashing the guy's kneecaps. The guy was grunting, squirming, howling, and trying anything to free himself from our chair, but that'd never happen. He was here until we'd finished—and finished him in the process.

Tyler took his turn next, lifting the cleaver up and bringing it down hard on the guy's thighs. He sliced into his flesh then yanked the cleaver out before slicing again. In this moment, seeing what we were doing, some might say we were like a pack of wolves. But to me, this wasn't savage, it was a process, and we were artists creating our masterpiece. The masterpiece that was justice in its truest form.

I walked over to stand in front of the guy, my soldiers stood to the side of me, and I bent down to tell him why I was doing what came next. For me, it wasn't about the act of violence or even revenge. I liked to add an element of irony to my contribution. An eye for an eye, perhaps. Or maybe, I'd had so many games played on me in the past, I liked to see the tables turned in the most specular and fitting way.

"You left that couple alone," I hissed at him. "That woman had to watch her husband die in front of her eyes and there wasn't a damn thing she could do to help him. All she could do was cry tears as he left her. Tears that she'll never recover from. Tears you put there. So, I think it's only fair you cry some tears of your own."

I took the scalpel and began my work, carving into his left tear duct, pressing until I drew blood. Then slowly, I cut a jagged line down his cheek, making tears of blood flow down his face. Tears that would never fade, just like hers. Once I'd done the left side, I moved to the right. Will stood behind, holding his head in place as the mark tried to pull away, screaming out in pain at every slice I made.

"I always thought an eye for an eye was a fair trade," I said over the noise of his howling. "And it will be your eyes next, but I'll choose a different tool for that job. Something that'll be slow and painful. Excruciatingly so." He squealed and howled like the piece of shit he was, and I smiled in satisfaction. "I bet you're starting to rethink your life choices now, aren't you, mate?"

I stepped back once I was happy with the effect I'd created. Will stepped up next with his hunting knife, but when we heard something crashing outside one of the windows of the warehouse, he stopped, and we all turned around.

Sensing what we were all thinking, Adam jumped to attention first, barrelling for the door with his baseball bat raised and ready to attack. We followed him, running towards the door to catch whoever was out there, because whoever it was must've had a death wish if they dared to interrupt us when we were

THE REAPER 159

working.

When we got outside, we saw Adam standing there, frozen in place, and under his breath he cursed, "What the fuck?"

When I looked past him, I knew why. There, dressed all in black with a hood pulled low to hide her identity, was Leah May.

CHAPTER SIXTEEN
Devon

She didn't move or try to run away. She just stood next to a pile of old milk crates scattered on the floor around her and stared at us, her eyes blinking, full of innocence and apprehension. I could sense that her fight or flight mode was engaging, and she was choosing to fight. Even though the raven was her spirit animal, she never chose flight, not from what I'd seen, anyway. My little raven was all about standing her ground in this life. It was another thing that I admired about her.

We pulled off our balaclavas, and her chest heaved as she took deep breaths. Her eyes remained stoic, strong, and determined, as she looked at each one of us in turn, until her eyes landed on me, and then they shone with something else entirely.

"What the fuck is *she* doing here?" Adam snapped, pointing

the bat at her.

She stood tall and squared her shoulders, but she didn't speak, just swallowed and kept her eyes fixed on me.

"Devon, deal with her. I don't have time for this bullshit today." Adam reached into his pocket and pulled out the car keys, throwing them over to me. "Get her out of here. We'll finish up inside." Then he glanced back at Leah May. "We have enough going on, we don't need any more loose ends."

Her eyes widened slightly at what he'd said, and I took a step closer to her as the others went back inside.

"What are you doing here?" I asked, stunned that I was having this conversation with her here after what I'd just done.

She gulped and looked down at the crates.

"I stacked them, but I lost my footing and fell off."

I took another step closer, treading slowly, carefully, afraid that the next step would push her too far and she'd run.

Would she run?

Did I scare her?

"Did you watch us? Did you see what was going on in there?" I asked, keeping my voice calm and steady.

She looked at me and nodded but didn't say a word.

Why wasn't she running?

Didn't it frighten her to see what we'd done?

"You shouldn't have been out here skulking around. How did you know we were here? What are you even doing here?"

She blinked, collecting her thoughts and then said, "I saw you loading up the van, back at The Sanctuary. I called an Uber, and when you set off, I followed. I didn't think you'd find me. I'm not usually so clumsy."

My head snapped back, hearing her veiled admission.

"Do you mean you've done this before?"

She opened her mouth then closed it, choosing to keep quiet instead of incriminating herself further.

And then, on a whispered breath she asked, "Are you going to kill me?"

My heart twisted when I heard her ask that.

"Of course I'm not going to kill you. Why would I ever hurt you?" I tilted my head, trying to show through my eyes that she was safe with me, always. I might be a killer, but I wasn't a monster, not for her. Never for her.

"Adam said to deal with me, he doesn't want any loose ends." As she spoke, her voice cracked slightly, and I could tell she was trying to hide her fear. She'd done a good job of concealing it until now.

"Adam wants me to take you home, that's all he meant. That's the only loose end there is. He'd never hurt you. None of them would. And me? I would rather hurt myself than ever do anything to cause you pain. You can trust me."

She stood still, watching me with those eyes of hers that seemed to call out to my soul. "I know," she said on a whisper.

I stared right back at her, not quite believing what was happening. She'd admitted that she'd seen what I'd done, seen the savage I could be, and yet she was looking up at me like I was her saviour. She wasn't scared. She wasn't threatened by me.

She was just here.

Accepting.

"Are you going to be okay getting into the car with me, so I can take you home?" I asked hesitantly. I was conscious of the fact that I didn't look my best, my hoody was blood-stained, and

THE REAPER

I looked like I'd walked off the set of a horror movie, standing here in this shitty run-down industrial estate, still holding my bloody scalpel.

"Yes." Her voice was quiet, and she cleared her throat before repeating herself louder and with more confidence, "Yes, I'm okay."

I nodded and headed to the car, taking my hoody off and throwing it onto the back seat along with the scalpel. It wasn't perfect, but at least my T-shirt was clean, no tell-tale splatters.

The sky was grey, and the clouds were circling, bringing with them the threat of an almighty downpour. I tilted my head back and felt the first drop of rain on my face.

"It's going to tip it down soon, get in," I told her, and without argument, she got into the passenger side and put her seatbelt on.

I got in too, and when I started the engine, she turned to me and said, "I'm not scared. I just wanted you to know that."

I didn't know what to say to her, so I kept quiet and drove slowly over the uneven rubble of the warehouse grounds, putting the windscreen wipers on a little faster as the drizzle became a steady beat of rain hitting the glass.

"And I want you to know," she carried on, turning in her seat so she was sitting to the side to face me. "I saw what happened, but I wasn't freaked out. I get it."

That caught my attention, and I glanced sideways at her and asked, "You get what?" before turning my attention back to the road.

"It's not a choice for you. This is who you are. Its your calling. You're like *Dexter*, you have a dark passenger. I've watched *Dexter* at least three times… okay, maybe more like four or five, but he was never a bad guy. He was the good guy doing bad things to make it all right. That's you. You're *Dexter*."

I sighed and ran my hand over my face.

"This isn't a fucking TV show, Leah. I'm not *Dexter*. I'm not some kind of hero. It's just my job."

"A job you have to do. Like a doctor saves people by curing them. It's your destiny. You save people too. You take the souls of those that don't deserve to be here."

I did. And I was also aware that ninety-nine percent of the population didn't see it that way, not like I did. But for some reason, she saw it that way too. Maybe she just watched too much damn TV and didn't see the harsh reality of what I did, but I stayed quiet and let her carry on.

"Not all heroes wear capes. Some wear a balaclava." She smiled and then added, "And some girls like a balaclava."

"You're not some girl, Leah. This isn't who you are."

"How do you know who I am?" she replied defensively, and I could feel her eyes boring into the side of my face as I concentrated on the road ahead.

I sighed, trying to choose my words carefully. Words meant a lot to Leah May. I could tell they held a lot of power over her.

"I know that this world I live in, my life, it isn't for you. You don't belong here. You're too good. You deserve better."

"Shouldn't I be the judge of that?" She sighed right back at me and turned her body so that she was facing ahead. "You see hell all around you, it's everywhere you look, but I don't. I'm not stupid, Devon. I don't use rose-tinted glasses in life, but when I look at you and your world, all I see are fragments of a twisted, contorted, self-inflicted hell that's scattered on the floor. Broken pieces from your life that made you who you are, but they're shattered and broken for a reason. You fought to make them that way. Scars show you've fought a battle and won. The destruction I see is beautiful, a beautiful chaos. I'd take those fractured parts a million times over some make believe heaven that doesn't make me feel anything."

She smoothed her hands down the thighs of her jeans, serenity and truth coming off her in waves. But in contrast, my heart was beating like a drum, my mind a ticking timebomb ready to explode after hearing her words. Serenity knew no place in my psyche.

"When I watch you," she added. "I see it. I see how it affects you. For the others, it's work, they're doing their bit. Adam loves the rush of it all, the buzz, you can see it in his face. He lives for the adrenaline kick. Colton is the same, but he isn't as serious as Adam. Tyler is precise in what he does, and Will is just… crazy." She shrugged. "But you? To you, it's like art. I see the concentration on your face, the satisfaction when it turns out the way you've envisioned it in your mind. You're creating art from what you do. You study your canvas, and every stroke, slice, whatever it is you do, it's done with thought and care. Meaning, almost. And I get it."

I didn't understand how she could get it. She was a vicar's daughter. Raised in a Christian household with firm morals and principles. How could she get what I felt? How could she get me? Where were all these words coming from that seemed to be taken right from my own mind. Carved from my own moral compass.

"You're painting me like I'm a character. But this is real life, Leah. Its dirty, filthy, savage—"

"And I've watched you long enough to know the difference

between real evil and a necessary evil done by a good person. You are good, Devon."

My heart stilled.

"What do you mean, you've watched me for long enough? How long has this been going on for?"

I felt her stiffen in her seat next to me.

"I don't feel comfortable answering that question."

"But you feel comfortable talking about torturing being art and necessary evils? What the fuck is going on here?"

"I'm just saying I know you, Devon. I see you. I'm not asking you to do anything with that information, but it makes me feel better to say it."

We turned into the country lane where her house was, and I pulled up a little further down the road, so we weren't right outside. I wanted to talk to her away from prying eyes. I wanted her to myself for just a moment longer.

I shut off the engine and we both sat in silence for a while.

Eventually, I was the one to break.

"So, I'm guessing you've been watching for a lot longer than I anticipated?"

She lowered her head, and stared into her lap as her hands twisted together. I wanted to reach over and take her hand in mine, but for the first time in my life, I felt something that made me second guess everything. I felt nervous.

"I'm not going to lie, not anymore," she said quietly. "Yes, I've watched you. I think about you a lot too." She looked up at me then and the sadness in her eyes made my heart feel like it'd been pierced by a million needles. "You're like a drug that I take every day. And you know what they say about addicts? The addiction is also the cure."

I couldn't speak. My throat had become painful, as if it was made from shards of glass and razor blades. How had I not noticed her before? Where the hell had my head been lately that I could let someone like her fade into the background, to remain unseen? Because I sure as hell noticed her now. She was everywhere. My mind couldn't focus on anything because it was drowning in her.

She took a deep breath and stared straight ahead, then said, "I need to forget about you, stop thinking about you, because I know you don't think about me."

She grabbed the door handle to leave but I shot my arm across to stop her.

"You're not leaving. Not like this," I told her, taking her hand in mine, fighting the nerves I felt and running my thumb over her knuckles.

"I have to," she replied sadly, looking down at where our hands were joined and covering my hand with her own.

"You're upset," I stated. "I'm not letting you leave me, not when you're like this."

She squeezed my hand, then pulled hers free, and turning to me with a sad smile she said, "It's okay. I'm used to it."

Those four words.

Four simple words were what broke me.

I'm used to it.

"You shouldn't have to be used to anything," I said, whilst my brain screamed at me to make this right. "You shouldn't be used to feeling upset. Not because of me."

I took a few deep breaths, trying to make sense of the feelings inside, feelings that I didn't fully understand, but they were warning me, telling me I couldn't let her walk away. I had to be honest, even if it put me in a position that I didn't feel comfortable with. She was opening up to me; I had to do the same.

"I know I've only just met you. And this is all going to sound weird. Hell, I don't even understand it myself, but I do think about you, Leah May. I think about you way more than I should. Just because I don't say it, doesn't mean I don't feel it too."

I expected her to look happy, be hopeful after what I'd said, but she didn't. Sadness still glistened in her eyes. Tears threatened to fall, and she was doing everything in her power to keep them locked up safely where they were.

"Of course I think about you," I carried on, wishing that she'd truly hear what I was saying. "And it makes no sense to me. All I know is you came into my life a few weeks ago, a little raven flapping her wings around me and tapping away. How could I not notice you?

"Some days, you're all I think about, and it's confusing because I don't really know you, but I feel like I need to know you, and I worry. I worry so damn much, because you're like a bird that doesn't want to be caged, but you're so small and gentle, so trusting. And I worry about the things out there in the world, things that could hurt you. I get scared myself, because I didn't know I could feel the kind of way I'm feeling right now.

"I didn't ever think I'd feel this way about another person, especially one I've only just met. It's like I'm going insane, and I can't control anything. When I asked Liv if you'd gotten home safely the other night—"

"You asked about me?" she said, quietly interrupting my rambled speech.

THE REAPER

"Of course I did. I wouldn't have been able to sleep that night if I hadn't known you were safe at home. I wanted to drive you myself but—"

"You care," she stated, and smiled as she looked at her lap. Then she glanced across at me and said, "It's enough. You see me too, and that's enough."

I didn't know what was going on, and I couldn't seem to form any meaningful words, but I did manage to say, "I don't understand."

"It's enough that you see me, Devon. That's all I've ever wanted."

I furrowed my brow, still no clearer about what she meant. I was opening up, telling her things I wouldn't dare tell another soul, so why did it feel like she was slipping away from me?

The rain was lashing down outside, and I watched as she put her hand against the passenger window, her fingers tracing the trail of water as it trickled down the glass, and on a whisper she said, "It can't rain forever, right?"

If I thought my heart hurt before, it was nothing compared to the crushing pain I felt in that moment. When she opened the car door and stepped out into the rain, leaving before I could stop her, it felt like my heart had been ripped from my chest. Lying battered on the floor, drowning in the gutter, all hope washed away by the rain. This girl saw me. She knew what I was, what I'd done, and she liked me anyway.

What sort of a fool lets a girl like that walk away?

CHAPTER SEVENTEEN
Leah May

I slammed the car door and put my head down. The rain soaked through my clothes almost instantly, but I didn't care. I felt numb, and no amount of rain could counter that. As I walked the short distance towards my gate, I heard his car door open behind me and his voice calling out for me to wait. I did. Because despite what I'd convinced myself in the car, that this had to end, I would still do whatever he told me to. The spell wouldn't be broken that easily.

Do you like being a doormat?

The voices in my head chastised me, but I ignored them. I wasn't a doormat; I was taking steps to get control back.

I folded my arms over my chest and turned to face him. He was only wearing a T-shirt, and the rain had already soaked right through it, making it transparent, but I wouldn't look at his

THE REAPER

chest. Instead, I kept my eyes on his and gritted my teeth. I had no idea how this would go, but I didn't want to lose myself. I'd lost enough over the years since my mum had died, and all that grief and pain had been channelled into him. My dark, broken heart had attached itself to his and he didn't even know it. My saviour who hid in the shadows. My reaper.

"Leah, please. Don't walk away from me like that. Don't tell me it's enough," he said, coming to stand right in front of me.

"But it is," I peered up at him from under my hood and he stepped right into my space, his face close to me, his eyes boring into mine. "It's enough," I repeated automatically, not believing the words coming from my mouth. "And now it has to stop. I have to stop."

"No," he barked, his eyes flickering between my mouth and eyes.

Tears started to fall down my cheeks, but I doubt he could tell the difference between them and the rain that was smattering my face.

"It might be enough for you, but it isn't for me." His brow furrowed in confusion.

It wasn't for me either, but what choice did I have?

"It's okay, Devon. None of this is your fault."

"What isn't my fault? I need to know exactly what you're saying because I feel so confused. I don't know what you mean."

"Me. That's what I mean. You don't have to feel responsible for me. I'm fine, I'll survive. I've done it before."

He reached up and grabbed my face in his hands, tilting my head so I had no choice but to look right at him. "Just stop with the whole martyr thing. The *'I'll cope,' 'I'm used to it,'* I don't want to hear that from you. Ever."

He panted out his breath as he held me. The warmth fanned my face, and his closeness made it difficult to breathe. His thumbs gently stroked my cheekbones, tears that'd trickled into the rain were wiped away with what felt like care. My heart swelled, the prickle of hope rippling under my skin. But I'd lived this life long enough to know that feelings like that couldn't be trusted.

"Don't make me promises, Devon. Don't touch me like there's something there when there isn't. I'm strong enough to walk away now. And besides, I hate promises. They only get broken."

He dipped his head, taking a moment to compose himself. And when he eventually looked up at me, the love that shone in his eyes made my breath catch in my throat.

"When I touch you," he said softly. "It's because I want to." He moved his face so that his nose touched mine. "When I touch you it's because I have to." He moved closer still, his cheek brushing mine, and he whispered in my ear, "I touch you because trying not to is like trying not to breathe. It's too hard, and after a while, it hurts."

I closed my eyes, feeling the warmth of his breath on my cheek, my neck, even in the coldness of my heart. I felt him everywhere.

"I don't know what's going to happen," he whispered. "I haven't done anything like this before. But what I do know is, I can't let you walk away without at least trying to work out what this is, this connection between us. I feel this pull deep inside of me whenever I see you. When you're not around, it's like the pull gets stronger and I can't settle, I can't think straight. And some days, you're all I see." He pulled back, keeping his hands on my face but staring straight into my eyes. "Why, Leah? Why do I feel like this?"

I wanted to tell him that I loved him, but I knew that'd sound crazy. He didn't know me, and he thought I didn't know him. So, I stayed quiet, giving him time to process his thoughts.

"I feel like I'm going crazy here," he carried on. "And yet, if I walk away now, I will never forgive myself. Who are you?" he asked, narrowing his eyes again and frowning. "Where did you come from?"

"I haven't come from anywhere. I've always been here."

He shook his head, a confused expression marring his beautiful face.

"I can't stand the thought of you walking away but I feel like my world is just so wrong for you. It's not the place for a girl like you."

He swallowed and I could see the war of emotions playing out in his troubled eyes.

"But don't you see? I'm already in your world. I've been here for a while; you've just never noticed me."

"Don't say it like that," he urged, holding my face closer as the rain beat down around us.

"Like what?"

"Like I ignored you."

"It's enough that you see me now." I gasped quietly and plastered a smile on my rain-splattered face, fighting off the shiver that wanted to break free. I wanted to let him know it was okay. I would be okay.

"There you go again, saying it's enough. It's not. Not for me."

We stared into each other's eyes, blinking away the rain that peppered our cheeks. Panting into the misty cold air, we breathed each other's breath as our own. My heart was thumping, my pulse racing, and every inch of me was drowning in him.

I waited, scared to move in case it broke the spell we were both under. I wanted to stay like this forever, close to him, held by him, hypnotised by him. And then, everything stopped as he leaned forward, and I felt the gentle brush of his lips against mine.

He was kissing me.

No warning.

No words.

Devon Brady was really kissing me.

Slowly, tenderly, his lips moved against mine like I was made of silk, and he was savouring the feel, the softness. I closed my eyes, wanting to experience him through every one of my senses. The way he smelt, the taste of his lips; it felt like he was gently bringing me back to life right here in this rainstorm.

I reached up, placing my hands on his hard, broad chest. His T-shirt was soaked but the heat of his skin through the wet fabric warmed my palms. I could feel his heart racing under my fingertips and his chest heaved as he kissed me with the kind of intensity I'd always dreamed of. After a while, he became more insistent and pushed me back against the wall behind us. His kiss deepened, his tongue tasting mine, and I sighed into him, losing all sense of place or time. When he pulled away, it felt like a loss that I couldn't bear, but he kept his hands on my face and then gently placed a kiss on my forehead and the tip of my nose. I felt like my heart was about to burst.

Devon Brady had kissed me.

"I know you don't want my promises." He whispered the words right into my heart, and I wanted to tell him that I did. I wanted them all, I just didn't want the rejection that would follow. But before I could reply, he added, "But I *can* tell you this. I'm not sure what's going to happen. Like I've said, I haven't done anything like this before. Relationships don't come naturally to me, not with anyone. But for you… with you, I want to try." He took a few more deep breaths and then he placed his forehead against mine and asked, "Can we try?"

I bit my lip and nodded. Like I'd ever say no to him.

"Leah May Johnson, I think you might be the strongest woman I've ever met," he said, a slow smile spreading across his face.

"What makes you say that?" I asked, reaching up on my tiptoes, daring to place a sweet kiss on his lips.

"Because you're willing to take on a lost cause like me."

"You're not a lost cause, Devon. You're just a lost soul. At least, you thought you were. But I've never seen you in that way."

"What did you see?"

"The other half of me."

The words were out before I could stop them, and I worried in that split second that I'd scared him off a little. But he gently rubbed his thumb over my cheek again and said, "You're right. It can't rain forever. But if standing in the rain with you makes me feel like this, I'm not sure I ever want it to end."

I'd told him I didn't want any promises, but in this moment, I promised myself one thing. No one would ever own my heart, because it was his. Forever and always.

CHAPTER EIGHTEEN
Devon

"You're loitering. Just come in and tell me what it is that's got you pacing in front of our door like a mad man."

The others were still at the warehouse, but I'd come straight back to The Sanctuary after dropping Leah May at home, and now I was pacing the hallway outside Adam's room, debating whether to talk to Liv or not.

"Your mind is procrastinating so loudly I can hear you from in here," Liv shouted from behind the door. "You're giving me a headache, so do us both a favour and get your ass in here."

Realising I probably had no choice at this point, I stepped in and closed the door behind me. Liv was sitting on her new black velvet sofa under the window. Something she'd bought recently to give Adam's room what she called her 'feminine touch'. Tyson was lying across the whole thing with his head in her lap, and she was scratching between his ears and gazing down at him like he was her baby. I moved some of the throw cushions she'd scattered all over their bed and sat opposite her.

"What's up?" she asked as she bent down to kiss Tyson.

I shrugged and tried to gather my thoughts.

"Adam texted me," she added, her eyes finding mine. "So, I know what happened back at the warehouse."

I nodded, still not sure if she knew exactly what'd gone on. It was always a grey area for us, guessing what Liv knew and what Adam protected her from.

"Do you want to talk about her?" she pressed, lifting her eyebrow in question, and I knew that grey area wasn't so grey in this instance.

"I'm confused." My honesty slowly seeped out of me, despite it being totally against my nature to show myself to the world. The real me, anyway. "I don't think this is something I can talk to the others about. I don't want them to think I've gone soft. I don't ever want anyone to think I'm losing my touch."

"I'm going to stop you right there, Devon Brady. One, you helped Adam a lot when he was going through what we went through. He told me. And not once did you make him feel any less of a man for how he opened up to you. If you want to talk to Adam about anything, he'll listen and he'd help. He probably wouldn't be as awesome at advice as I am, but he'd never think less of you.

"Two, addressing the way you feel and your emotions is never a sign of weakness. Avoidance is weak. Not taking a chance is weak. But facing things? That takes courage and strength.

"You know, you can be different things to different people.

Look at Adam. He's the sweetest, kindest, goofiest goofball with me. He tells me all the time how much he loves me, and he shows me too. But with you guys, he's a moody, mean motherfucker who gives no shits. I know exactly what he's up to today, and I know why. You all think he shields me, but he doesn't. He tells me everything, because that's what being in his world and accepting him for who he is is all about. The good, the bad, and the ugly. I'm not some pampered princess that needs to be protected from life… and neither is she. She's stronger than you think."

I knew what Liv was saying was right, but the thought of sharing everything the way she described was something I would take a long time to get my head around. That's if I ever could get my head around being that open.

"Her life is so different from mine."

"Is it? Is it really? Have you walked a day in her shoes? I don't know her, but from what I've seen, the girl has got some serious balls on her. She came to the club to see you. Came on her own too and stayed. You know how that worked out when I tried to do that. She watched you kick off, but it didn't put her off. She saw you today and she's still standing there begging you to notice her. And she's sweet and caring, she could be the best thing to ever happen to you, Devon."

I could hear what Liv was saying, but deep down, I felt like I wasn't enough, and I doubted I could change or mould myself to become the kind of man worthy of a girl like Leah May.

"I can't change who I am." I spoke candidly, knowing that the morals rooted within me were there for good. She might've seen what I was, what I'd done, but to live with that… that was something else entirely.

Liv sighed and shook her head, the exasperation in her tone told me she thought my arguments were unfounded, flimsy excuses.

"She doesn't want you to change. If she did, she wouldn't be the girl for you. Relationships, love, all of that, it isn't about change, it's about growing together. And you won't know if that's something you can do until you try." Liv's candour was like a mirror reflecting all of my fears, reminding me that I needed to see the bigger picture, and not become overwhelmed by it.

"From the moment I first laid eyes on her, she's been open and honest, sometimes too much. She's like a fountain pouring out all these words and emotions whenever I see her. Sometimes, it's not even the words, just a look, a sigh, and it breaks me apart. I don't know how to handle it. It feels like it's too much."

After surviving a childhood where I had to learn to control and even fight my emotions, I was aware that facing them might prove somewhat of a problem for me. It was a tap that'd grown rusty and stiff from lack of use. To try and turn it on again wouldn't be the easiest thing in the world. It might not even work anymore. Or worse still, I might not want it to work.

"You're feeling like that because its new. You haven't felt this way before, and it can get overwhelming when you find that one person in life who means more to you than anything. You rip yourself open, tear yourself apart, but at the end of the day, you love them because it's impossible not to. Eventually, you'll realise that you can't fight this. Sooner or later, you will have to own up to how you feel, because if you don't, it'll eat you alive."

It was already eating me alive. I was second guessing every

word, every action, every thought I was having because I didn't want to hurt her. I didn't want to let her down. Could a killer like me ever be a good man for a girl like her?

"I've told her I want to try. But what if I fail, Liv? What if I can't give her what she wants, or I can't open up enough to keep her? I don't want to let her down. What if I'm not enough?"

As a soldier, as the self-proclaimed reaper, it was hard to admit to anyone that I didn't feel like I was enough. I'd even berated Leah May for using the word. But for me, it was a shadow that loomed in the dark corners of my life. An echo of a voice I'd banished to my nightmares, telling me I wasn't worth shit. That I was a burden to my mother. That I'd never be good enough for this world. The voice that I'd buried at the bottom of Brinton canal all those years ago, but it never seemed to stay silent for long.

"You can't worry about what ifs. You'll drive yourself insane. All you can do is try, and the fact that you've told her that you will is a massive step, Devon. I could be wrong, but I think you're being too hard on yourself, and you worry too much about what other people think."

"I don't give a fuck what people think of me." And I didn't, at least I thought I didn't.

"I don't mean just anyone," Liv chastised, the roll of her eyes telling me she knew me better than that. "I mean these guys; Colton, Tyler, Will, even Adam. You want to preserve that persona you've worked so hard to cultivate here; the strong, silent reaper. I know you take pride in that being who you are, but it doesn't have to be all you are. I understand it's where you feel at home and what gives you that control you crave, but your relationship, and whatever you build with Leah, its fresh and new, a clean slate, and quite frankly, none of anyone else's business. It's between you and her. You can still be a soldier and be her everything."

Could I?

Did I have the capacity to add another facet to my life; soldier, brother, son, friend.

Could I also be more?

More to her?

"Maybe I should talk to Adam? He managed it with you." I felt that talking to Liv today had helped, and I knew there were things that I could work on within myself. If Adam could do it, why couldn't I?

"I really think you should," Liv replied. "He thinks the world of you, Devon. We all do."

Liv bit her lip, then reached over to the drawers by the side of the sofa. She pulled open the top drawer and took out a flyer.

"After I dropped Leah off the other night, we swapped numbers and I started to text her. She told me about this gig she has tomorrow at Merivale town hall." Liv leaned forward and passed the flyer to me. "I really think you should go. I told her me and Adam would be there, but I think it'd mean the world for her to see you there too."

I turned the leaflet over in my hands, reading the tagline for a night of local musical talent, and when I saw her name right up there in bold letters, a spark of pride ignited inside me.

"She never told me about this," I said, focusing on my feelings of pride and fighting the twinge of my bruised ego that seemed to follow the initial elation.

"Maybe because she's embarrassed about you seeing her, or maybe she doesn't think it'll be your thing. Maybe," Liv sighed dramatically, "she just plain forgot. Don't overthink it, Devon. It is what it is."

"She might not want me there."

Liv huffed and threw her head back in exasperation.

"Don't make bullshit excuses. Just come with us. She's shown you she wants to step into your world, now make the effort to step into hers."

I stammered, stalling to give my brain time to take it all in.

"I don't have a ticket."

Liv let out a frustrated growl, and Tyson's head jerked from her lap in annoyance at being disturbed.

"Jesus. Now you're just scraping the barrel of shitty excuses. Its pay at the door, dumbass, and I hardly think they'll be turning people away, it's a charity night at the town hall."

I glanced down at the flyer I was clutching in my hands, toying with all the pros and cons flying around my head.

"You need to stop holding back," Liv blurted out, pulling me from my thoughts. "Go to her. Lose yourself in her. Watch her play for you and burn in her flames. And maybe, just maybe, if she's the one, you'll rise like the phoenix you are, that you both are. You never know unless you try. That's all you can do, Devon… *try*."

Enough.

I was using that word again, but this time to tell myself that I'd done enough procrastinating. Enough arguing. Enough driving myself crazy about things that might never happen.

"I want to try." I did. Trying felt like the only thing I was sure of.

"Then do it," Liv stated. "You don't have to tell the others anything until you're ready. Keep Leah to yourself and see where it goes. Just know, we'll always be here for you, whatever happens."

Talking to Liv was cathartic, and it'd helped me voice some of the things that were eating away at me. I'd given myself a few hours to act like an idiot, but I was done. Life wasn't about playing it safe. I knew that. Now, I was about to embark on another adventure. I needed to grab it with both hands and see where it took me. Enjoy the ride and to hell with the consequences. To succeed, you had to be willing to take risks. This wasn't even a risk, it was an experience; a life experience that I didn't want to miss, not if I was truly honest with myself.

"Thanks, Liv," I said as I stood to leave. "I feel better for talking to you."

"That's what I'm here for." She winked, and I left feeling lighter and more confident than I had done when I'd first arrived.

I could do this.

CHAPTER NINETEEN
Devon

It was the night of Leah May's performance, and I was eager for the hours to move faster than they were. I showered and stood staring at my wardrobe like a bloody woman for far too long, trying to decide what to put on. I finally settled on the same black shirt and black jeans that I always wore if we were going out. It didn't really matter what I wore, all that mattered was getting to that town hall to see her. Eight o'clock couldn't come fast enough.

After checking myself in the mirror one last time, I went out to meet Adam and Liv, who were waiting for me in the hallway. Liv smiled a knowing smile and Adam just patted me on the back.

"You're doing the right thing," Liv said, her eyes twinkling with excitement. "This is going to mean the world to her."

"I hope you're right," I replied, stuffing my hands into my

pockets and trying to fight my nerves.

She was right though. How could I not turn up? This night would mean everything to Leah May, I knew that, and I had to be there to witness it.

"I'm always right." Liv smirked and Adam gave her a sly smile that told me he knew it too.

I walked in step with them both, heading towards the back stairs. It was crazy to think I could kill a man and not break into a sweat, not even give it a second thought. But the idea of seeing my little raven, sitting on a stage being vulnerable, that damn near terrified me. To think she was brave enough to go up and play in front of all those people told me all I needed to know about her. She could be fearless. She had guts. She was strong enough to deal with a man like me and my baggage. I felt ashamed that I'd ever doubted that, even for one second.

"Do you think I should call or text her? Give her a heads up that I'll be there?" I asked as we made our way down the stairs.

"No. I think it'll be a nice surprise for her to see you there. Anyway, she might get more nervous if you call. Let her do her thing and then go to her. You'll forever be her hero for doing this off your own back. Trust me."

I did trust Liv.

I also trusted my instincts that told me after tonight, my life would never be the same again.

***

Merivale town hall was one of those Greek style buildings, with white pillars and statues of guys no one had ever heard of placed at the entrance and scattered throughout the hallway. It was a far cry from the venues we'd usually go to on a Saturday night.

Adam had suggested we hold back and let the crowds go in first. I agreed. It was better to keep a lower profile when you weren't on your own hunting ground, and we were a few miles away from Brinton Manor. But we had no beef with Merivale, so we weren't overly concerned.

Once inside, we headed towards the main hall and found three seats towards the back. Liv sat in-between us, and I took the aisle seat, giving me a perfect view of the stage.

The place was fancy, albeit with a nineteen-eighties vibe. Plush red velvet was everywhere; on the seats, the stage curtains, even the walls had red panels painted sporadically around the hall to add to the effect. On the ornate ceiling there were chandeliers that'd seen better days, but they still managed to sparkle through the dust that'd settled over the years. And then, as I was trying to scope the crowd and see if I recognised any faces, the lights dimmed, and the compere welcomed everyone over the loudspeakers. When he said, "Ladies and gentlemen, please give it up for our first performer of the night. A uniquely talented star of the future, our very own, Miss Leah May Johnson," a wave of nausea coursed through me.

This was it.

The curtains opened to reveal a single chair in the middle of the stage, a microphone placed in front of it, and the spotlight shining ready for her.

"Here we go," Liv leaned over and whispered.

I couldn't reply even if I wanted to. I had no words. No breath left in me. And then she appeared, drifting on from the side of the stage, holding her acoustic guitar and smiling timidly at the crowd.

Her hair hung in dark waves, and she wore a black dress that came to her knees—she looked fucking stunning. She smiled at someone in the front row, and when I strained to look and see who it was, I noticed her father sitting there next to her cousin, Jodie. Leah May sat down on the chair as the hall held their breath, and she placed the guitar strap over her head, settling the guitar on her lap. Then, she looked up one last time and her eyes met mine. Even from this distance, I could see her chest heave as she gave a surprised gasp, and her eyes widened. Then she smiled, closed her eyes and opened them again, looking right at me, like she'd expected me to be a dream not a reality, a mirage or a trick of her mind. I smiled back at her, to let her know I was here. I'd got her.

"See? Totally the right thing," Liv whispered and patted my knee.

Leah started to strum the guitar, but she never took her eyes off me, and when she started to sing her version of *Radiohead's 'Creep'*, her voice haunting, soul-stirring, I knew she was singing those words to me.

The hall, the people, damn, the whole fucking world fell away as she sang each word. Fragments of my dark heart falling away and floating like that feather she sang about to attach itself to her soul.

This girl was mine.

She was meant for me.

I didn't need to question whether this was right, because it felt right. It felt like nothing else mattered other than what she was saying to me through this song. She wanted me to notice her. Notice when she wasn't around. All I did was notice her. It might've taken me longer than she hoped, but I did.

I sat mesmerised by her voice, her words, her music, and I never wanted it to end. But then, a guy around the same age as me walked onto the stage with an electric guitar, and as the second chorus hit, he started to play, turning her haunting melody into something more like the original version, and I didn't like it. She didn't need him to stand out or to make herself heard. She was good enough to carry this performance on her own. He sauntered forward with a cocky swagger as he played his loud-ass guitar riff over her delicate voice, then he looked at Leah May, and the fire he had in his eyes made me want to burn the fucking world down.

Liv must've felt me stiffen in the seat next to her because she leaned over and whispered, "Calm your demons. He's a nobody. She hasn't taken her eyes off you once."

But my demons weren't aimed at Leah May. I knew she was an angel, my little raven. But him? He needed to be put in his place.

With every strum of his pointless electric guitar, my anger ranked up a notch. With every heated glance he threw her way, my muscles tensed. My brain went into overdrive, imagining all the ways I could eliminate him from the face of the earth. His closeness made me clench my fists and grind my teeth. And in my mind, the same word repeated over and over again like a mantra.

Mine.

Mine.

Mine.

***

A few hours later, after all the acts had finished, we made our way to the foyer. I could see Leah May's dad talking to a group of men in the corner, and Jodie chatting to some girl I didn't recognise.

"Wait here for her," Liv told me. "She'll want to see you."

I didn't intend to go anywhere else. I wanted to see her. I also had someone else I wanted to have a few choice words with.

"I'm not going anywhere," I replied, "Don't feel like you have to wait for me. I can get a taxi home."

Adam fished the car keys from his pocket and said, "I'm taking Liv for a meal and then we're going to have a few drinks. You take the car; we'll get a cab."

"Are you sure?" I asked, taking the keys off him.

"Yep." He patted my shoulder then put his arm around Liv to pull her closer to him. "Don't wait up." He winked, then they both walked out.

I stood against the wall, my arms folded over my chest, waiting for her to come out. When I saw the blond-haired guy, who'd duetted with her on stage, come sauntering out first like he was a fucking rock God, my back went up and I pushed myself off the wall, ready to go and have a little chat with him.

He was talking to a group of girls when I approached, and as he saw me, he smiled and put his hand out to shake mine.

"Hey, man. Did you enjoy the show?" I just stared down at his hand and smirked at his audacity. Did he really think I was a fan coming to talk to him?

"I enjoyed watching Leah May own the fucking stage," I hissed, and sensing my animosity, the group of girls stepped out of the way. "Not quite sure what your role was though."

The guy gave an awkward chuckle and ran his hand over the back of his neck nervously.

"Leah was awesome. I really enjoyed duetting with her."

"I bet you did." I stepped into his space and looked him dead in the eyes. "But if you ever look at her again the way you looked at her tonight, I will gouge your eyes out and shove them up your ass." I saw his Adam's apple bob as he swallowed, processing what I'd said. "I'll snap every single one of your fucking fingers, so you never play another fucking note again. And—" Just as I was about to tell him what I had planned for his dick, I heard her breathless voice.

"Devon. You came."

I narrowed my eyes at him for just a second longer, and then I turned to look at her, to see her gazing at me in wonder.

"Of course I came. Where else would I be?"

She smiled wide and the guy next to us, the blond fucker, cleared his throat and said, "It was a great night. I'll see you around, Leah. And mate" —he turned to me—"I heard you loud and clear. You'll get no trouble from me."

The guy left us, striding away like he couldn't escape fast enough.

"What happened with Niall?" Leah May asked, frowning at him as he attached himself to another group of girls in the farthest corner away from us.

"Nothing. I just told him I didn't think you needed him up on stage with you tonight. You carried that performance all on your own." She turned away from Niall and looked at me as I added, "You were fucking amazing."

"Do you really think so?" She smoothed a strand of stray hair behind her ear, and her cheeks grew pink as she blushed. "I wasn't sure whether I did it justice. Everyone loves the guitar in the original, that's why I went with Niall's suggestion. I prefer the acoustic version myself though, but sometimes, I'm not always right. You have to think about the audience, and—"

I put my hand on her cheek and ran my thumb over her bottom lip to stop her talking.

"Trust in yourself," I urged her. "Listen to what your heart tells you."

But she shook her head slightly and replied, "The voices I hear aren't always right. I get confused sometimes."

"Then next time, ask me. Trust me."

I kept my thumb on her lip, desperate to kiss her again and taste her sweetness when I heard a gasp coming from behind.

"You have got to be shitting me?" Jodie was standing right next to us, and reluctantly, I dropped my hand, but I reached forward and pulled Leah May towards me. I needed her closer.

"Hey, Jodie. Did I do okay?" Leah asked, and instantly I wanted to tell her she didn't need to ask that. She didn't need Jodie's approval. She didn't need anyone's approval.

"You knocked it out of the fucking park, just like you always do," Jodie replied, still glaring at me, and even though I knew she was here to show her annoyance at my presence, she did go up slightly in my estimation. "But what the fuck, Leah? What's going on?"

I didn't want to make Leah May feel uncomfortable, so I spoke first.

"I came to see Leah May play. Not that it's any of your business."

"I couldn't care less about that," she spat. "I want to know why you're mauling her face in the middle of the foyer." Then she turned to Leah and added, "Your dad is standing right over there. He could've seen you."

I felt Leah reach for my hand and take it in hers, and I couldn't stop the smug smile from spreading across my face.

"I really couldn't give a shit," Leah said on a whisper that I found cute, endearing even. She was cursing but trying to hide it. Even in anger, she kept her sweet side. "Devon and I, we're together. So Dad will just have to get used to it. You all will."

Jodie bit her lip, smiling. Deep down, I guessed she liked that Leah was showing more of a rebellious side.

"Leah, if that's what makes you happy, then go for it." She looked me up and down then added, "No matter who it is you choose. I just thought I'd give you a heads up, that's all. I know what your dad can be like."

I felt my hackles rise.

Was her dad controlling?

Did he hurt her?

But before I could question her, Jodie gave one more parting shot as she turned to leave.

"Devon, you seem like a great guy, all things considered. I was really grateful that you looked after me a few weeks ago. But I swear, if you ever hurt my cousin, I will hunt you down, cut your balls off, and feed them to my dog. Do you understand?"

I laughed. I couldn't help it. I threw my head back and laughed out loud, drawing the attention of the people around us.

"You've got nothing to worry about from me," I told her, and she nodded, then grinned.

"Hi, Uncle Nathan," she sang, her mouth twisting into a tauntingly teasing, smug smile. "I'll leave you three alone." She spun around and scuttled away like a rat from a drowning ship.

THE REAPER

Leah May's dad, Father Johnson, came to stand in front of us. I didn't let his presence unnerve me. I'd dealt with scarier men than him. Father Johnson was a pussy cat compared to the men in my life.

He leaned down to place a kiss on Leah's forehead and said proudly, "You were amazing up there, sweetheart. Absolutely spectacular, and I felt her, you know. Your mum. She was sitting right with me, watching you."

Leah squeezed my hand as she replied, "I know, Dad. I felt her too."

He schooled his expression as he looked at our joined hands and then back up at me.

"I don't think we've been introduced," he said, holding his hand out expectantly.

I took it and shook his hand, noticing that he had a limp, weak gestured handshake.

"Dad, this is Devon, my—"

"Boyfriend," I cut in, wanting to make sure he knew exactly who I was.

His brow furrowed in confusion, and he said, "Devon, as in the Brinton Manor Devon? The one who runs that new club, whatever it's called?"

"The Sanctuary," I corrected him. "And yes, that's me."

"Then I believe we've already had dealings with one another over the chapel."

He was cutting right to the chase.

"Yes. You contested our use of it, and we conceded. The chapel remains empty." A little white lie never hurt anyone. "It shall forever remain sacred ground."

Sacred in the way that I choose.

He smiled, but I didn't trust him. Something felt off about the way he was carrying himself. Maybe it was a front he was putting on after finding out his daughter had a boyfriend he knew nothing about, or maybe he was simply a shady fucker. Only time would tell.

"I hope you don't take what happened back then personally," he stated. "You see, that chapel holds a special place in my heart. Years ago, my mother was a patient at the asylum. When I used to visit her as a boy with my father, we'd sit in that chapel and pray for her recovery. It was where I found my faith. It set me on the road that led me to my calling with the church. I would've hated to see it destroyed or desecrated in any way."

I'd be lying if I said I didn't feel some compassion for the guy. He must've had to deal with some shit too when he was growing up.

But then he added, "I'd really love to come and see it sometime. Maybe we can arrange that?"

He glanced between Leah May and me, and I knew she was thinking the same thing that I was.

Over my dead body.

"I'm sure we can work something out," I replied, knowing that would be the last thing to ever happen. I glanced down at Leah and asked, "I have the car parked outside. Can I take you home?" Then I gestured to her dad. "Unless, of course, you have other plans."

"No," they both answered, and Leah gave a little laugh.

"You go on ahead and have fun. I'll see you when you get home, love." Father Johnson gave Leah one last kiss on her head and then said his goodbyes to me. "It was nice to meet you, Devon. Look after my girl, won't you?"

THE REAPER 195

"Always," I replied.

CHAPTER TWENTY
Leah May

I held Devon's hand as we left the venue and all the way to his car that was parked around the corner. I didn't want to let it go, but he opened the passenger door for me and gestured for me to get in first. So, reluctantly, I dropped his hand and climbed into the car. I'd left my guitar behind with my dad for him to bring home, and I suddenly felt self-conscious and unsure about what to do with my hands as he got in beside me and started the engine.

"Are you okay?" he asked, reaching over to squeeze my knee before focusing his attention on pulling out into the oncoming traffic.

"Yeah, I'm still buzzing. I can't believe you came."

He smiled and gave my leg another squeeze.

"I'm glad I did. I wouldn't have missed it for the world. You owned that stage."

"I'm sorry I didn't tell you about it. It wasn't that I was trying to keep it a secret, I just wasn't sure if it was something you'd be interested in." I knew I was rambling but I couldn't stop myself.

"Anything you do is something I'd be interested in." He turned to look at me and gave me a warm smile before turning back to focus on the road ahead.

I smiled too, but deep down, I felt a twinge of unease. I knew something had gone on between Devon and Niall back at the town hall. Niall could be an overconfident ass at times, and I guessed he'd rubbed Devon up the wrong way. Knowing that might've been the case, I started to witter on to avoid overthinking and worrying about something I couldn't change.

"Did you know that Thom Yorke wrote the song Creep because he really liked someone but he didn't feel good enough?" I was going to say that it was someone he loved, but I felt a bit weird using that word in the car. I don't know why, but liked came easier. "He originally recorded it as an acoustic song back in nineteen-eighty-seven when he was studying at Exeter University. He hadn't even formed the band Radiohead back then."

"Cool. I think he'd like your version," Devon said, navigating his way around a slow driver and letting me ramble on.

"The guitar blast, the one you hear on the version they released for radio, that was all John Greenwood. That was his contribution because he thought the song sounded weak and needed a stronger vibe. I guess Niall thought the same about my version," I joked, giving a hollow laugh that I didn't fully mean.

"Niall is an asshole," Devon spat, and I fought down the

butterflies that fluttered inside me as he spoke passionately about something I'd felt strongly about too. I didn't want to lose the emotions of the song, but Niall had said people wanted the theatrics and excitement that'd come from his electric guitar. I'd disagreed, but my opinion hadn't been loud enough to make a difference. I needed to rectify that. I should've stuck to my guns and kept things the way I wanted them.

"In the original" —I kept going, my brain in overdrive and my mouth working overtime to catch up—"they sung, *'You're so fucking special,'* but they felt like they had to rerecord it to make it consumer friendly. I sang their cleaner version tonight because I didn't want to upset my dad, but I agree with Thom, ditching the swear word made the song lose its anger. I like that it's an angry song, you shouldn't have to alter your art to please others." I knew I was contradicting myself. I'd compromised my art in the same way, but I hadn't liked doing it.

"I totally agree," Devon said. "You don't need to water anything down or change your art to suit anyone; your dad, Niall…"

He got me. More than anyone else I'd ever met, Devon got me. I loved that about him.

"And did you know that Thom Yorke received fan mail from murderers who wrote to him saying they could relate to the lyrics of the song? Well, so could I. So what does that say about me?"

Devon laughed, a kind, warm laugh. He wasn't mocking me; he agreed with me.

"No, I didn't know that. And it tells me you have empathy for people in all walks of life." He rubbed his chin and asked, "Leah, is there anything you don't know? Because I swear it's

THE REAPER

like sitting next to the Encyclopaedia Britannica whenever I'm with you."

I chuckled, he was right. I did have a thing for pointless knowledge. If I was working on something, I had to research and find out everything I could about it. I'd always been that way.

"I guess I just like to know about stuff. If I'm doing something, working on a new song or writing about something, I like to find out everything I can."

"You're like Tyrion Lannister," he said, giving me a sly wink. "Only you sing, play, and you know stuff. Less of the drinking."

I loved that he referenced that book and the show. I'd watched it so many times. Dad hated it, but I'd watched it in my room alone. I'd read the books too. It seemed like there were so many levels that connected us. Okay, so it was only a story, but to me, it was so much more. He liked what I liked.

"I love Game of Thrones," I stated, unsure how to tell him that he'd just touched another string in my heart.

"Me too," he replied. "But if I was in Game of Thrones, I wouldn't be like the others, I'd be like the Hound, or I'd run with the brotherhood with no banners. That's the kind of family I'd be a part of. A badass brotherhood."

"You already are." I laughed.

I didn't know I could love this man anymore.

I was wrong.

He'd been made by the Gods, especially for me.

It was official.

Devon pulled into the country lane where I lived, but I didn't want the night to end.

"Have you ever seen my dad's church?" I asked, clutching at straws, trying to think of some way to make him stay a little longer.

I wasn't sure when my dad would be home, and I didn't want to bring Devon into the house, not yet. I wanted him to myself. I wasn't ready to share, and I knew my dad would have a million questions. I was surprised he'd seemed so relaxed about me having a boyfriend in the first place. That wasn't like my dad. He'd always told me how much he'd hated the idea of me finding a boyfriend or ever leaving him.

A boyfriend.

It didn't feel real, and yet when I said it, I couldn't stop smiling. I felt like a kid at Christmas.

"No offense, but I'm not really a church person." Devon drove a little further down from my house and parked up at the kerb. "But the graveyard… maybe that'd be more my thing?"

I grinned back at him. Yes, the graveyard was definitely more like Devon.

***

We got out of the car and walked the short distance towards the graveyard beside my dad's church. It was a full moon, and the shine of light that cast over the gravestones gave it a gothic, eerie feel. I loved it. Like darkness was shrouding us but the moon was guiding our way.

I lifted the metal latch on the wrought-iron gate and stepped through. Devon followed me, his eyes burning into me as I picked my way across the grass to walk between the graves. I turned to look at him and the moon's reflection on his pale skin made him look other-worldly, haunting but beautifully so. His eyes were hooded, as his stare pierced me with the level of intensity I saw there. If I didn't know any better, I'd say he was transforming into a hunter, a thief in the night, and I was about to become his prey. His steps were measured, predatory, long and sure strides, as if he was gaining on me, moving with slow determination as I tiptoed away.

"So, tell me what you know," he whispered in a gravelly voice that made my insides clench with anticipation.

"What do you mean?" I asked, my head lost to the effect this night, this moon, and this man was having on me.

"What do you know about the graveyard?" He took another long slow stride towards me and lifted his chin. "You know everything." He dragged his fingers over the top of one of the gravestones and added, "What's the oldest grave you have in here?"

I stared at him, not even daring to blink in case I lost this connection we seemed to be forging in amongst the shadows of the gravestones. The way he stared back at me, standing a few feet away, and yet feeling like every inch of his soul was clasped tightly around mine made me shiver.

"Are you cold?" he asked, and then shrugged his coat from his shoulders.

"I'm fine," I replied, but when he came to stand next to me and draped his coat over me, I couldn't help but pull it tighter around myself. The warmth of the heavy fabric and the scent of him everywhere made me take a deep breath, desperate to fill my lungs. I'd always found certain aromas could soothe my soul. The scent of my mum, my dad, our house. But now, I had a new favourite—him.

I burrowed my face into the collar as he stood close to me, his warm breath on my face suddenly made me aware of how close we were and how much I wanted to lean forward and kiss him.

But I didn't.

Instead, I stepped back, nervous about making a fool of myself, and I started to walk through the graves, zigzagging between them slowly as I told him, "The oldest grave in here belongs to Arthur Mabberley. He died in eighteen-sixty-two, aged twenty-six, a loving father, son, and husband to Mary, who was buried in the same plot a few years later. Church records show he died of consumption."

"I've never understood what that means," he replied as he followed my steps like my forbidden shadow.

"Today, consumption is known as TB, tuberculosis. Back then it was called consumption because it consumed the whole being of the person who contracted it. It was an agonisingly slow death. Bacteria would burrow its way into your lungs, eating away at the tissue from the inside out until your chest began to fill with blood as the destroyed lung tissue turned to mush. Eventually, the lungs would totally liquify, meaning the patient couldn't breathe anymore, and then they'd drown inside their own body."

Devon hissed and shook his head.

"And they think we're twisted for what we do. I think God invented some pretty sick ways to kill people. If there even is a God."

I didn't want to get into a discussion on faith, so I changed the subject.

"My favourite gravestone is Penny Picker's. She died aged

THE REAPER

eighty-two, and her headstone reads, 'I told you I was sick'.

Devon laughed. "If I were buried here, not that I would be, but I'd have to have something like, 'Here lies an atheist. All dressed up and nowhere to go'."

I laughed at his dry humour, and then remembering my own experience of settling on a headstone and all the crippling emotions that came along with it, I gave a weak smile.

"My mum wanted the recipe for her favourite fudge carved into hers, but when the time came, Dad couldn't bring himself to do it." I sighed. "They were like chalk and cheese, my mum and dad, but it didn't matter. Their love always won out in the end."

They were the reason I believed true love could conquer all. Their relationship, the closeness they had, it had been the benchmark that I'd always aspired to. The love that I wanted for myself.

"She sounds cool," Devon said with a quiet reverence. "I wish I could've met her. You'll have to tell me more about her one day." Empathy shone from his eyes, but that wasn't what I wanted to see. I wanted the fire that I saw before.

"One day," I replied. "But not today." I wanted this night to be about us. Exciting, new, an adventure that I would always remember. Those memories had no place here, no matter how precious they were.

Suddenly, I felt self-conscious, so I turned away, creeping further into the heart of the graveyard.

"Did you know that in the olden days, the type of stone used to make your grave used to represent how wealthy you were?" Devon hummed something that sounded like he was feigning interest. "If you had marble or granite, you were rich, but poorer people had sandstone, lime, or if they were really poor, wood."

"Or a ditch." He shrugged, and I carried on, each step feeling like I was luring him into an abyss, with no idea what the outcome would be. But the excitement I was feeling, firing up inside of me, only spurred me on even more.

"Early gravestones were rumoured to face the east. They said you had to have the feet pointing east, and the head towards the west, that way, on the rise of a new day, you'd be facing the sun, ready to be reborn."

"That sounds like a crock of shit," he spat back, and I could hear the playfulness in his voice as he said, "Are you trying to get away from me?"

"No."

I was, but only because I felt nervous, and I couldn't seem to stop my feet from wandering deeper into the darkness.

"I think you're lying to me. I bet if you stopped and turned around to look at me, I'd see the truth in your eyes. I can always see what you're thinking in those eyes of yours, Leah May."

My heart fluttered hearing his gravelly, seductive tone, like liquid velvet making my body melt and yearn for him. The way he spoke, knowing that he saw through all the bullshit, created a warmth inside of me. In my eyes, he noticed the real me, the one I kept hidden from the world, locked behind closed doors. No one had ever found the key before, the key to my soul. But here, in this graveyard, I felt like he'd taken ownership, changed the locks and woken up a side of me that I never wanted to lose again. He'd breathed life into me and made me feel excited for what was to come. I hadn't felt alive like this for a long time.

"They call Mount Everest the 'Graveyard in the Clouds'." I don't know why I was still talking. It was like my mouth had bypassed my brain that was currently screaming at me to shut the hell up and throw myself at this man and climb him like a monkey up a tree. "So many hikers have died up there—"

"I couldn't give a rat's ass if the bloody pope died up there." He laughed. "Come here."

He reached forward to grab my arm, and I don't know why, maybe because in that moment I felt playful and wanted to tease him, but I turned and started to run away, dancing through the graves and panting as I laughed. I could hear him behind me, hot on my heels, the heaviness of his breathing as he picked up his pace made my skin prickle in excitement. He'd catch up to me, capture me, and what then? What would happen when he had me?

I glanced over my shoulder to see how close he was and didn't notice the stone jutting out of the ground. My body twisted as I fell onto the grass, landing on my back. I was lucky I hadn't injured myself, and as I lay on the ground, he came to stand over me, and I couldn't stop the laughter from breaking free.

But he didn't laugh.

He just stared down at me. A storm was brewing in his eyes, darkness clouding his vision as a veil of wicked intent seemed to fall over him. Right before my eyes, the reaper everyone had spoken about from Brinton Manor appeared. Only my reaper wasn't here to take my soul, he was here to own it.

"You're more like me than I ever thought possible," he whispered, his rasping voice sparking every nerve in my body to come to life. "I always said I never liked doing things the easy way. Seems you're the same, if that little chase you just made me do was anything to go by. Do you like me chasing you?"

I nodded, struck dumb, and slowly he knelt on the grass

beside me. Then, like a tiger, he crawled over my body, his arms holding the weight of his upper body, but his legs and his hips sliding over mine.

"I like chasing you too." His voice was like a seductive wave warming me from within, making me crave what was about to happen.

His face hovered over mine as we both stared, savouring the moment, and yet, pining for more.

Then he lowered himself and whispered in my ear, "You want to talk to me about death, but right now, the only thing I'm interested in is this very alive, very beautiful creature lying underneath me." His nose grazed my neck as he inhaled and then gruffly, he added, "I have dark thoughts too. Is that something you want to explore? With me?"

I nodded again, feeling no need for words.

He lifted his head, and then his hand skimmed up my side, over my chest, and he placed his hand at the base of my neck.

"I love how smooth you are. You're so soft," he said, his thumb brushing over the pulse in my neck.

My heart was beating furiously out of my chest, and I held my breath as he gripped my neck, squeezing lightly, but I wasn't scared. I lifted my chin, exposing more of myself to him, and he smiled.

"You like my touches, don't you?" he whispered as I shivered from the contact.

"I like everything you do," I replied, surprised I could form words.

Smiling, he leant down, licking over the pulse in my neck and then kissing up to my jawline. When he reached my mouth, I opened to him, hungry for his kiss. He was hungry too, and he took what he wanted, kissing me hard, desperately. Tongues and teeth clashed as we writhed on the ground, devouring each other. The taste of his mouth, minty and deliciously him, was a drug I'd always crave. I couldn't get enough. The warmth of his kiss, his body, all of it was so much more than I'd ever expected. Devon's kisses had always been the stuff of my dreams. Thoughts of being his were what had fuelled every single one of my fantasies. But now that I'd experienced the real thing, a fantasy would never be enough. I'd always want more.

His hand moved from my neck to grab my waist and pull me closer to him.

"Use me," he urged, and instinctively, I opened my legs, knowing that I needed him closer. I bent my knee, lifting my leg so I could wrap it around his waist, and he reached down to grab my thigh, pulling me further into him and grinding his hips against me.

"That's it," he said in a low growl as he broke our kiss to nibble on my earlobe. "Rub yourself against me, do what makes you feel good." And then he bit my neck gently and moaned. "I'll make you feel good, baby."

I angled my neck, loving how feral it made him to kiss and tease me there. He licked over the skin he'd just bitten, and I hissed and moaned. There was a yearning, aching burn in my gut, and wetness between my legs. Everything he was doing was driving me crazy, and I felt like I'd die if he ever stopped. My fingers scraped the back of his neck, scratching, clawing, needing, and my hips circled against his, grinding to create the friction I craved to ease this ache inside of me.

"Devon, please don't stop," I begged as we lay together in the middle of the graveyard, in the dead of night.

Darkness was all around us, the moon and stars the only witness to the lust that was consuming our souls. Devon's hips were rocking against mine, moving in a way that made me cling to him like he was my anchor. Faster and faster, he moved, kissing me, moaning, consuming me. I could feel how hard he was as he rubbed and ground himself against me. I ran my hands down his back, grabbing his jeans and pulling him closer, and as his kisses moved from my mouth back to my neck, I cried out into the night, feeling a burning, tingling sensation building. I felt like I was chasing something, something I didn't understand yet, but I knew I couldn't stop. I couldn't stop my hips from grinding into his.

"I want you," Devon groaned, and his hand stroked over my hip and then grazed along my thigh.

Tentatively, he brushed his fingers across my skin, tracing gentle circles under the skirt of my dress. I could tell he was holding back, and I didn't want that. I didn't want him to treat me like I was something fragile. I wanted to be owned. I needed him to take charge, and when I groaned into the night and begged, "You have me. Please. Touch me..." he heard me.

His fingers dug into my skin, his hand palming my thigh with rougher, more insistent strokes, and then he reached around to grab my ass and squeeze hard. I cried into the darkness, and he moaned too, moving his hand to rest in-between my legs, and then gently, he stroked his fingers over my knickers.

"So wet for me." He gasped, and when his fingers teased the lace of my underwear, moving them aside, I felt like I was ready to explode. I had to feel his fingers on me, inside me. I couldn't stand to be teased any longer. "I love the sounds you make, the feel of you under me, but this," he said, slowly running his finger along my pussy. "This feels like fucking heaven."

The moment I felt him touching me there, I moaned, pushing forward onto the palm of his hand. He stroked along my pussy, circling my entrance, and then trailing his fingers up to my clit, rubbing and stroking in delicate flickers that made me cry out in ecstasy. He rolled my sensitive nub between his fingers, and then circled it, drawing out the most delicious sensations from my body. Heat, desire and need coursed through me with an urgency I'd never felt before. His touches lit me up, turned me inside out, and as he slid his fingers lower to push one inside me, his thumb still circling my clit, I clung to him, desperate with a frenzied desire I couldn't contain.

"Oh, Devon. Please don't stop," I cried, and he buried his head in my neck to kiss me as his fingers fucked me hard. My legs were shaking, and my body didn't feel like mine anymore. I had no control. I belonged to him. He commanded me.

The burning intensified, the tingle became too much but not enough, and then, just as Devon lifted his head to look at me, I felt a burst, a spark between my legs, like a firework had gone off inside my body.

"Holy fucking fuck." I gasped as my legs started to quiver. "What the fuck?" I'd never had an orgasm before, even when I tried on my own, and lying there, seeing stars dancing before my eyes and feeling the gentle pulse as my soul drifted out of my body, I knew I would never be the same again.

Devon placed his forehead against mine as he panted, trying to catch his breath. His hand was still between my legs and his fingers were massaging, caressing, exploring and making the explosions that I'd felt before flicker and spark back to life.

"That's it, baby, close your eyes and ride it out. Feel what

I'm doing to you. Squeeze my fingers and soak me with your cum."

I'd never heard him talk like this, but I couldn't deny it did things to me. I loved his dirty words, but the intensity of the moment and the feelings were becoming overwhelming. It was too much; I was too sensitive.

"I can't," I whimpered, and sensing what I needed, he slowed his strokes, bringing me back down to earth.

"Fucking hell," he rasped. "That was the most intense, fucking unbelievable, mind-blowing, non-sex, sex ever. If it's like that for us when we've got our clothes on, we are in for a crazy ride, and I am so here for it." He smiled and slowly pulled his finger out of me. I gasped at the loss of him, but when he brought his hand up to taste me, licking and then putting his finger in his mouth, I felt my core clenching all over again. "You taste incredible." He moaned, and I sighed. I never thought seeing something like that would be so sexy but watching him taste me was like nothing I'd ever seen before. It was dirty, taboo, filthy, and I loved it.

"Are you okay?" he asked, cradling me in his arms.

I nuzzled into him, knowing I'd found home in this man, and I replied, "More than okay."

We lay together for a while longer, holding each other. I could've stayed in the graveyard all night, but as I began to stifle my yawns, Devon lifted himself off me and said, "I need to take you home. It's been a long night."

He held his hand out and I took it, letting him pull me from the ground. Then I melted into him as he put his arm around me to lead me back to the vicarage.

Once we reached my door, he grabbed my face in his hands.

THE REAPER

"My little raven needs her rest." He smiled and gave me a gentle, loving kiss.

I felt the tears well up in my eyes, and he frowned. "What's the matter?"

"You called me little raven," I whispered, holding back my tears. "That's what my mum used to call me."

Concern etched his face as he asked, "Do you want me to stop? I didn't mean to upset you. It's just that in my head, I've always called you my little raven."

"No." I placed my hands on his cheeks, stroking his face, so the frown lines would disappear. "I love it. You just caught me off guard, that's all. I love that nickname."

He gave me one last smile, placed a gentle kiss on the tip of my nose and said, "Well then, goodnight, little raven."

Hearing him say that name again made gentle waves of warmth and comfort flow through me. Reluctantly, I shrugged his coat from my shoulders, already missing the smell of him. Then he waited for me to open the door and step inside before he walked back down the path to his car.

Why did it feel like my heart was twisting in an unforgiving way every time he left me?

Inside, I could hear my dad clattering around in the kitchen, and the whistle from the kettle told me he was making a cup of tea. I popped my head around the corner of the door to let him know I was home safe.

"You did well tonight, sweetheart. I was so proud of you."

"Thanks, Dad. I'm going to head straight to bed if that's okay. Goodnight," I said, turning to leave.

"What's that in your hair?" he asked, making me stop and run my fingers through the strands. I felt a crisp leaf entwined in the curls at the back of my head and I used my nails to entice it out.

"It's just a leaf. Its windy out there tonight." I knew I was blushing, but I put the leaf in the bin by the door and walked towards the staircase.

"So windy it blew the mud from the floor and plastered it to the back of your legs too from the look of it." I pretended I hadn't heard my dad berating me. That was a conversation I was not willing to have tonight. But I couldn't keep the smile from spreading across my face and a quiet laugh from breaking free.

Devon had made me dirty in more ways than one, and I loved it.

When I got to my room, I turned the lights on and closed the door, ready to get cleaned up and enjoy a night of dreaming about him. And there, sitting on my pillow, waiting to show me how proud they were of my performance tonight, sat a single black origami raven.

"Thanks, Dad." I sighed as I picked it up and ran my thumb gently along the delicate wings. "And thanks for making these for the future you couldn't be a part of, Mum."

I was truly blessed.

Life was starting to look up for me.

The raven was finally flying high.

CHAPTER TWENTY-ONE
Devon

Walking back into The Sanctuary, I could already feel a sense of foreboding threatening to burst through the bubble of euphoria I was revelling in after my night with Leah May. I took the back stairs, and with each step, a darkness began to engulf me. When I finally reached our floor and walked towards the living room, the hushed voices warned me I was about to embark on something I wouldn't like.

I strolled through the door to find them all sitting together, and when they saw me, they glanced between themselves with a mixture of trepidation and guilt.

Adam was the first to speak, holding up a familiar white envelope then throwing it down on the table. Gravely, he announced, "You've had another one."

Tyler piped up next, not even giving me the chance to open

the letter and read what it said.

"We checked the CCTV. It was a guy that delivered it to the back door about two hours ago. We couldn't identify him though. Maybe you might, if you take a look?"

"Can I open the letter first?" I snapped and stalked over to the sofa where Liv and Adam were, snatching the envelope from the table and ripping it open.

Adam stared straight at me as I read, anger making his face burn red and a snarl curl his lip. Liv sighed and rested her head on Adam's shoulder, trying to calm his demons. The others sat quietly and waited.

> Oh, Devon. You won't get away with what you've done. You're a fool to think you ever would. I'm coming for you.
>
> Do you remember what happened after our darts match? I think I'll have a better aim this time, when I have you chained up properly. That bullseye will be the least of your worries.
>
> So, if you know what's good for you, you'll run. Run away like the coward you are and never come back to Brinton Manor. This is your final warning.
>
> Vinnie.

The screech of white noise in my head resonated through my brain, piercing my ears and shattering my heart. I crumpled the paper and threw it across the room in anger. How fucking dare they do this to me. Dragging up all the bullshit about the darts game they'd played when I was chained to the radiator as a kid. I guessed that was this fucker's way of showing me he knew all about me. Making sure I knew it wasn't some chancer doing this—coming at me with empty threats. Whoever it was, they knew their stuff, I'd give them that. But I knew stuff too. I knew how to fight back now. I'd always fight back.

The demands that I leave Brinton were laughable. Like that'd ever happen. I wasn't a coward, not even as a kid who was being beaten and abused. Backing down wasn't in my make-up. My DNA had fighter embedded deep within. And besides, I had more than enough reasons to stay—Leah May being at the top of that list. If he thought this crap he was pulling would scare me, he had another thing coming.

"When I finally catch him, I'm going to enjoy tearing this guy apart with my bare hands," I hissed, fury blinding my reasoning, venom tainting my resolve. "I won't need weapons for this one. I want to use every ounce of strength I have to send him back to hell."

Adam stood up, stalking over to where the letter lay discarded in the corner of the room, and he picked it up. Smoothing the crumpled paper, he read what was written, then snarled and glared at me.

"Do you think it's him? Vinnie?" Adam asked, passing the letter to Tyler to share with the others.

"No, I don't. But it's definitely someone who knew him. They want me to know that too, that's why they added all that shit about the darts game."

"Who else was there that night? Who played that darts game?" Will questioned, and I sat down, running my hands over my face, wishing that the high from my night with Leah May had lasted a little longer.

"There was Ray, Nigel, and Vinnie. That's it. No one else was there apart from me."

"We took care of Ray back at the old meat factory." Colton grinned and added, "That was a hit I'll never forget. The slicer, the bone saws…" He screwed his face up, then remembered Liv was in the room and looked apologetically at Adam, then he shrugged like it was nothing. "Best use for any meat grinder if you ask me."

"Nigel was the one we strapped to the chair in that abandoned barber's shop, am I right?" Will asked, and Colton started to nod, his reminiscing turning from meat grinders and slicers to cutthroat razors, straight-bladed scissors, and scissors with serrations that for the barber would've been used to cut finer hair, but we used them for the finer touches of our torture plan.

"There isn't a chance in hell either one of those guys is behind this. Ghosts don't talk. So that leaves stepdaddy dearest," Colton announced.

It was true that Ray, Nigel, and all the other men who'd been a part of Vinnie's crew had been killed by all five of us. Taunted at first with our game of consequences, then put down like the dogs they were. Vinnie was the only one I killed alone. But I knew he was dead. There was no way this was him.

"Show him the CCTV," Adam cut in, knowing I was about to lose my shit over them questioning my murder skills again.

Tyler placed the laptop on the table in front of me, and I leaned forward as it played out. A tall, dark figure dressed all in black was videoed posting the letter and walking away. Nothing stood out. Nothing looked out of the ordinary. The cap that he wore, a cap that most of the men in this area owned, was pulled low over his face so no features could be identified. It was the most pointless piece of evidence. It gave nothing away.

"It's not him. For a start, that guy's a scrawny sack of shit," I stated, feeling pissed off.

"Maybe a few years at the bottom of the canal did wonders for his figure?" Colton joked, but no one laughed.

"He's too tall as well. Did the water give him a few added inches in that department?" I slammed the laptop shut and cursed under my breath.

I hated not knowing who this was, and from the grimaces that I saw on the faces that surrounded me, they felt the same way. There was no chance that this could be Vinnie or his mates. Anyone that he had dealings with, everyone in his fucked-up crew, we'd already dealt with.

All except the one person closest to him.

Stella.

"It's got to be Stella." I gritted my teeth, eager to face-off with her and stop this bullshit. "She's the only person that's still alive that might know about all this. Maybe she hired someone to deliver the letters?"

"You need to go and talk to her, man. Have it out with her. Let her know you're on to her and she can't fuck you about like this anymore." Adam was right, and the murmur of agreement around the room told me what I had to do.

"Oh, I will. Tomorrow, I'll pay her a little visit. Let her know what's what. She might think she's smart, but I'm smarter."

"We'll come with you," Tyler added. I appreciated the sentiment, but this was something I had to do on my own.

"No need. This is a cat I want to skin all by myself."

CHAPTER TWENTY-TWO
Devon

The next morning, I stood on the step of Stella's small terraced house, and when she opened the door, she smirked at me then appeared to bend forward, looking for something on the floor.

"What are you doing?" I was irritated enough without her adding to it with her bullshit tricks.

"I'm looking for the cat that dragged you here."

I didn't laugh. Her use of pointless sayings was pitiful humour at best.

"Cut the crap, Stella." I stepped over the threshold, and she didn't stop me, just looked me up and down like I was a piece of shit. "The less time I spend here, the better. Let me say my piece, then I'll leave. You don't want me here anymore than I do."

"You've got that right, tin soldier boy." She slammed the

door behind me and walked back down the hall. "So, to what do I owe the pleasure?"

I followed her into her pristine living room full of cabinets of china ornaments and weird creepy-ass porcelain dolls. It was like walking into the horror museum in the film, *The Conjuring*. It wouldn't surprise me if she had a few voodoo dolls stashed away behind the freaky-eyed Annabelle that stared at me wherever I walked.

"I would offer you a cup of tea, but I don't want to." She smirked, inwardly congratulating herself on putting me down.

"I wouldn't drink it anyway. It'd probably be laced with arsenic."

She didn't deny it, just sat down in her recliner chair and lifted her chin defiantly to give me an evil grin.

"It'd be no worse than what you did to my boy. I reckon an eye for an eye would be apt in this instance."

I wasn't going to beat around the bush, so I cut to the chase and came right out with it.

"It's you, isn't it?"

She swivelled slightly in her chair to face me and gave me one of her deadly stares.

"What's me?"

"The letters. You sent them, didn't you?"

Her frown lines deepened, but she gave a low chuckle.

"I haven't been sending you any letters, boy. Why would I waste valuable stamps and paper on you? Let alone the time it'd take to write down all the reasons I think you deserve to go to prison for being who you are."

"You didn't waste money on a stamp though, did you? Just sent your errand boy to hand deliver your vile bullshit."

She sat up straighter and lowered her gaze, glaring at me through her horn-rimmed glasses.

"Let's get one thing straight, soldier boy. I haven't sent you anything. If I wanted to tell you what I thought of you, I'd do it to your face. You should know that by now. Second, I can't say I'm all that disappointed to hear that someone else is onto you. I hope they pin your ass to the wall. And last but not least, do not ever curse in my house."

It didn't matter that she'd said the word ass. She was no lady, no matter how much she tried to convince herself otherwise.

"I don't believe you," I stated, folding my arms over my chest. I wasn't leaving this house until I'd gotten what I came for.

"And *I* will not lose a minute's sleep over that. So, if that's all you came here for, to accuse me of sending you some nasty letters, you can leave."

I pinched the bridge of my nose, trying to relieve some of the tension that made it difficult for me to focus clearly.

"Every Saturday we do this." I gritted my teeth, squeezing my eyes shut and willing myself to keep my cool and still get the results I wanted. "Let's have it out, right here, right now."

"You really want to do this? Because I have a whole fricking folder of stuff on you. And don't think I haven't given copies to the police too. I have and I'll keep doing it until they sling your ass in jail."

With dogged determination, she hauled herself out of her chair and went over to her sideboard, opening the drawer and taking out a large box folder. When she sat back down with a heavy sigh, she opened the box and started listing all the evidence she had.

"I've got all your school reports in here. Every single one of those teachers told your poor mother what a reprobate you were. You terrorised the other kids and the staff. You were a menace. I've got the notes from your counselling sessions that your mum took you to as well, although God knows why she bothered. When my Vinnie left, she thought she could help you with those children's mental health groups that referral unit you attended had suggested she use, but that was pointless. All you did was waste their time and spout crap, tainting my Vinnie's good character."

She started rooting through old papers, shuffling through it all like she was some mediocre Poirot on a mission to prove I was the villain.

"These pictures you drew in school, they show what a head case you were. I mean, what eight-year-old draws pictures like you did, of torture and death? I always knew you were a wrong 'un."

It was starting to become glaringly obvious what was going on here. She had no fucking evidence at all, and no idea about who I was, or her precious Vinnie.

"Stella," I scolded sharply, cutting her off and forcing her attention back on me. "I get that you hate me. I don't like you that much either. But what the fuck is all this?"

She gazed at me with her mouth open, then said, "It was you. You're the whole reason I lost my Vinnie."

"How? Spit it out, woman." I was losing my shit and fast.

"You drove him away."

I took a moment to take in what she was saying.

"He never could stand to have you around. Every time he used to come to visit me, he'd tell me all about the trouble you were in at school, the trouble you caused at home. You made his life a misery. He couldn't stand it anymore. If it wasn't for you, he'd be right back where he belongs."

Was she really as clueless as she was pretending to be?

"And you think threatening me, sending letters telling me to leave Brinton Manor is going to bring him back?"

"I haven't sent you any bloody letters," she shouted. "And regardless of whether you leave or not, he will come back. Your mum rang me just this morning to say she'd seen him again, on the corner of her road." She waggled her bony finger at me. "Mark my words, when he does come back, he's gonna whoop your ass for the way you've spoken to me over the years."

She knew nothing.

She could be bluffing, but I doubted it.

Her evidence was a ridiculous folder full of childhood bullshit. Her accusations were all flimsy threats centred around what she saw as my misbehaviour. As performances went, this one would be Oscar-worthy if she did know about Vinnie's death and was covering it all up to trick me. Stella was an evil bitch, but she wasn't that good. In front of me was a woman who thought I'd driven her son away. Nothing more, nothing less. My paranoia about her knowing more was just that—paranoia.

"Bring it on," I snapped sarcastically, knowing a reunion with a dead man wasn't on the cards, not until I finally rocked up in hell, and that wasn't happening anytime soon.

Stella tutted and got busy rearranging her valuable evidence back into her folder. I didn't bother saying goodbye, I just stalked out of there, slamming the door behind me.

So, if it wasn't Stella, who was it?

I got on the phone to my mum, still wracking my brains,

THE REAPER

trying to think why someone was watching her house, sending me letters, trying to pretend that Vinnie wasn't dead at all. Mum was no use though, she was even more blinkered to the truth than Stella, so I hung up. Maybe I had missed something all those years ago? But whatever it was, I needed to get a hold on it, and fast.

Desperate to pull myself from the dark headspace I was trapped in, I tapped out a text message to the one person I wanted to see above anyone else. The one who always quietened the noise in my life. I needed a fix of my little raven, and nothing and nobody would ever get in my way of that.

CHAPTER TWENTY-THREE
Leah May

I couldn't stop thinking about him. All the voices in my head had been replaced with thoughts of him; what he was doing, what he was thinking. When he messaged me and asked me to come to the club to see him, I almost couldn't contain myself.

I put one of my short black dresses on and styled my hair, so it fell in loose curls down my back. I applied light make-up and spritzed myself with perfume. All the while, nervous butterflies danced around in my stomach, as desperate to get to the club and see him as I was. When I emerged from my bedroom and walked downstairs, I could see the living room door wide open. Dad was reading the newspaper, and he peeked his head over the top when he heard my footsteps.

"Are you off out?" He closed the newspaper, folding it and putting it on his lap so he could give me his full attention. I

THE REAPER

stood in the doorway, debating whether to tell a little white lie to appease him, but I couldn't. It was time he started seeing me for the adult I was.

"I'm going out with Devon."

He nodded and steepled his hands under his chin.

"Is he picking you up?" He gave me a stern, knowing look and added, "A gentleman would pick a lady up. I hope he isn't asking you to meet him on some street corner somewhere."

"Of course he isn't." It bugged me that he'd think that low of Devon. "He's picking me up, but I wanted to go out to the car as soon as he got here, save him parking up and getting out." Truth was, I still wasn't ready for Devon to come in and get the third degree from my dad.

Dad mumbled something and screwed his nose up to show he didn't think much of my plan. I didn't care. Nothing was going to sour my good mood tonight.

When I saw headlights reflecting through the glass in the front door, I headed over to the window and saw Devon parking the car.

"I won't be too late," I told my dad, kissing him on the head as I rushed for the door. I heard him mutter about the shortness of my dress, but I just smiled, imagining Mum telling him to mind his own business.

Once outside, I climbed into the car, and as I shut the door, Devon asked, "Do you want me to come in for a while and talk to your dad?" The way I shook my head must've startled him because he added, "Is everything okay? Is he being all right with you?"

"He's fine." I smiled to let Devon know there was nothing to worry about. "It's just that my dad can be a bit full-on. If you go in there, you may not come out this side of Christmas."

Devon laughed and put the car into gear. "Like father, like daughter, hey?"

He pulled off and we drove towards The Sanctuary. Every now and again, he would reach across to put his hand on my knee or squeeze my thigh. Every time that he did, the butterflies in my stomach would multiply. But tonight, I didn't feel the need to fill the silence with pointless words or facts. I was enjoying being next to him. That was enough.

When we eventually pulled into the grounds of The Sanctuary, he parked the car and we both got out at the same time. Devon grabbed my hand as I headed to the front doors where the people had started to form a queue to get in, and he steered me towards the back door.

"We don't queue," he said, smiling at me.

We walked through the back entrance and into the main dance floor area, making our way through the crowds to get to the bar. Once there, Devon gestured to the barman, and without even asking what we wanted to drink, he poured a pint of lager and a vodka and coke and put them down in front of us.

"How did he know I'd want this?" I asked, lifting the glass and sipping my favourite drink.

"He didn't," Devon replied. "But I saw what you ordered the last time you were here, so I took a guess."

"Are you trying to impress me?" I gave him a sultry look and twirled my hair around my finger.

"Is it working?" The heat in his stare made my butterflies transform into fireflies and I took another sip of my vodka and coke to hide my blush.

"You know you never need to do anything special to impress

me, Devon. You won me over years ago." The words were out before I could stop them. From the startled look on his face, they'd surprised him too.

"Years?" He stared at me, waiting for a response.

"Mmhmm," was all I could manage in response.

"So, let me get this straight…" He put his lager on the bar and turned to face me, pulling my hips so I was in his line of sight. "I have wasted years? Years where I could have been getting to know you better?" He shook his head. "Damn that's a depressing thought."

"We can't change the past," I said. "All we can do is right the wrongs."

"And it is a wrong that I'm going to enjoy putting right."

***

We stayed at the bar, drinking, talking, and feeling so at ease in one another's company that it wasn't like we were standing in the middle of a club. It was as if no one else existed.

Our world.

Our bubble.

Our heaven.

"Am I going to get that dance you didn't give me the last time I was here?" I asked, feeling my confidence grow by the minute. The alcohol had helped to lower my inhibitions as the night wore on. That, and being in Devon's company. He made me want to be a little reckless. But only for him.

"I already told you," he whispered in my ear, making the skin on my neck prickle from his closeness. "I don't dance. Not in public, anyway."

"Then let's dance in private." A bold statement, but I liked being bold with him.

"I think I can do one better than that."

He took the drink out of my hand and placed it on the bar, then he took my hand and led me through the crowds towards the stairs. Once there, he greeted a security guy and we started to walk up to the next floor. I'd only been inside The Sanctuary once before, but even I'd heard the rumours about the second floor. But I wasn't fazed by it. I trusted Devon, and wherever he was leading me, I wanted to follow.

The second floor was less crowded than the first, with a few people mingling in the corridor. Down the hallway, I could see closed doors, a mystery that called to my inquisitive side.

What were those doors hiding?

There was music playing up here, but it wasn't as loud and booming as downstairs. It was piped through a sound system, not from a DJ set like the main floor.

I felt a shiver as Devon leaned into my neck and said, "I know you like watching. My little raven is also a little voyeur in her spare time."

I grinned, telling him, "I've always liked watching you."

The look on his face told me he liked it too, and then he whispered, "I'm going to show you something, but I need you to make me a promise."

"What?" I'd promise him the world if he asked for it.

He stopped in front of a door and pulled me towards him, holding me in his arms.

"I need you to promise that if you don't like what you see, you'll tell me, and we'll leave. No questions." I nodded. "I need you to promise that if you feel uncomfortable for even a second,

THE REAPER

you'll let me know." I gave another nod. "And I need you to promise that despite drinking with me downstairs, you're not too drunk to know what you're doing. To trust that I will look after and protect you, but also, to trust yourself."

I placed my hand over his heart. "I trust you, Devon." He took a deep breath, like he was giving himself one final chance to back out of whatever plan he had in his mind.

"You're in control," he stated. "Whatever happens, you get to call the shots."

He gently kissed my nose, and I couldn't help but wrinkle it and giggle from the tickling sensation. Then he leaned down and kissed me on the lips, slow and seductively. I wrapped my arms around his neck, but after a few seconds, he pulled away and asked, "Are you ready?"

"I was born ready."

CHAPTER TWENTY-FOUR
Leah May

He took my hand and led me towards the door we were standing in front of. When he opened it and walked in, I followed him, curious to find out what was inside. The room was darkly lit, with dimmed spotlights overhead. There were black leather sofas and a few tables dotted around the room with couples sitting together having a drink. Some people appeared to be on their own, but they didn't seem too bothered, they were quite happy to sip their drinks. But that wasn't what made this room special—it was the huge window that ran along the full length of one wall, showcasing an adjoining room. A dark room with a single spotlight pointed at a padded bench in the middle.

Devon led me towards the wall opposite that window and we stood next to a tall table. He leaned against the wall and pulled me to stand in front of him, my back to his chest, and his arms wrapped around me like a comfort blanket. Leaning down into my neck, he breathed deeply.

"Do you remember your promises?"

"Yes," I gasped, staring straight ahead at the window to the other room.

"Good, because the show is just about to start."

I held my breath as a man and a woman walked into the room on the other side of the window. The woman was wearing skimpy black underwear, but the man was completely naked, and both wore black masks over their eyes in an attempt to hide their identity. Devon's hold on me tightened as the woman crawled onto the bench on all fours.

I wasn't sure my voice would work but I had to ask, "Can they see us?"

"No. It's a two-way mirror. We can see them, but they can't see us."

The man knelt behind her, and I froze as he slowly peeled the woman's G-string down.

"Do they know we're watching?" I could feel my pulse quicken as I watched, and I couldn't take my eyes off them.

"Oh yes. They're regulars in this room. They like to be watched."

The man started to stroke himself as he leaned forward and darted his tongue out, licking the woman's pussy in long, slow licks from behind. I swallowed, feeling my body react at what I was seeing. My skin puckered with goosebumps, my breathing became shallow, and wetness pooled between my legs as heat and a gentle pulse made me squeeze my thighs together.

Devon nuzzled into my neck, kissing me softly as I watched what was happening. He didn't seem to be bothered by the couple in front of us. From the way he held me, and his panted breath as he kissed me, I could tell he was more turned on by my reaction. He was getting lost in me.

The woman was writhing on all fours, and we could hear her moans as he worked her with his tongue and mouth. When he thought it was getting too much for her, he pulled away, then stood up and slapped her ass, telling her, "You don't get to come yet. You have to earn it."

He strolled around the bench with his dick in his hand, and then on a growl, he told her, "You're going to take every fucking inch and enjoy it."

He rubbed his thumb over her lips then forced her mouth open and pushed his fingers inside, pressing them to the back of her throat. Playing her part beautifully, she opened her mouth and sucked greedily.

"Good girl," he told her, then removed his fingers, lifting his dick for her to take. Eagerly, she sat up, licking the head of his dick, swirling her tongue around the tip, but he wanted more. So he grabbed the back of her head and guided himself into her mouth, angling her so that she could take him all the way down her throat before he pulled out again and thrust back in.

His hand gripped her hair, his ass clenching as he thrust into her mouth. She was moaning and taking it as she stroked his legs, his ass, then reached underneath to cup his balls. I squeezed my legs together again, feeling the pressure building inside me.

"They like to use toys and... other stuff. That'll come later," Devon whispered, then kissed behind my ear, his nose grazing my skin as his hand slipped from around my waist to tease the hem of my skirt. I liked the feel of his fingers on me, but I wanted more. I needed more.

THE REAPER

I let him stroke my thighs with his fingertips, then I reached down, threading my fingers through his as I watched the guy groan and pull his dick out of the woman's mouth. The guy said something, but I couldn't make out what it was. My ears started to ring, my senses were being drowned by the presence of Devon all around me, invading my mind, making my body yearn for more.

The guy moved to stand behind the girl and forced her back onto all fours, making sure her ass was at the right angle so the people in this room could watch. Then he took his dick and slid it up and down her pussy, slowly sliding inside her, grabbing her hips as he pulled out then slid back in again. The movement, the sounds, the heat that'd built up inside my own body as a result of watching, it all became too much, and when she turned to the window with a look of sheer ecstasy on her face, I couldn't hold back anymore.

I turned my head to the side, moving my hand up to touch Devon's face, then, I grabbed the back of his neck and pulled him to me, and I kissed him, releasing all the passion I'd been holding inside. My lips were hungry as they devoured his, my tongue desperate to taste him. I couldn't get enough, and I turned my body to get closer—press myself against him and melt into him. His hands threaded into my hair, gripping, pulling, angling me so that he could deepen the kiss. Then I felt him grow needier too, and his hands moved to my waist and then down to grab my ass.

I was feverishly grinding into him as he lifted me up. Instinctively, I wrapped my legs around his waist, and he turned, placing me onto the table next to us. Then he pulled away, breaking our kiss but gasping as he stared with desperation into my eyes.

"Everybody out," he shouted, and there was a low murmur around the room, but nobody moved. "I said, GET OUT!" he bellowed, his chest panting as he kept his eyes on me, shameless, wicked intent glaring back at me. Promises that I was all too willing to cash in on, because he wanted me, and I wanted him so badly.

There was a ripple of discontent amongst the group, but they didn't argue. Every last one of them stood up and walked out. Devon's reputation preceded him, and in this instance, I was grateful for it.

Once the last person had left and the door had closed, Devon stalked over to lock it. Then, like a predator moving towards his prey, he came back to me. The couple in the next room were still fucking, but I didn't care; all I could focus on was him.

"I need to taste you," he said, his voice gruff and demanding. "Tell me now if you don't want that."

I nodded, but he shook his head.

"I need words, Leah. Tell me."

"I want that," I answered, my voice shaky from nerves that were laced with desire.

He came to stand in-between my legs as I sat on the table. Our eyes fixed on each other as we breathed shallow, lustful breaths. Tenderly, he grazed his hands slowly up my legs, along my thighs until they reached the hem of my dress, and then, a little more forcefully, he pushed the material up, over my thighs. I held onto his shoulders so that I could lift myself and let him pull my dress right up to my waist. Exposed to him, wearing only my black lacy knickers, I shuddered, savouring every second. His fingers skated over my stomach, then slowly

THE REAPER

he ran his finger along the seam of my knickers, touching but not enough. Never enough.

"Don't play with me," I moaned, and he smiled.

"But playing is the best part." He leaned by my ear, and when he spoke, I closed my eyes and gave a low moan. "I can't wait to play with you, Leah." I held the back of his head, my nails scraping him as he hissed, "Keep moaning like that and I won't be able to control myself."

"I don't want you to. I want you to lose control."

He moved to press his forehead against mine, his eyes penetrating my very soul as he said, "Be careful what you wish for."

Then he pulled back slightly, and I felt his fingers sliding down to my knickers, easing them down. I placed my hands either side of me and held onto the table as I lifted myself up, then I watched as he pulled them right off, holding them in his hand and running his fingers over the lace before stuffing them into the pocket of his trousers with a wicked glint in his eyes.

I was naked from the waist down, exposed to him in the most delicious way, but for him, it wasn't enough.

"Lift your legs. Put your feet on the table," he commanded, and I did.

My shoes got in the way, and seeing that, he took them off, placing them carefully on the floor. Then, standing in front of me, he moved my legs the way he wanted, my knees falling open, my pussy glistening and on show for him. I could barely breathe, I felt vulnerable sitting on the tabletop ready for him; vulnerable but powerful.

"So fucking beautiful," he whispered, staring between my legs and licking his lips, his eyes burning like a starving man ready to feast.

He reached forward, and with his finger he touched me, feeling my wetness and running his fingers along my pussy, circling my clit, and then he pulled away. I sighed, missing the feel of his touch, but when he put his finger in his mouth to taste me, I felt like I was going to explode.

"I need you, Devon," I cried, wanting more.

"You've got me," he replied, and he knelt in front of me.

He started with gentle kisses along the inside of my thighs, and I squirmed, needing more, so much more. His hands held onto my legs as his mouth travelled higher, teasing me with the desperation I felt for him to reach his final destination. I couldn't take my eyes off him as he reached the apex of my thighs and he licked slowly, tantalisingly along the inside of my leg, stopping just short of my pussy, his breath teasing my clit.

"Oh, please…" I gasped, and then he put me out of my misery.

His tongue licked from my pussy right up to my clit. He circled his tongue, flickering it over where I was so sensitive, and then his lips closed over me, sucking my clit into his mouth and making me cry out. I threw my head back, wanting to focus everything I had on the feel of him. The warmth of his mouth, the friction from his tongue, the suction, all of it was driving me crazy. He ran his tongue over my clit and then he moved back to my pussy, pushing inside of me, fucking me with his tongue. I became frantic, gripping the table as I felt the waves of pleasure build. I was so close to orgasm, and I could feel my body taking over, rubbing against him, desperate to find that release—chasing the high.

I glanced down at him through my lust-filled hazy eyes, him

on his knees before me as if I were his queen and he was bowing to me, worshipping me. We were in a voyeur room, but the only thing I wanted to watch was him. I noticed his shoulders moving, the muscles flexing, and I leaned forward to get a better view of him. When I saw that he had his dick out and he was stroking himself while eating my pussy, the sensations spiralled and multiplied. It was the hottest thing I'd ever seen; he was so turned on he couldn't wait any longer, he needed the release as much as I did. Long, firm licks matched his strokes. As he ate me faster, he pumped his dick faster, harder… everything was becoming too much.

"Oh, Devon," I cried. "I'm gonna come."

He moaned into me and then his body jerked, and I watched as he squeezed his dick and came in white-hot spurts. It was the hottest thing I'd ever seen, watching him come undone like that and all because of me. His moans grew louder as he rubbed himself, riding the high. And all the while he still kissed, nibbled, sucked, and fucked me with his mouth, never stopping. He wasn't going to stop until he'd brought me to my climax.

Seeing him lose control like that sent me over the edge, and I gripped the edges of the table as I came hard. My legs shook furiously as my pussy clenched and my clit exploded with sensations that made me imagine I was floating from my body, God himself staring right back at me as I lost myself in the heaven he'd created. Time stood still. Nothing else mattered. And when I eventually came back down to earth, I gave the biggest, most satisfied sigh.

"Oh my God. That was so fucking good." I smiled and opened my eyes, feeling the gentle kisses Devon was giving me between my legs, and the look of pure adulation in his eyes made my heart swell.

He peered up at me, his face glistening, his skin glowing, and whispered, "So fucking good. But, baby, this is only the start."

CHAPTER TWENTY-FIVE
Devon

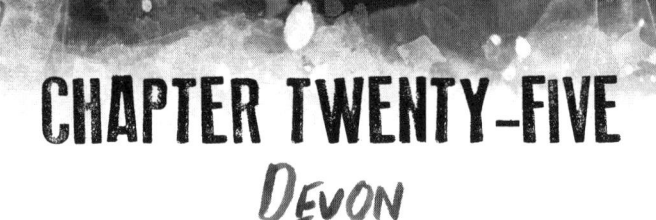

I couldn't get enough of her. I always knew she'd taste as sweet as she looked, but I had no idea how fucking sweet. Having my head buried between her legs had driven me crazy. I couldn't control myself. I had to get some relief too, so I'd jerked off as I tasted her, tongue fucked her, and made her come. It'd helped to ease the frustration a little, but not much. I was a man on the edge, desperate to sink inside this goddamn angel that had flown into my life.

I stood up and put my hands on her face, cupping her cheeks and staring into her eyes. Her pupils were dilated, her breathing ragged, and I could see the glow of satisfaction burning right back at me. A swell of pride burst through my body, knowing I'd done that to her. She was flushed and sated all because of me.

"I should really take you home," I told her, knowing that was the last thing I wanted to do. "I know your dad will worry about you, but I can't, Leah. I can't let you go yet. I haven't finished with you."

Her eyes became hooded as she replied, "I don't want you to take me home. I want more. I want you."

She leaned forward and kissed me, tasting herself on my lips and groaning. I lifted her from the table, and then, like the gentleman I wanted her to believe I was, I pulled her skirt down to cover her up. Reaching into my pocket, she slid out her G-string and pulled it back on, blushing as she did. I wanted to call her out, let her know those belonged to me now, but her shyness in the moment did something to me. It made me feel primal. Most people had an angel and devil on their shoulders, but not me. I had a demon and a devil, and both were screaming at me to take her to my room and show her what it meant to be mine. To own her the way I wanted to.

"We need to go upstairs," I said, my voice sounding gruff from the want and the sheer craving that I felt. I had an overwhelming need to touch her constantly, and I wrapped my arms around her. "I don't want to share you with anyone else."

She smiled a wicked, seductive smile that I hadn't seen from her before, but I liked it.

"The voyeur room was... something else," she whispered. "But I think your room is going to be my favourite."

I took her hand and led her to the door, unlocking it. Then I pulled her towards the staircase that would take us to the third floor. Every thought was focused on what I wanted to do to her, how I would devour her, and then it struck me like a thunderbolt.

Was she a virgin?

When I'd first met her, I'd assumed she was a sheltered, inexperienced vicar's daughter. Getting to know her, I could sense the purity within her. She had a darker, sexier side, a side she'd shown me more than once, but was that something she'd only ever explored with me? I could be a bastard sometimes, but not with her, not about this. I needed to know how to play it.

We came to the door to my room, I unlocked it, and we walked through. The tension in the air was electric, and I closed the door behind us, grabbing her for a kiss as it slammed shut. I wrapped my arms around her, and I kissed her like she was the last thing I'd ever taste, the only thing I ever wanted to taste. The way she kissed me back, with her arms around my neck and her lips as desperate as mine, made it feel like she was my life source. The one thing that ignited me into a frenzy of want and need. Her arms loosened their grip around me, and her hands travelled down my back, gripping my ass, and then she moved to stroke my dick through my trousers. I was rock hard and straining in my boxers, but I pulled back.

She frowned, and instantly I regretted what I'd done, so I took her hand and led her to sit on the bed.

"I know you might not want to tell me," I explained, trying to be careful with the words I used. "But I have to know. Is this your first time?" The fear in her eyes affected me on a deeper level and made me want to take back what I'd asked, so I added, "I don't want to hurt you, and I know it's none of my business, but I feel like I should know. I want to make this good for you too. Make it special."

I'd expected her to blush, maybe stutter through her response, or even blurt out all the facts she knew about it, like she'd studied it along with her ravens, graveyards, and popular culture from the nineties. What I didn't expect was for her to put her head in her hands and burst into tears.

What the hell had I done?

"Leah, please don't get upset." I turned to face her, using my thumb to stroke her tears away, but more fell in their place. "I don't want you to cry."

I opened my bedside drawer and took out a box of tissues, handing them to her and sitting back to give her time to calm down.

She took a tissue out and wiped away her tears, hiccupping as she said, "It's always been you, Devon. I always wanted it to be you."

"That's okay," I told her gently, wanting her to realise that there was no shame in her waiting.

"But it wasn't." She sniffed, staring into her lap. "It wasn't you. And every day since it happened, I've regretted it. I've never regretted anything in my life, but that, I do. It was… awful."

I could feel the fury bubbling up inside me at her words. 'It was awful' played over and over in my head as my rage began to take form.

"Who hurt you?" I said through gritted teeth.

She turned to look at me and the sadness in her eyes damn near broke me.

"No one hurt me. I made a mistake."

I took her hand in mine to try and show her I was here, I was listening. She hadn't done anything wrong.

"You're crying and I've never seen you this upset. You're obviously thinking about what someone did to you. I need to know, Leah."

She squeezed my hand, but her shoulders sagged with regret.

"I'm crying because I'm pissed at myself. I never thought

THE REAPER

you'd notice me. I didn't think it would ever come to this. And now it has, I feel… disappointed… in myself, that is."

"Talk to me. There's nothing you can say that'll make me think any less of you. That's a promise I *will* make, and I'll keep it."

She sighed, twisting and scrunching her tissue in her fingers nervously as she began to talk to me softly, sadly. With words that I knew were about to break my heart.

"I was nineteen, and there was this church club outing, a camping trip. Eight teenagers stuck in the woods with shitty tents and marshmallows to toast while we sang around the campfire. Or at least, that's what my dad thought it was.

"One of the girls had brought wine and beer with her and we all figured, why not? There was fuck all else to do and the peer pressure got to all of us. To cut a long story short, I got drunk. This guy had been paying me attention and no one ever did that. My dad always scared guys away, so when this guy started to talk to me, I felt… flattered."

"And he took advantage. He hurt you. Tell me who he is, Leah, because I'm going to fucking kill him."

"No. He didn't take advantage. We were both drunk. I let him come into my tent, one thing led to another and… *fuck*. I hate that I'm telling you this. I lost my virginity in a fucking tent in the middle of Trowley Bridge Woods to a guy who didn't even remember my name the next morning." She put her head in her hands to avoid looking at me. "I feel utterly mortified. It should've been you."

I was angry.

I was beyond pissed off.

But not because she wasn't a virgin. No. I wanted to rip

that guy's head off for using her like that. He'd had someone as bloody amazing as her right there, and he'd treated her like she was nothing. Not even remembering her name. Well, I'd find out his, and I'd make him pay.

"I made a mistake," she whispered, like she felt ashamed, and it hurt me to think that she thought badly of herself for something like this.

"No, you didn't," I stated. "He made a mistake, treating you like that and then letting you slip through his fingers. I made a mistake by not noticing what was right under my fucking nose all this time. But you? You did nothing wrong, Leah. I wish it had been me. And I'm sorry he treated you so fucking shitty the next morning. But just know, we're not all like that. I'm not like that."

She huffed a gentle laugh, and I saw the hint of a smile on her face that she tried to hide from me.

"I know you're not. That's why I have all this regret eating me up inside."

"Well, that stops right now. No more regrets. Yes, I wish it had been me. But, Leah, I've been no angel in the past either. There's regret on both sides. Hindsight is a wonderful thing, and it helps no one. All it does is give you more excuses to beat yourself up." I put my finger under her chin and turned her face to look at me. "If I could go back and change things, I'd notice you sooner. You'd be my first too. But we can't do that. I seem to remember a very wise woman telling me not so long ago that we can't change the past, we can only right the wrongs. Well, this here, us, it's our way of righting the wrongs. As far as I'm concerned, you are my first. The first girl who's ever made me feel like this. The first girl who's shown me that I can be a better man, for her. You're the first girl I've ever opened up to, and I want you to be the last. I hope you feel the same."

"I do." More tears began to fall, and I leaned forward, kissing her cheek and kissing them away.

"Forget what happened," I told her, pulling away to stare into her eyes. "This is a fresh start. Our story. It begins right here with us. Nobody else matters. The past doesn't matter. Damn, Leah, you know me better than my own family. You've seen me in ways no one else ever has, even my brothers. If that isn't the best start, the best first for both of us, then I don't know what is."

"You're right. I love that. A clean slate." She sniffed and nodded.

"A new beginning," I said, shuffling closer to her.

"Just me and you."

"No one else matters." I wrapped my arm around her to pull her against me.

"No, they don't." She smiled, her hand coming up to stroke my cheek, and I turned to kiss the palm.

"I have to ask one question, though." I knew I had to get this last worry off my chest. "I promise that after this, I'll never mention that night ever again."

"Okay." She swallowed nervously.

"Was it Niall? The guy in the woods?"

She gave a sigh of relief.

"No. It wasn't Niall. The guy left Brinton about two years ago and moved to Australia with his family. I didn't hear from him after that night, but Jodie told me about him emigrating."

"Good riddance," I replied, but the cogs in my brain had already started working. I knew that was something I could do some research on, find out which fucker from around here had left for Australia. It wasn't like that was something that happened often in Brinton. Someone was bound to have a name. I'd find him one day, and he'd pay for making my special girl feel like crap. No one would ever get away with hurting her or making her feel less than she was.

"So, you're not mad?" The trepidation in her eyes made me reach forward and pull her down to lie on the bed with me.

"How could I ever be mad at you? You're my little raven. My soulmate."

"But you're going to start treating me differently, aren't you?" She moved back and gave me a pointed stare. I knew she was worried that what she'd said might change things, but I was confused. I'd already explained to her that I didn't blame her.

"I've told you…" I placed a gentle kiss on her nose. "You did nothing wrong. It's all forgotten."

She narrowed her stare and with a hint of accusation she said, "That right there, that little kiss, that's exactly what I mean."

"What?" I shrugged, having absolutely no idea what she was on about.

"You're treating me like some china doll. Like I'm fragile. That isn't what I want. I don't want some watered-down version of you, Devon. I've watched you for long enough to know who you are. That darkness, the side of you that you keep hidden, I want that. I want it all."

I took a moment to look at her, watch her, and take in what she was truly saying to me.

"That girl you caught watching from outside the warehouse, that's me, Devon. The real me. A little crazy sometimes, a desire to be reckless maybe, and no one to take my hand and show me the way. And you? You're the boy with the devil in his eyes, a darkness in his heart, and a wicked streak running right through his soul. The one I've always dreamed about. It's you I've craved all these years. Not a version of you that you think I can handle. The real you. Don't hold back on me now. Please."

"Do you really think you can handle me?" I joked, giving her a side grin and squeezing her thigh.

"I want to at least try," she said, then with more confidence she added, "Do you think you can handle me?"

"Oh, I can handle you." I leaned to her ear, rolling towards her and pressing my whole body over hers. "I can handle you exactly the way you need to be handled. Hold on tight, baby."

CHAPTER TWENTY-SIX
Devon

She'd just given me the green light to unleash every bit of the pent-up frustration I had scorching through me. Every inch of my body was burning for her. I would show her what she meant to me, but at the same time, I had to let my demons out to play. They couldn't be tamed anymore.

I knelt on the bed and stared at her, lying there, panting like the innocent angel she was. I couldn't wait to ruin her in all the ways that would make her scream.

"You need to take off that dress," I commanded. "Nice and slowly. Show me what's mine."

She bit her lip and then sat up, wriggling the dress up and over her head.

"And you need to lose the shirt," she responded boldly. "Show me what I own."

I chuckled at her. I liked that she was being daring too, but I could do better than that.

"Oh, I'll show you what's yours, baby." I smirked, sliding off the bed and standing in front of her. With a cocky grin on my face, I took my shirt off, then I undid my trousers and pulled them—along with my boxers—right off. I kicked my shoes and socks off, and then, standing completely naked in front of her, I said, "Do you like what you see?"

My dick was rock hard, standing to attention, and all she could do was nod and then clear her throat to say, "Hell yes."

"Good, because I plan on making you a satisfied girlfriend. Very satisfied."

I sauntered over to the bed and crawled onto it, stopping right at her feet. She was fucking stunning, wearing nothing but a black G-string. Her perfect tits were swaying slowly as she took long deep breaths, her nipples puckered, making my mouth water—desperate to suck on them. I wanted to have my mouth everywhere, my tongue exploring every inch of her, and my dick inside her, bringing her to orgasm.

"Take off your knickers and show me how wet you are," I ordered. My eyes focused on her fingers as she slid them into the side of her G-string and pulled it slowly down her legs, and then off. I could see her blushing slightly, but I pushed harder, keeping her in the moment with me. "Legs open, Leah. Show me how much your pussy wants me."

She moaned quietly but did as she was told, opening her legs so that I could see that pretty pussy I'd enjoyed tasting only moments ago. I reached forward, using my finger to trace along the seam of her pussy, coating my finger in her wetness. She wriggled and hissed, her head moving back against my pillow as she closed her eyes and enjoyed the feel of me touching her.

"Don't close your eyes, baby. I want you to watch everything I'm going to do to you."

Her head snapped up at my command and she opened her eyes.

"Good girl," I said as I took my finger away and slid it into my mouth, sucking her sweetness and moaning with how good she tasted.

"I want to taste you too," she whispered, and the thought of her doing just that made my dick throb. So, I gave her what she wanted. What sane man wouldn't?

Stroking myself, I crawled over her, and when I reached her face, I teased my dick against her mouth.

"Taste me," I told her, running the tip along her bottom lip, desperate for her to open to me. Like the good girl she was, she opened her mouth, her tongue darting out to swirl around the head. "Suck me, beautiful girl. Make me come."

I leaned forward, pushing into her mouth, hissing at how good it felt to be inside her this way. I held onto the wall with one hand to give myself leverage and placed my other hand behind her head, guiding her.

She lay on the bed, propped up on my pillow as I was suspended over her, fucking her face in slow, steady strokes. The warmth of her mouth, the swirl of her tongue, all of it was sending me over the edge, but I needed more. Fuck did I need more. More sucking, deeper penetration. I wanted to fuck her hard.

"I need you to take me deeper, baby. Tap me if it gets too much."

I pushed further into her mouth, sliding down her throat

THE REAPER 251

until she took every goddamn inch. She choked a little but not for long. I could feel wetness as the spit ran down her chin, but she didn't tap out. My girl was willing to try anything, that much was becoming clear. She sucked me like I was the tastiest goddamn lollipop she'd ever had in her life, and when she grabbed onto my ass, pulling me to her as I fucked her face, I knew this girl had been made for me. She was perfect.

Long strokes became faster, more furious, and I became frantic as I began to chase that high. The suction of her mouth, the tightness of her throat, and her tongue rubbing against my shaft became too much. When she reached to cup my balls, her nails gently tickling and caressing me in the most sublime way, I lost it. My balls tightened, my spine tingled, and I knew I was close—so close.

"I'm going to come, Leah." I gasped, but she took hold of my ass to let me know she wanted me to come down her throat. She wasn't going to pull away. And so I did, groaning as hot spurts of cum slid down her throat. The sensation of her swallowing as my dick throbbed in her mouth was fucking heaven, indescribable heaven, and I closed my eyes, savouring every second of it.

When I eventually pulled my dick free, she gasped, wiping her face a little, and then she smiled up at me.

"You are fucking unbelievable." I groaned, moving back to sit between her legs. When I looked down and saw how wet she was, how turned on sucking me off had made her, I growled, "You've got my bed sheets all wet, baby. That's so fucking hot. Did you enjoy that as much as I did?"

"You know I did." She grinned shyly.

I leaned down, taking one long slow lick of her wet pussy,

and then I moaned. "The sweetest honey, that's what you are. Once I'm finished with you, these bedsheets will be soaked through." I crawled back up to her. "Kiss me," I whispered. "See how good you taste on my tongue."

She did as she was told, her tongue tangling with mine as we tasted each other. I could feel myself getting hard again, and I broke the kiss, kneeling in-between her legs.

"I need to fuck you hard, Leah," I told her, running my fingers along her pussy and loving how soaked she was because of me. I rubbed and teased, exploring her with my fingers, pushing gently inside her but only enough to coax out more moans from that gorgeous mouth of hers. The sounds she made were the biggest turn on, and my dick started to throb again, desperate to be inside her and feel the tightness of her pussy gripping me. Taking my dick in my hand and pressing it against her clit, I used the head to circle and rub against her. I wanted her desperate for me; on the edge, out of her mind with desire.

"Fuck me anyway you want." She sighed, and with my free hand, I slapped the side of her ass.

"That's my girl. Always ready to give me what I want."

Firmly, I grabbed both of her legs, putting them over my shoulders as I lined myself up against her.

"I'm going to fuck you so good, baby, so hard. I want to hear you scream for me. Scream my name and let everyone know whose pussy this is."

I didn't give her time to reply, I thrust forward, impaling myself into her, and hissing at how tight she felt. Her cry of ecstasy as I pulled out to the tip then thrust back in hard spurred me on. I held her legs, ramming into her, watching her tits bounce, her face contort, her cries grow needier, wilder, as I

THE REAPER

slammed my cock into her tight warm pussy over and over again.

"Do you like that?" I asked as I thrust hard. "Do you like the feel of my big cock stretching you, baby? Does it feel good?"

She nodded, unable to form words. But the room was filled with her moans, her cries, the sound of our bodies slamming together, and me groaning as I ground into her, wanting to give her the best orgasm she'd ever had.

My thrusts sped up and she gripped the headboard behind her, screaming, "Oh, Devon."

I smiled.

"That's it, baby, scream my name. Let everyone in this building know I'm fucking you. Let them know you're mine."

"Devon," she repeated over and over as I rammed into her.

I watched her swallow, and her head fell to the side as she started to lose control.

"Eyes on me," I ordered, and she turned her head back to look right at me.

I leaned forward, my hands moving from her legs to rest either side of her head, and then I put my hand against her neck. That feeling of having power over her, being able to control her high made me pulse and throb harder. I held onto her throat, squeezing gently as I asked, "Do you trust me?"

She nodded and I squeezed a little harder, choking her as I fucked her, swivelling my hips and grinding into her as the compressions on her neck added to the high.

Her pupils dilated as she stared right at me, her mouth in the perfect 'O' as I felt her pussy start to tighten around me. She was close, so I gripped harder for one last time, and then as she came, contracting hard around my dick, I let go of her neck, watching as she screamed out her orgasm. Ripples of pleasure coursed through me as she came and then came again and I kept thrusting into her—I couldn't stop. Her back was arched off the bed, her legs shaking from the intensity of her orgasm, and it was the sexiest thing I'd ever seen. Then, when she cried out my name one last time, I came too, spilling everything I had into her and falling forward onto her body as I got lost in the intensity, the emotions, and the sheer ecstasy of what I was feeling.

She wrapped her legs around my waist as I lay over her, both of us panting as we recovered. Slowly, I turned to whisper in her ear.

"You were made for me, little raven. That was fucking incredible."

"I didn't know it could be like that," she replied breathlessly.

"Me neither. But with us, it always will be."

"Promise?" she asked, nuzzling further into me and holding me as tightly as I held her.

"I promise."

CHAPTER TWENTY-SEVEN
Devon

Sunday morning, and I was sitting in the living room with the biggest shit-eating grin on my face. Images of the night before flashed through my mind, reminding me of all the ways I'd fucked Leah. Thinking about it made me want to stalk back round to her house and do it all again. The way she'd sat on me, riding my dick like she couldn't get enough. How she'd held onto me as I fucked her hard against the wall, her cries still ringing in my ears. But my favourite had been when I fucked her from behind. Her hands holding the headboard as she was on all fours on the bed. Me, watching my cock sink into her tight pussy over and over again as I pulled her hair back.

I hadn't noticed anyone walking into the room, but when something landed in my lap, I was jolted out of my daydream. Liv was getting things ready to make breakfast, and Adam was standing over me with his arms folded.

"You've got another one," he said, gesturing to my lap.

I looked down and saw the white envelope.

"Before you ask, I've already checked the CCTV. It's the same as before. Fucking useless."

I gripped the envelope in my hand, debating whether to burn the fucking thing. I was getting pissed off with these games, and I didn't want anything to sour my awesome mood from last night. This was bullshit I really didn't want to deal with this morning, and it angered me that even in death, my step-fuck-up was still goading me. Why couldn't the fucker just stay dead?

Eventually, curiosity got the better of me, and I had to see what was written inside. I always had been a glutton for punishment.

"I thought we were upping our security?" I asked as I ripped it open.

"We have," Adam snapped back. "But obviously we need to do more. Maybe Colton's suggestion of setting up your crossbow to fire at the letter box isn't such a bad idea after all?"

I rolled my eyes and scoffed. "The postman will love that."

"Maybe that's what we need to solve this, a little collateral damage." Adam shrugged.

"No one is shooting the postman!" Liv turned, pointing the butter knife she was using right at us. "I'd rather do a stake out myself and catch this fucker than resort to that. I mean, Jesus, Adam. First its pizza delivery guys, and now the postman? Do you really have it in for anyone involved in home delivery?" I assumed that was some private joke, but I was too riled up to ask.

"I do when they threaten the people I love," Adam said

THE REAPER

through gritted teeth.

"You have a warped view of what's a threat when it comes to some of us, but I'll let it slide… for now." Liv grimaced at us and then turned around to carry on buttering her toast. Adam went over to hug her from behind and whisper in her ear, and I sat where I was, reading the next instalment of utter bullshit from my fake-ass stalking dead stepfather.

> Devon,
> I see you have a little more to lose now. She's pretty. I don't know what she sees in you, though. Maybe I need to do her a favour? We never did get round to playing that game of Russian Roulette that I promised you. Good job I have a bullet right here with your name carved into it.
> This is your last chance.
> Leave, or I will make you.
> Vinnie.

My heart froze in fear in my chest. I threw the letter onto the table, picked up the TV remote and smashed it against the wall. Liv squealed and they both turned around, but I didn't apologise. I didn't care about anything except protecting Leah and bringing this fucker to his knees. The other letters had fucked me off, but this one? It was the icing on a really shitty cake. The fact that he'd mentioned her made me rampant with fury. This guy had made my life hell growing up. He'd destroyed my past, but I was damned if I would to let him obliterate my future. He knew about Leah, but I'd rather die than let him get anywhere near her.

"This stops. Now," I shouted. "This ends today."

"Too fucking right," Adam said in solidarity. "Whatever you need, brother, just let me know and I'm there. We all are." Adam stood tall, radiating anger, but mine was off the charts.

Was he watching her?

Was he a threat to her?

Because if this guy hurt one hair on her head, I would annihilate him in this life and the next. My fury would be like nothing he'd ever seen before if he pushed me that far. She was untouchable.

"I need to see Leah, check she's okay. Then I'm going to my mum to find exactly who else knew about this sick bastard. I have to be missing something." I charged for the door, but Liv calling out stopped me in my tracks.

"No, Devon. Not like this. Go to your mum first. But please don't go to Leah all angry and worked up. You need to calm down, and anyway, it's Sunday morning. She'll be at her dad's church, won't she? Ring her, talk to her, put your mind at rest that she's safe. But don't go to her raging like this."

I wouldn't believe she was safe until I'd seen it with my own eyes, but I knew what Liv was saying was right.

"I think Liv's right," Adam added. "See your mum first. Get all this shit out of your head. Then go to her if that's what you need to do."

I didn't know what I was going to do. All I knew was that I couldn't stay here and do nothing. So I walked out, grabbing my jacket from the door as I left.

"I'll text you later," I told them, my mind already debating which of the two destinations would be my first port of call.

THE REAPER

***

Ten minutes later, I was knocking on my mother's door, eager for answers so I could leave and get to where I really wanted to be; with Leah.

"Okay, I'm coming." My mum cursed from behind the door. "Enough with the knocking, it's Sunday morning for Christ's sake." She started to work all the locks free, and when the door swung open, she narrowed her eyes at me, peering at me as though she was seeing things. "Devon? What are doing here so early?"

She smoothed her hair down and wrapped her dressing gown a little tighter around herself as a cold gust of wind blew into the house.

"Well, don't just stand there, come in. You're letting all the warm air out," she chastised, and I walked in, giving her a peck on her head as I slid past her and down the hallway.

She shut the door behind me and followed me into the living room.

"Do you want a cuppa? I could put some bacon and eggs on for you?"

"I'm not here for a social call," I snapped and then regretted it when I saw the look on her face. "Sorry, Mum, but I'm in a hurry. I'll pop round another day when I have more time. But for now, I need to ask you about Vinnie."

It pained me to say his name, but I managed to swallow it down.

"What do you want to know?" She sank into the nearest armchair, but she didn't look comfortable as she sat forward with her arms wrapped awkwardly around herself.

"I need to know if there are any of his friends or family still around here. And by friends, I mean close friends, people he spoke to regularly and told stuff to."

"Why do you want to know that?"

"I can't tell you right now, but I need you to trust me."

Her eyes glistened with hope, and inwardly, I cursed.

"Is it because I thought I saw him a few times on the corner out there?"

"Kind of." I clenched my fists, wishing I could tell her the truth. He wasn't coming back, but his ghost was fucking me right off. Instead, I sighed and said, "Look, Mum, one day I'll be able to explain, but for now, I just need names."

She bowed her head, and I could see from the expression on her face that she was wracking her brain for anything that'd help.

"There's no family. No one we spoke to anyway, only Stella."

Yeah, that'd been a dead-end I wasn't prepared to wander down again.

"As for friends..." She stood up and walked over to the cabinet in the corner of the room, taking her wedding album out and clutching it to her chest as she went over to the dining table. She placed it on the table and began flicking through the pages, and I stood next to her, watching her skim over her memories. Memories she clung to and ones I'd rather forget.

Eventually, she stopped on a group photo and started to point from left to right, listing the whereabouts of each person.

"He's dead. He went missing a few years ago. I haven't seen him for ages. I think he might have died too." I knew the dead ones because I'd been there when most of them took their last breath. I was just about to state that it was pointless me being here when she stopped and hovered her finger over a man in the photo. "Now, Eddie Hall, that's a face I haven't seen in a long time. Him and Vinnie used to be quite close. Went drinking together, played on the same football team if I remember right."

It wasn't the golden nugget I was looking for, but it was something.

"Is there anyone else on there who might still be around?"

She shook her head. "Not that I know of." She looked up at me sadly. "I'm sorry I can't be more help, Devon. And I'm sorry that you're still taking your dad's disappearance so badly. I always focused on Brooke. I thought she was the one who'd taken it the worst, but maybe I should've given you more support. You were always so quiet and just got on with things. I never stopped to think you might be hurting too. I'm sorry."

"I'm not suffering, Mum," I told her to put her mind at rest. "And he wasn't my dad. I just need to get to the bottom of something."

She smiled and nodded.

"You want to find out where Vinnie is. We all do."

I knew where Vinnie was, but that was a conversation I wasn't willing to have on a Sunday morning. Not in my current frame of mind.

"You've been a lot of help, Mum. I'll let you go back to bed," I said and kissed her. Then I walked out of the living room, down the hall, and back out onto the street.

I pulled my phone out of my pocket and sent a message to the soldier group chat.

Look into an Eddie Hall for me. He used

to be friends with Vinnie. That's the only name I've got right now.

Then I pocketed my phone and got back into my car. I wouldn't rest until I'd seen her, and I didn't care if I had to go to her father's church to do that. No one was going to keep me away from my little raven.

CHAPTER TWENTY-EIGHT
Devon

I parked up around the back of the church. When I got out, I could hear the church organ playing and the sound of the congregation singing a hymn. I headed to the rectory first, thinking she might've given the service a miss this morning after our heavy night last night, but when no one answered, I knew I should have trusted my first instinct. She'd never let her father down. She wouldn't let anyone down.

I picked my way across the soft grass, still wet from the morning dew, making sure to avoid trampling on any wildflowers that grew there. Flowers that I knew she'd love. She loved anything wild, reckless, and full of beautiful chaos—a little like me.

As I approached the imposing double doors that led into the church, the congregation reached their crescendo, belting out their love for God on this windy Sunday morning. My trainers slipped on the flagstones at the entrance, so I wiped my feet on the mat and strolled in with my hood pulled low and my hands shoved deep into my pockets. I hoped they were all still standing up because I didn't want to draw attention to myself, and thankfully, luck was on my side, because not only were they all standing, singing, shielding me from view, but I spotted Leah May right away, sitting on her own in a pew at the back of the church. The nearest parishioner to her was three pews down.

Perfect.

I sidled into the pew to sit next to her, and she jumped slightly and turned to face me. I grinned a wicked grin from under my hood and she reached up to pull it off my head.

"Devon? What are you doing here?" she asked, nervously glancing around to see if anyone had noticed my presence, then shyly looking back at me.

"I missed you. I wanted to see your beautiful face." I went to lean forward and kiss her, but she flinched, and shaking her head said, "Not here. My dad might see."

The church organ played its final extended dour note and the congregation sat down. Over their heads, I could see her dad at the pulpit, ready to give his sermon. He was smiling, but when his eyes landed on mine that smile faltered. He righted himself soon enough, but I noticed it. He didn't like that I was here.

Leaning my head to the side until it touched Leah's and keeping my eyes on her father, I whispered, "He can't see everything."

I peered down and thanked my lucky stars that she was wearing a dress. A pretty, cotton white sundress that she'd paired with a little blue cardigan to keep herself warm. She was

THE REAPER 265

the picture of innocence, and I couldn't wait to corrupt her.

My heart was beating out of my chest as I reached down to pull her skirt up a little. Then I placed my hand on her bare knee, squeezing and smiling as I felt her looking at me out of the corner of her eye. She knew me well enough now to know what my intentions were.

"Devon," she whispered in an accusing tone, trying to deter me. But it was weak and sounded more like a 'What are you doing? Be careful you don't get caught,' kind of warning. To me, it was an invitation to push a little further.

I stroked her knee, my fingers tracing a delicate pattern on her skin, and I felt her relax a little in her seat. But I wasn't going to stop there. I wanted more. So, I tickled the side of her knee with the tips of my fingers, then grazing slowly up the inside of her thigh, I left a trail of goosebumps on her skin as I headed to where I desperately wanted to touch. She gasped, looking down at where my hand was and her skirt bunching further up her leg.

I leaned close to her ear.

"Be quiet, little raven. Focus on the service. Let me take care of you."

She pulled her skirt down to try and hide my hand, and I grinned at her attempt to retain some decorum. I knew I was pushing my luck, with this being her dad's church, but I also knew my girl loved to be tested. An angel to the world, but a devil for me. A dirty girl when I wanted her to be.

My hand moved higher, already feeling the heat between her legs as I rubbed the top of her thigh, gripping and massaging her there. She didn't stop me, only bit her lip and opened her legs a little wider to give me better access.

"Good girl," I whispered back, the sense of euphoria at

being able to dominate her like this rippling through me, making my heartbeat even faster.

I slid my fingers into her knickers and sighed when I felt how soaked she was. She gave a whispered moan too and leaned back a little, angling her body so I could touch her the way she wanted. Her legs opened wider still as her eyes became hooded.

"I'm going to make you come on my fingers," I whispered. "Don't make a sound, or I'll stop. Do you understand?"

She nodded.

"You don't want anyone turning around and seeing what I'm doing to you, do you?" I added, and she bit her lip and shook her head.

I started to slowly circle her clit with the tip of my finger, using gentle swirls and strokes, and she gave a little moan that made me stop.

"No sound, remember?" I stated, and she closed her eyes for a second, gave me another slow nod, and then opened them, staring straight ahead at the pew in front of us, not daring to look elsewhere. She was focusing, preparing herself. She was perfect.

I began stroking her again; small circles around her clit, delicate brushes across it, then I rubbed down to her pussy and pushed my finger inside. She didn't make a sound, but she held onto my arm as I started to pump my finger in and out. Her wetness coated me, so I added another finger, curling them inside to tease her G-spot. My thumb pushed on her clit, and she breathed a little heavier, but she kept quiet.

"Good girl," I said, struggling to steady my breathing as my fingers fucked her soaked little cunt.

I pumped faster, my thumb rubbing and stroking to bring

her to climax. I could tell she was close by the way she clung to my arm. Then, her legs started to shake, and I felt the walls of her pussy tighten around my fingers as she came, wetness flooding onto my hand and her knickers as she squeezed her legs together, milking her orgasm for as long as she could. Her walls clamped down on me as she contracted, and her head fell forward, unable to retain the composure she'd held so well. But she didn't make a sound. Not once.

Eventually, her legs relaxed, and she lifted her head.

I leaned over and kissed her forehead, and she didn't stop me this time.

"You did good," I told her. "You are such a good girl."

Then she hissed as I removed my hand from between her legs. My fingers were wet, glistening with her cum, and she looked up at me, her pupils dilated and her skin flushed. When I put my fingers into my mouth and sucked them, she grabbed my leg and whispered, "Fuck. Devon. This is a church and I'm not supposed to swear, but watching you do that, and what you've just done… Fuck, that was so hot."

We stared at each other, lost in our world, but we were abruptly pulled back to reality when the congregation in front of us started to stand up and shake each other's hands. Leah stood too, smoothing her skirt down and blushing as some of the parishioners turned to shake hers. I stood back, not wanting to be a part of it, but then I felt a presence standing beside me, and judging from the looks I was getting, this wasn't a normal occurrence. Father Johnson, Leah's dad, was standing right next to me with his hand outstretched.

"Welcome to our church," he said, pushing his arm forward to encourage me to shake it. "Peace be with you."

I took his hand, and I gave him my sturdiest handshake. And all the time all, I could think was, *I've just fucked your daughter with this hand. She just came on my fingers*. I was such a smug bastard.

Did I feel like a piece of shit?

Absolutely not.

She wasn't his girl anymore; she was mine.

"I hope you'll be coming to join us more, now you and Leah are... *friends*." I didn't like how he used the term friends, and I really didn't like the self-satisfied grin he had on his face, but I let it slide. I did have the upper hand, after all.

"Oh, I'll be around an awful lot. The more time I get to spend with my girlfriend, the better... no matter where I have to come to be with her," I shot back smugly.

Leah slid her hand into mine, no doubt sensing a little tension between the two men in her life. It wasn't that I didn't like her dad. We had a history, but that'd been put to rest. What I didn't like was anyone belittling her or what we had. When it came to Leah, I was a fierce protector. A warrior for my girl, who would go up against anyone I saw as a threat, even her father.

"Well, I for one am glad she has you," he said, throwing me for a loop. "Take good care of my girl," he added, kissing her on the cheek before walking away. It didn't go unnoticed that his swift exit meant he got the last word.

"Come on, let's get out of here. Let's go home," I said, leading Leah out of the church.

"Home? As in, my home? Or The Sanctuary?" she asked.

"The Sanctuary. Our home," I replied, like it was a stupid question, and then I winked and she smiled, shaking her head at my assertiveness.

THE REAPER

I felt my phone vibrate in my pocket with a few incoming messages. The signal in the church must've been low and they were all flooding onto my phone at once, so I pulled it out to see what was happening.

> **Adam: We found nothing on an Eddie or Edward Hall. We did track down an Edwin Hall to a halfway house on the other side of Brinton. According to the records Tyler hacked, he got out of prison about three months ago. He did time for armed robbery and assault. Sounds like the kind of man we need to pay a visit to.**

It had to be him. I could feel it in my bones.

> **Me: Don't do anything yet, not until I get there. I'm bringing Leah home with me.**

> **Adam: You call the shots on this one. We'll hang fire until you say otherwise.**

I slid my phone back into my pocket and put my arm around Leah May.

"I've got a feeling things are about to come good for us," I told her, and she laughed.

"Things are already good."

I pulled her closer to me and kissed her head as we walked towards my car.

"They are, but it's about to get a whole lot better."

"It gets better?" She peered up at me, quirking her brow.
"It does. Hold on tight, baby."

CHAPTER TWENTY-NINE
Leah May

"Tell me about the first time you saw me," Devon turned to ask me as we were sitting on the grass at the back of the asylum. "I know the first time I saw you—on your doorstep, when I brought Jodie home that Sunday morning. But I want to know about when you saw me."

Tyson was running around like a mad dog, chasing leaves that were swirling in the air and occasionally coming back to us with a stick that he'd drop at our feet for us to throw. I watched as he spun in circles, barking and then rolling over in the mud without a care in the world.

"It was years ago," I said, playing with the hem of my sundress and smiling to myself at the memories. Memories that I kept locked up in a special box in my head—not just because of Devon, but for my mum.

She'd been so proud of what she'd pulled together that day at the coffee morning. The images of her beaming as she chatted to the community, her brightness helping to lift others was seared into my brain. It was one of my favourite images of her.

"It was at a coffee morning my mum had organised through Dad's church. Who knew that a windy, April Saturday morning at Brinton Manor Community Centre would change my whole life?"

I started to fill him in on all the details about the event, the special things my mum had organised, and what I'd been doing there. Devon listened intently, furrowing his brow as he concentrated, and then it was like a lightbulb went off in his head.

"The coffee morning with the church? I remember that. My mum took me and Brooke because she thought it'd be good for us to mix with the other kids from the neighbourhood. I'd been excluded from school for something, I can't remember what, probably fighting, but I really didn't want to go to that cake and coffee morning. I remember telling her I thought it was lame and I wanted to stay at home, avoid seeing any of the kids from my school, but she had her ways of talking me round." He smiled fondly, then added, "I don't remember seeing you though."

"Probably because you spent most of the time outside, hiding down the bottom of the gardens, sharpening the tool you were crafting out of a branch." I picked up one of Tyson's sticks and gave Devon a playful poke in the arm.

"Hey." He frowned, pretending to look hurt and rubbing his arm. "I'll have you know that was a bit of master craftsmanship going on there. I transformed that branch into a weapon any samurai would be honoured to wield." Then he shook his head.

THE REAPER

"Damn, you have a good memory. I can barely recall that day."

He rubbed his chin in thought then added, "There was one part of the day I remember. Brooke came outside to play a game of pass the parcel with some of the younger kids. I always got nervous when she wasn't with me or Mum, but she was holding a girl's hand."

"Dark hair, wearing a black pinafore dress?" I asked, feeling my heart begin to race in my chest.

"I don't know what she was wearing, all I know is she was holding Brooke's hand."

"And she did the music for pass the parcel?" I added.

"Yes."

"That was me." I gasped, surprised that he'd remembered. "I took Brooke out to play with the others. She was so shy, and it took me ages to gain her trust and get her to leave your mum's lap, but she did."

"That was you?" He stared at me wide-eyed, not quite believing what he was hearing.

I nodded and added, "I rigged the final go so it'd land on Brooke. She was so sweet, and I wanted her to win, but some kid reached over and snatched it off her."

"And I went to storm over and punch him for doing that to my little sister, but I didn't get chance—"

"Because I snatched it back," I answered for him. "I gave it to her." My heart was doubling in size with every word, every snapshot we were piecing together of our shared past. "Her face when she opened the wrapping and saw that cuddly panda inside. I'll never forget how tightly she hugged me after that."

Devon took a deep breath to right himself.

"You know, she still has that panda."

"Really?" Hearing that made a rush of warmth flow through me.

"Yeah. She keeps it on the pillow on her bed. She always tells people it's the only thing she's ever won."

My heart swelled a little more.

"That's so lovely."

"That was you." He shook his head in disbelief. "The one who was kind to my sister. My memory is hazy, but that I'll never forget." He kept his eyes on mine for the longest time, not saying any words—he didn't need to. He'd noticed me. He just wasn't ready back then to acknowledge me. It wasn't our time.

"My mum said she thought you needed a friend," I explained. "I wasn't so sure. From what I could see, you didn't want anyone around you, but she asked me to look out for you, so I did. That's how it all started."

"You watched over me." He smiled a cheeky smile and moved closer to me, his head touching mine. "My little guardian angel, hiding in the shadows."

"You weren't ready for me to come into the light. The shadows were the better option back then."

"I'll have you in the light, the shadows, and every damn place in-between," he whispered, leaning further down to kiss my lips.

"Graveyards, secret rooms, church pews, you really aren't fussy, are you?"

He gave a wicked laugh and added, "And fields behind the asylum. I'm only fussy about who I spend my time with. As long as it's you, that's all that matters."

He went to put his arm around me, pulling me closer to him, but when the first spot of rain hit, he reared back and said, "It's about to tip it down. We need to get inside."

He whistled to Tyson, who bounded over to us then headed straight past us into the open back door.

"He'll be off to Adam's room. His favourite bed and blankets are in there," Devon said, watching him leave.

The rain started to come down a little heavier and Devon stood up, putting his hand out for me to take so he could pull me up and lead me inside. But I wasn't ready to be locked up with him and the others yet. I loved being out here alone with him, and the rain didn't bother me. In fact, it made me feel exhilarated.

I pushed myself to stand, then raced off into the middle of the field, putting my arms out as I twirled in the rain, lifting my face to catch the drops as they fell.

"Dance with me," I shouted over to him. "Dance with me in the rain."

I knew he was about to say no and give me an excuse about how he didn't dance, so I pushed a little further.

"No one's watching. Its only you and me. Dance with me, Devon. It can't rain forever. Let's make the most of it now."

The way he smiled at me like I'd just given him the world made my already swollen heart burst open. And when he walked over the grass towards me, shaking his head and pretending to look harassed by the thought of it all, I laughed, grabbing his hands and pulling him closer to me.

"We don't have any music," he said by way of a weak protest.

"There's music all around us," I told him, and then I giggled as he spun me out in his arm and reeled me back in.

The rain was heavy, and I had to blink fast to keep it out of my eyes and focus on him, but I did, because I didn't want to miss a second. This was a side to Devon I'd rarely seen before––a vulnerable, open side. One that felt uniquely mine. I couldn't quite believe that he was all mine.

I wrapped my arms around him as we swayed in the wind and rain. And he held me in his arms like I was that angel he'd talked about on the step. His guardian angel. Closing my eyes, immersing myself in the whole experience of what dancing with Devon in the rain felt like, I began to sing.

CHAPTER THIRTY
Devon

The rain was soaking through our clothes, the wind blowing a gale, but I didn't care. Neither did she. This was our world, and nothing would stop me from holding her in my arms like this. I buried my face in her hair, the scent of vanilla and everything that was uniquely her made me hold her even tighter. If I were a religious man, I'd thank God for bringing her into my life. I'd praise the heavens for making her so perfect for me. And I'd worship for every goddamn day of my pitiful life if it meant I got to hold her like this in the rain. Soaking her up, getting lost in her, feeling like the whole world was in my arms and nothing else mattered. She made the rest of the world appear blurry, bland, pointless. And she was the one beacon of light that I clung onto. My little raven, my beautiful Leah May, and now, as she started to sing, my songbird.

At first, I couldn't make out the gentle words she was singing as we swayed in each other's arms. But then I heard her mention being brave and afraid to fall. And then my heart stilled, an ache growing in my chest that I almost couldn't bear. She sang words about dying every day, waiting for me. Told me she'd loved me for a thousand years. I wasn't normally emotional, but damn did I have tears in my eyes, and I hugged her as close as I could, breathing her in, wanting to consume every inch of her and be a part of her forever.

She hugged me back and I listened to every word she sang in a state of absolute wonder at this amazing woman. How the fuck had I gotten so lucky to have her in my life? To hear her tell me she loved me, and I hadn't even said it back. She was so fucking brave, so strong to put herself out there for me. But then, hadn't she always done that? Right from the moment she met me, she took a chance on a skinny little punk from the wrong side of the tracks, and she locked me in her heart. Never knowing if I'd ever feel the same.

I did.

I loved this girl with everything I had, and she needed to know it.

I stood tall, peering down at her and taking her face in my hands so I could look at her—look right into her eyes as I told her what she meant to me. I needed her to hear it and I wanted to see the look in her eyes as she did. Her eyes always told me so much, and this was something I didn't want to miss.

"That song," I said, my voice cracking from the emotions. "Those words, they're… everything."

"I always listened to that song in my room and thought of you. It's from the movie, Twilight." She was breathless and her cheeks were flushed, but the love she'd sung about glowed in her eyes.

"I've never watched it, but that song has just become my new favourite." She smiled at my words and her eyes dipped, but I brushed my thumb against her cheeks and said, "Look at me. I need you to look at me when I say this."

She was always my good girl, and just like I'd asked, she looked up at me, her eyes wide and her lips slightly open, like she wanted to say something but didn't know how.

"I might have taken a little longer to notice you, Leah. But trust me when I say, you are all I see now. You're my first thought when I wake up. You're the person I long for throughout the day and I feel like I can't function until I've seen you or I know where you are. You're my person. And I never thought I'd find anything like this, this bond that we have. When I'm with you, it's like there's this invisible connection from me to you and it doesn't matter who else is in the room, or what anyone tries to do, because nothing can sever it. I look at you and whole conversations pass between us, and we haven't even said a word. Like that night, at Merivale town hall, when you sang *Creep*. We looked at each other and I knew you felt it too. That I was there for you. I'll always be there for you. And I know I'm not good with words, but what I'm trying to say in a really bad way is that I love you, Leah. I love you so fucking much."

Our breaths mingled as one as I held her face and watched, waiting for her reaction. Her eyes softened then filled with tears I didn't want her to shed. The gentle pants she took as she processed what I'd said, and the way her body leaned further into mine, all of it spoke volumes to me. This was exactly what I'd meant. Whole conversations without words. We didn't need them, because right here, holding each other, we were saying it all.

It was always you.

I'd wait a lifetime to find you.

I'll love you until my last breath, and even then, my love will go with me, into the afterlife, forever etched into my soul.

This was meant to be.

The Reaper and the raven.

Two halves of the same whole.

Forever.

"Devon," she whispered, her voice full of emotion. "I love you, Devon. I always have and I always will."

My lips crashed onto hers, and all the love I felt poured into her. She was the fire that lit my dark, empty soul alive. She was the warmth that made my once stone-cold heart simmer with need. The spark she ignited in me was like nothing I'd ever felt before. Fireworks were too weak to describe it, even dynamite. She was a fucking nuclear blast that'd torn through my world in the best way and made me see what was always right there in front of me, waiting.

Her.

Our tongues teased as we tasted. Our lips fused, and the want, the need I felt for her became too much.

I pulled away first and placed my forehead against hers saying, "Love feels like it isn't enough." She frowned at me, so I added, "I meant the word. It doesn't seem strong enough to describe what I feel. Addicted, maybe? Consumed? Crazy and insane?"

She laughed and added, "Those too, all those words are perfect. I'm addictively, crazily, insanely consumed by how much I love you, Devon Brady. I'm also a little crazy about the ways you show me that you love me. I like your creativity, to put it politely."

"You like my dirty mouth."

"That too."

I grinned like a goddamn fool, and I pulled her to me, walking us back towards the asylum.

"Maybe, after we've dried off, I can show you some other ways I can use my mouth…"

"Why stop at the mouth?"

"Oh, I won't. That'll be just the warmup act." I slapped her ass as we got to the back door and she ran in giggling, heading up the stairs. I slammed the door shut, about to run up after her, but my heart stuttered in my chest when I saw what had been forced onto an old nail on the back of the door for me to find. I pulled it down, shoving it into my back pocket, before schooling my features so she wouldn't guess anything was wrong. But that ball of fire that I'd felt only moments ago had turned to unbridled fury.

He was here.

CHAPTER THIRTY-ONE
Devon

I took the steps two at a time, following her laughter as she sprinted ahead of me, but all the emotion I'd felt earlier had become clouded. Smothered under a swirling smokescreen that was fogging my brain, making it difficult to focus on anything other than the rage that was spreading through me. My vision was blurry, and my body was numb. I was going into defence mode. Next up would be attack, but I needed to get her somewhere safe before that happened, because the way I was feeling, I was about to go nuclear, and I had to protect her at all costs.

The sound of her laughter as she headed farther up the stairs penetrated through my dark thoughts. She thought this was a game, but I wasn't chasing her. I was desperate to get inside, upstairs to where the others were. The games were over. This was war.

Once she reached the second floor, she stopped, bending over and gasping to catch her breath. I caught up to her and plastered on a fake smile. Wrapping my arms around her, pulling her to me, I whispered, "I need to go and speak to the others about something. Would you wait in my room? There's towels in the drawers under the window so you can dry off."

"Okay," she replied, but there was a hint of disappointment that she tried to hide with her sweet smile. At least, she probably thought she did, but I could see the truth. I could always tell what she was thinking just by looking into her blue eyes. I hoped she couldn't see the anger and unbridled fury reflected in my own.

"I won't be long, and when I get back, I'm going to show you just what it means to be loved by me." I leaned closer and growled, "I'm going to fuck your tight little pussy until you're screaming my name. You'll be begging for more. I'll show you how good I can make you feel, baby."

She blushed and bit her lip in reaction to my filthy promise, slapping her hand on my chest as if she disapproved of what I'd said.

"I shouldn't find that so sexy, but I really do." She sighed, giving me a peck on the lips, and then turned to head towards my room, shaking her ass in the dripping wet sundress that was clinging to every curve. When she looked over her shoulder and said, "Don't be long. It's more than my sundress that's wet right now." The fire inside of me ignited. No one was ever going to take her away from me, and I knew I had to take drastic action. I had to protect her.

I waited until she was in my room and the door had closed behind her, then I stormed off in the opposite direction, heading for the living room. When I burst through the door, I found all of them sat around laughing without a care in the world. Adam was the first to see me, and instantly, he scowled. "Is everything okay?"

"No, it's fucking not!" I hissed, letting the anger flow freely now.

I took the Polaroid out of my back pocket and slammed it onto the table in the middle of the room. The laughter that I'd walked into died and every eye was on me.

"What the hell is that?" Liv asked, picking it up.

"You tell me," I snarled, turning my anger on her.

Adam didn't like that, and he came to stand by her side, taking the photo out of her hand and glaring back at me.

"Watch your tone. You might be my mate, but I don't like the way you just spoke to my wife."

"And I don't like being taken for a mug," I shot back.

He snarled, his eyes burning as he said, "Who exactly is taking you for a mug?" He shook the photo in his hand, then threw it back down onto the table and added, "I take it this is another one of your stepfather's calling cards? Not sure why that makes you think you can speak to my wife like a piece of shit, but I'm going to put it down to the pressure you're under and let it slide." He took a step closer to me. "But do it again and I won't be so understanding."

I stepped away from him, my demons tempting me to go toe-to-toe with Adam, but my mind was begging me to keep my cool. Of every person in this room, he's the one I trusted the most. I'd trust him with my life.

It couldn't be him.
Could it?

I grunted in frustration, grabbing the back of my neck with

THE REAPER

both my hands and gritting my teeth. I needed to relieve some of the pressure that was building inside me like a fucking pressure cooker. I was about to explode, and I gave a feral growl in an attempt to hold on for just a little longer.

I stared at the photograph lying discarded on the table. The image of Leah and me sitting on the grass outside had been taken moments ago, just before it had started to rain. My head was leaning against hers, but whoever had taken the photograph had used a black marker to scribble me out. They were erasing me from the picture, but that was never going to happen.

On the back of the photo there was one word written in capital letters.

LEAVE.

But I would never go. Not now. I'd never leave her.

I took a moment to look around the room at my fellow soldiers. All this time, they'd tried to convince me that it was my stepfather. They'd doubted me, challenged my memories and slowly twisted the knife. They had me questioning my sanity, and the more I thought about it, the clearer their intentions became. Thinking about it made me unhinged, anger was morphing into a need for violence. This had to end, and it would, at my hands. They needed to know that the game was up. I wasn't going to take their bullshit anymore. Whoever the guilty one was, their sick joke was over.

"We all know this isn't the work of my stepfather, don't we? Let's not kid ourselves." I stared at each one of them, waiting for a reaction. Studying the tell-tale signs that I'd learned over the years, but they all looked clueless.

"Let's get the van loaded up. I think we need to pay this Eddie Hall guy a visit," Adam stated, moving purposefully towards the door, but I stopped him.

"I think we all know that's a fucking pointless idea." I saw Will's eyes widen as I spoke, and he glanced at Colton to gauge his reaction. "Why haul ass all the way over town when someone in this room has got all the answers?"

Colton stepped forward, frowning in confusion. "What the hell are you smoking, Devon? What the fuck is all this about?"

"I'll tell you what its about." This was it. No more fucking about. I had to cut off the head of the snake to bring this to an end. "I don't think it's some random guy called Eddie who's been sending these. I don't even fucking know that guy. But I'll tell you what I do know."

"Please do," Colton added, coming to stand next to Adam and giving me a look that dared me to go there. "Because the rest of us haven't got a fucking clue what you're on about. So, tell us, what is it that you know?"

I stood my ground.

"There are six people, other than those sick fuckers that Vinnie was friends with, the ones we took care of, that knew about what my stepfather had done to me. And by that, I mean knew details, proper details like the ones in these letters I've been getting. The darts, the bullseye, his threats about Russian roulette. Six people." I held up my fingers to count them off. "Adam, Colton, Tyler, Will, Vinnie and me." I took a breath, letting it sink in, and from the flared nostrils and venomous glares, they didn't like what they were hearing. "Maybe I should make that seven." I nodded to Liv. "I bet he tells you everything."

Adam darted into action, pulling Liv towards him, his eyes boring a hole right through my soul. "Say it," he hissed, daring

THE REAPER 287

me to jump off the cliff I was teetering on. "Just fucking say it!"

"I know I'm not sending this shit to myself. Vinnie is dead. And that leaves you lot." I gave each one a pointed stare. "So, who was it? Who thought they'd fuck with my head for some sick fucking joke?"

"Jesus fucking Christ." Colton threw his head back, exasperated at what he'd heard. "Are you fucking kidding me right now?"

"Do I look like I'm kidding?" I narrowed my eyes, my brain spiralling into a vortex of insanity. "Was it you? Are you getting some sick kick out of this? I mean, I know you like to be the joker, but has life began to imitate art? Do you think we're in some twisted Batman shit? Have you taken the clinically insane angle a little too far?"

He shook his head and laughed, but his eyes were deadly. He didn't find it funny.

"Me?" He smacked his fist against his chest. "Why me? Why the fuck would I do something that shitty? I might be the joker, but I'm not a fucking snake. If that's what you really think of me, then let's deal with this like real men. Let's take it outside."

The twitch that Colton sometimes got in his eye when his anger surfaced had made an appearance.

"No one is sorting anyone out," Adam piped up, putting a hand on Colton's chest to keep him in place. "Devon," he growled, stabbing his finger towards me. "I don't know where this bullshit is coming from, but trust me, you need to stop. There's only so long I can hold my temper and you are pushing every fucking button and grating on my last fucking nerve."

"I really couldn't give a shit," I argued back. All rational thought had now evacuated my brain. "Someone did this, and I think that someone is in this room."

"Why would any of us do that?" Tyler announced, throwing his hat into the ring.

I turned, focusing my attention on him.

"That CCTV you keep showing me is really fucking convenient, Ty. No face shots, always angled to hide everything. I'm pretty sure I've seen a Polaroid camera in your room too." Liv groaned, but Adam shushed her. Seems he wanted me to say my piece, get it all out in the open. "Did you take that photo? Do you think its fucking funny?"

"No! I didn't! I've no idea when that was taken," he spat angrily, pointing at the Polaroid sitting on the table. "But I've been up here with these guys all afternoon. They can all vouch for me." He folded his arms over his chest, his muscles tensing as he too tried to rein in his fury. "Do you honestly think one of us is doing this? What the hell is wrong with you?"

Colton shook his head and with a face full of deathly hatred he added, "He's in love. It's fucked with his brain. He's obviously not thinking straight."

I flew across the room, ready to take his fucking head off, but Adam grabbed me, slamming me against the wall and pinning me in place. We were nose-to-nose as we both panted out our aggression, his face red with anger, mine hot with fury. This was it. No retreat, no surrender.

"Let's get one thing fucking straight," Adam hissed through his teeth. "Every single fucking person in this fucking building is on your side. We'd go to war for you. We'd die for you. Do you understand what I'm fucking saying?"

I took deep breaths and after a few seconds I gave a slow nod. I didn't believe it, but I'd let Adam have his say.

"You're our brother. More than that, you're a fucking part of us. You hurt, we all hurt. Someone comes for you, they come for all of us." His hold on me loosened a little and then he added, "And now, that includes Leah too. She's yours and that makes her a part of this family. It's a fucked-up family, but it's ours and I will die before I see anyone destroy it."

His words stung me. The sentiment behind them made it hard for me to reason with the warped reality that had taken hold of my mind. I didn't know who to trust. Everything seemed twisted, distorted, fractured beyond all recognition. I heard what he was saying but could I really trust that it was true?

Adam took a step back, dipping his head for a moment before looking back up at me.

"We've let you down. I know we have. It shouldn't have gotten this far. We should have shut this shit down the moment you got that first letter. And all I can say is I'm sorry. I'm so fucking sorry, but it isn't happening again. From this moment, we are in lockdown." He glanced around the room, and everyone nodded back at him in agreement. Everyone but me. "No one leaves this building unless one of us knows about it. No one enters without our say so. The club is closed until we find this guy, and if he so much as sneezes within a five-mile radius of here, we will know about it."

The room fell silent, and all I could hear was the whistle of the wind through the windows. Every one of us was lost in our thoughts, and the anger and hatred I'd harboured only minutes ago turned to a gnawing confusion, an ache that wouldn't let up.

"We'd never do anything to hurt you," Will said, breaking the silence. "We fucking love you, man. You keep us grounded. You're like the heart of this unit. The brains, even. No offence,

Adam."

"None taken," he replied, keeping his eyes on me.

"That goes for all of us," Colton added, looking contrite. "I'd rather hurt myself that do something to any of you. This is my family. My chosen family. Fuck the blood line, those fuckers mean nothing to me, but you..." He stuttered as if he was caught up in his emotions. I still had my guard up though.

"I agree." Tyler was next to step up. "We're here for you, mate. Whatever it takes to catch this fucker, we'll do it."

"Good," Adam announced. "So, we're all in agreement. Nobody makes a move unless we're all onboard. This asylum is closed to anyone who isn't part of this family." The knot in my throat tightened. I didn't know how this was going to play out. All I could do was wait.

"Tyler, Will, can you check the CCTV is fully functional and operating where we need it, and maybe get some sensors set up around the perimeter?" They both nodded as Adam made his plan. "Colton, you can come with me to pay this Eddie Hall a visit. It might be a dead end, but we have to check all avenues. No stone unturned, am I clear?" He switched his focus onto me. "And, Devon, stay here. Calm the fuck down and get your head straight. Is Leah May still here?"

"She's in my room."

"And does she know anything about this?"

"No."

"Then we keep it that way until Devon tells us otherwise. Devon, can you get her to stay here for a while? Olivia has spare clothes and stuff she could borrow. It'd be easier to have her under our roof. We can protect her better if she's here."

Wherever she was is where I'd be. No one would protect her

THE REAPER 291

as well as I could.

"She'll stay," I stated, but I wasn't happy. Not really. I felt like I didn't know which way was up.

"That's settled then. Let's get to work." Adam marched off, ready to fulfil his part of the bargain.

Me?

I was so wound up and there was only one way I wanted to deal with that.

By losing myself in my little raven.

CHAPTER THIRTY-TWO
Leah May

I was sitting on the bed, towel drying my hair and humming to myself when the door swung open. Devon wasn't happy. He could try to hide it with his devilishly seductive smile, but I knew him, and I also knew the minute he'd walked in here that he wasn't right. There was an edge to him, like a darkness had fallen over him. In his eyes, I could see that dark passenger I'd recognised all those years ago. Sometimes, it was hidden deep within him, and other times it shimmered beneath the surface, but right now, it was clawing, spitting, fighting to get out.

I shifted slightly to face him, and I was about to ask him what was wrong, when he slammed the door shut, locked it and said, "No words. I need you naked and face down on the bed. Now."

I didn't argue, I didn't want to because the way he spoke,

demanding what he wanted sent a ripple of excitement through me. If Devon needed me, he could have me, any way he chose.

I smiled shyly and stood up, sliding my fingers underneath the straps on my dress and letting them fall to the side. Then, I shimmied out of my wet dress, watching as it dropped to the floor, pooling around my feet. I was still wearing my white lacey underwear, but from the heavy breaths and pants I could hear coming from him, he wanted those off too, and now.

I unhooked my bra and took it off, keeping my eyes on his as I did. He looked feral, hungry, and for a moment, he let his attention waver from my eyes to my breasts, his stare becoming hooded and wanton as he drank me in, but he didn't move.

"Everything, Leah," he urged, his need growing like a rampant thunderstorm—dark, desperate, and greedy to devour whatever was in his path. "Take it all off and crawl onto the bed."

I slipped my knickers down and left them with the rest of my clothes. Then I stood for a moment, naked and vulnerable in front of him. I was surprised that being exposed to him like this didn't make me feel shy or embarrassed. Instead, it made me feel powerful, desirable, and wanted.

I couldn't keep the smirk off my face as I got onto the bed, crawling on all fours and peering over my shoulder to where he'd positioned himself right at its foot. The perfect view to see my ass. I felt brazen and opened my legs slightly, knowing it'd please him. His expression darkened even more, and he hissed.

"So fucking beautiful. I can't believe you're all mine."

"All yours." I gasped, and he nodded his approval.

"You know I love you, don't you?" he asked, and I nodded. "And you know I respect you so fucking much." I gave another nod. "But right now, I need to fuck you hard, dirty… I need to fucking own you, Leah."

I loved the way that sounded. Even more, I loved the way it made my stomach twist with excitement and tingles spark between my legs.

"Then own me," I told him.

There was a second where he stayed still and just watched me, like he was hypnotised, lost in another world in his mind but desperate to use my body to claw himself back to this one.

"I need you, Devon," I said on a whisper to break through whatever walls were locking him in.

When he climbed onto the bed behind me, I knew I'd succeeded. He needed me too, and he was about to show me exactly how much.

"You might want to hold onto the headboard," he commanded. "I can't promise I'll be gentle."

I did as I was told and was rewarded with a "good girl."

I closed my eyes as I felt him hovering near. Every sense in my body focused on him. His hot breath on my thighs, travelling closer and closer to where I needed him to be made me shiver, and quietly, I urged him on.

"There. Right there. Touch me."

He didn't speak, but he grabbed my legs and forced them further apart, commanding my body like it was his and placing me exactly where he wanted me; ass up, legs wide, upper body dipped.

He put his hand on my back and pushed my head down. All the while I played my part. I was his doll, his to use. I always would be.

His fingers stroked my inner thigh roughly, but it wasn't

long before they were in-between my legs, rubbing my clit, swirling and then pushing inside of me. He stroked my inner walls and then pulled out again, working my clit, teasing me, making me push back into him, wanting more of what he was giving me.

"Such a greedy girl." He tutted, but he didn't stop. My eagerness only seemed to spur him on.

He fucked me roughly with his fingers, his thumb pressing on my clit then releasing, building the pressure inside me. I reared back, grinding onto his hand, and he groaned.

"You're going to come on my fingers, my tongue and my cock. I'm going to make you come so many times, baby. All for me."

I moaned back, loving the sound of being dominated and owned by him.

He slapped my ass hard, then used his other hand to rub the soreness. All the time curling his fingers inside me, stroking me to orgasm. I was so close and began writhing against him, wanting more—more friction, more fingers, more of everything.

"Touch yourself," he commanded, and I took my right hand off the headboard, reaching between my legs and rubbed over my clit, circling and stroking until I was there.

"I'm coming," I cried, feeling my walls start to contract around his fingers, the pulse of my clit, then explosions, mind-numbingly amazing explosions that made my legs quiver and my body shudder. All the while, he kept pumping in and out of me, his fingers rough and demanding, his aggressive grunts adding to the sexiness of it all. I'd never been this turned on, and I couldn't get enough.

He didn't give me chance to come down from my high, he

didn't let up for one second. He'd made a promise and he was going to keep it. One orgasm wasn't enough.

I felt the hotness of his breath and then I cried out as his mouth clamped over my pussy. I was so sensitive that I almost couldn't take it, but I clenched my eyes shut and lost myself in the sensations of his tongue pushing inside me, licking my orgasm and teasing another one right from my very soul. Then he moved to my clit, flickering his tongue over it and sucking it into his mouth. I pushed into him, loving the feel of his mouth on me, driving me wild as the next orgasm began to build. I tilted my hips, moving against his mouth and tongue, creating a rhythm that my body knew instinctively. The sparks were firing inside of me, and there was a delicious tingling between my legs as he ate me like I was the best thing he'd ever tasted. And then he stopped, sat back, and with his hands he spread me wider and sighed a wicked, tempting sigh.

"I want all of you, Leah," he growled.

"You have me," I said on a whimper, wanting him to get back to licking me. I didn't ever want him to stop. "I'm yours."

The moment I said that I felt his tongue lick my clit, along my pussy, and then he was on my ass. Holy fucking hell, that was somewhere I never thought I'd ever want him to go, but fuck me, the feel of his tongue on me, rubbing, pushing inside, teasing nerve endings that I didn't even know could feel so good made me scream out in pleasure. He held my ass and ate me, his fingers on my clit, and I came so hard, waves stronger than the last as he lapped it all up, groaning and licking, he pulled every drop of ecstasy from my body. It was all too much. I was a mess of smouldering limbs, and I didn't think I could take anymore.

"So perfect. You taste like heaven," he said, and gave my

ass another smack before I felt the pressure of his dick. He was rubbing the head against my clit, coating himself in my wetness and then running it up and over my ass. I felt his fingers there too, and slowly, he pushed inside, but I lurched forward and gasped.

"We'll work up to this," he said, fingering my ass, and I liked the way it felt. I wanted to be dirty for him. "I need to get you ready to take me here." He rubbed a little more, then his attention was back on my pussy, his dick sliding over my clit, spreading my wetness, and I pushed back into him again, desperate to feel the stretch of him filling me, fucking me.

"You like the feel of my cock on you and inside you, don't you? Say it, Leah. Tell me how much you love my cock."

"I love it." I gasped, wanting him so badly I couldn't think straight. "I love all of it. I love you, Devon."

He didn't wait a second longer, just plunged his cock into my pussy hard and grabbed my hips with both hands. I held the headboard as he started to slam into me with punishing thrusts, pulling out to the tip and ramming inside me, making my whole body jolt from the impact. Grunts accompanied each thrust as he filled me hard and fast. Then, once he'd set his punishing pace, he reached forward, grabbed a handful of my ponytail and pulled my hair, making my head jerk back.

He held my hair in one hand as he wrapped the other around my waist, lifting my hips so he could slam into me harder, faster. And then, when I thought I couldn't take anymore, he commanded, "Sit back on me. Ride my cock."

He sat back with his dick still inside me, pulling me back to sit on his lap, his knees bent and his arms wrapped around my waist. I let go of the headboard and held onto his thighs, lifting myself up and then slamming back down onto his dick.

"Oh, baby, that's it. Ride me. Fuck me." He groaned, and he pulled my back to his chest, his hot breaths fanning my neck as he panted and moaned in my ear. "Make me come, Leah. I need you to make me come."

I wanted to please him, and even more, I wanted to come again. I could feel myself about to fall, teetering on the edge of an orgasm that would probably kill me with its intensity, but I didn't care. All that mattered was getting there and bringing him along with me.

He held me close to him, thrusting upwards as I bounced on his dick, using him to give us both pleasure. Then one hand snaked up my body, caressing my breast and pinching my nipple. I pushed my chest into his hand, wanting more, and he reached up with the other hand, kneading my breasts, playing with my nipples and making my pussy clench tightly around him. I let my head fall back, resting on his shoulder as I got lost in all the sensations that his touch evoked. I heard a growl from deep within him, then I felt his hand move to my neck, holding tightly and squeezing, keeping my head in place as he thrust his cock into me, his fingers pinching my nipple and his other hand clamped tightly around my neck.

"Fucking come, Leah." He grunted, thrusting hard. "I need you to fucking come. Come on my cock."

He squeezed a little harder on my neck and I ground myself over him, rubbing my clit as I rode his dick, and then the stars that were dancing in front of my eyes burst into the most mind-blowing explosion, and I came hard, so hard I felt my body convulse and lose all control as it rode out wave after wave of the most intense orgasm I'd ever had. Devon held me up, still

THE REAPER

pounding and grinding into me, then he cried out too, his cock thickening inside me as he came.

I turned my head, kissing him as he panted, his eyes closed too as he lost himself in me. The swell of my heart as my body slowly came back down to earth made me whisper, "I love you so fucking much."

He buried his head in my neck and gasped. "Me too. So fucking much."

He held me close as we both struggled to regain our breath and control over our bodies. Then slowly, he lowered me to the bed and turned me so that I was on my back and facing him. Love burned in his eyes, but when he looked down at my pussy, that burn began to smoulder. He opened my legs, and I felt the warmth of his cum as it trickled out of me. He stared transfixed, then ran his fingers along my pussy, through his cum, gathering it and pushing it back inside me as if he didn't want me to lose a drop.

"Seeing my cum dripping out of you is the hottest thing ever." His fingers teased my sensitive throbbing pussy as he spoke. "I love the thought of being inside you. Hold me inside you, Leah." I lifted my hips and clenched, wanting to do what he asked. "You're such a good girl. I hope you know this was just the start. I intend to have a night of dirty, filthy sex with you. I want you here all night, so whenever I wake up, I can fuck you any way I want."

I held my breath, loving the words and the filthy promise behind them.

"I'm here for you too," he said, crawling over my body and pinning me down as he lay above me. "I'm yours. If you want me, have me."

"You want me to stay?" I asked, placing my hands on his face to look at him.

"I do. Would you do that? Tell your dad you're staying here and let me hold you and love you all night?"

I knew my dad wouldn't like it, but I wasn't a little girl anymore; I was a woman. I was going to be twenty-three next month. I had a right to spend time with my boyfriend. Surely, even my dad would accept that? Okay, well, maybe not. He was a very religious man with more principles than the lord himself, but that was his life, and this was mine. I had to live it the way I wanted to.

"I'd do anything for you," I said, nuzzling into Devon's neck and breathing him in. "I'll text him after we get cleaned up. I'll stay as long as you want me."

CHAPTER THIRTY-THREE
Devon

I heard a tapping, and feeling disorientated from being woken up, I prised my eyes open. The room was in complete darkness, and I felt the warmth of Leah May lying in my arms, breathing slow and steady.

Tap, tap.

There was someone at my door.

Gently, so as not to wake her, I pulled my arm free and got up off the bed. I slipped a pair of joggers on, all the time watching her to make sure she didn't stir, then I padded quietly across the room to the door. When I unlocked it and pulled the door open, I found Tyler standing there, looking like he hadn't slept in a week. His eyes were bloodshot and ringed with dark circles. Lines that I hadn't noticed before were on his face and there was an air of defeat about him. An air I'd probably put there after what had happened earlier when I called them all out.

But when he spoke, I knew exactly why he was so weary.

"We've got him," he said, and my heart stopped.

"You've got him?"

Tyler nodded and then he hung his head. "He breached the fence I'd rigged with a motion sensor earlier and it set off the alarm on my computer. I didn't want to wake you, so I went straight to Adam. He woke the others and the four of us went down and caught him. We've got him, Devon. He's waiting for you in the chapel."

The pounding in my ears made me question what I was hearing.

"You caught him? He's downstairs? You did it without me?"

Tyler sighed.

"We all owed you that much. We wanted to do it for you."

I took a moment to compose myself, then it started to sink in.

"You did that for me?" Tyler looked up and nodded gravely.

"We had to. We hadn't done enough before. We all wanted to fix this for you. You're our brother."

"Thank you," was all I could think to say. I knew I had a lot of grovelling to do. I'd lost my mind and blamed my brothers. I'd been a dick, and I needed to put that right.

I glanced over my shoulder into the darkness of the room where Leah was sleeping.

"What if she wakes up?" I asked myself, but a smaller voice behind Tyler spoke up and answered me.

"I'll be here." I saw Liv standing in the doorway in her pyjamas, her arms folded over her chest and a look of concern etched onto her face. "I'll watch the door, and if she wakes up and comes out, I'll keep her up here with me."

THE REAPER

I knew I could trust Liv. I'd always known. Why had I been such a dick earlier?

I started to speak. "Liv, I'm so sorry for—"

But she held her hand up to stop me and smiled.

"Family means never having to say sorry, Dev. I think that's from Lilo and Stitch." She gave a humourless chuckle. "But you get what I'm saying. You don't need to say anything, just go down there and show this fucker that he can't play with you anymore. Give him hell."

Nodding, I grabbed a T-shirt from the chair behind my door and pulled it on, then slid my feet into my Nikes.

"I'll do more than that. He'll wish he was in hell when I get hold of him. Hell will be a fucking walk in the park." I closed the door behind me, the lock clicking quietly into place, and headed for the stairs.

Tyler followed me down, and when we came to the ground floor and turned the corner towards the chapel, I saw Adam and the others standing, waiting at the door. They looked up as they saw me approaching, but the triumph I expected to see on their faces wasn't there.

"Devon, mate, I think you'll want to take care of this one yourself," Adam stated, with regret laced heavily in his tone.

"Are you sure it's him?" I asked.

Adam took something out of his pocket, and when he handed it to me, I saw it was a Polaroid, like the one left on the back door earlier. This time, the image was of Leah and me dancing on the grass, my arms wrapped around her as she looked up at me and smiled. On the back, in the same lettering it said, leave. I didn't need any more proof.

"We'll be out here if you need us," Adam stated. "All you

have to do is shout and we'll be by your side. We're here for you. But trust me, I think you need to see this for yourself."

Hearing him say that made the nervous energy inside me flicker with apprehension. What the hell was I going to find behind those doors? Was it really my dead stepfather? Or some long-forgotten friend of his? What if it was my own family? The twist in my gut made me want to double over, but I had to stay strong. What the fuck was I about to walk into?

Without speaking, I moved past them and gripped the door handle.

"You've got this," Colton said, patting me on the back. "Whatever happens, remember that. You are stronger than him. He can't beat you down anymore. You're the one in control now."

I swallowed, unable to form words, and pushed the handle down, walking into the chapel and shutting the door behind me.

In the corner, I could see a dark figure slumped into the chair, tied to it with ropes and chained with handcuffs. He had his hood up and I stepped forward, to get a better look and finally find out who it was. When he lifted his head and the moon's glow shone through the stained-glass windows of the chapel, I felt every muscle in my body freeze. My breath caught in my throat, and my brain screamed, refusing to believe what was right in front of my face.

"You?" I croaked, feeling like the walls of my whole life were crumbling around me. Devastation that I was petrified I'd never come back from clamped around my soul. It was like hell's deathly grip had its hold on me, and I was powerless to it, ready to be dragged down and kept locked in its depths forever.

How was I ever going to recover from this?

THE REAPER

"Me," he stated, lifting his chin defiantly. "It was all me."

CHAPTER THIRTY-FOUR
Devon

From the moment I'd received that first letter, even when my mum had told me about the stranger on the street, watching her, saluting her as he walked away, I never thought that it would bring me to this.

I took a few steps closer to him, my mind whirling with questions, doubts, and anxiety to find all the answers, because looking at the man sitting in front of me, I had no fucking clue what the hell was going on.

"Why?" I asked, because seeing his face, I couldn't fathom it. Well, there was one glaringly obvious reason why he'd targeted me, but so much didn't add up. There were so many things I didn't understand. How did he know about the specifics of my childhood? Where did he get it all from? What drove him to do this? Why? Just, why?

"You couldn't stay away, could you? You had to step into my world, and so I stepped into yours."

The face that had greeted me warmly, shook my hand like I might one day be an equal, now scowled at me like I was the devil incarnate. A father, a holy man, Nathan Johnson glared at me like he was on a mission from God, and I was the demon he was here to exorcise. All this time, he'd been right under my nose, playing out his role for the world and his daughter, but in the shadows, he was another man entirely. He intended to destroy me, and from the venom burning within him, nothing was going to get in his way.

"You need to start talking." I gritted my teeth, anger coursing through me as I tried to make sense of this. Tried to imagine what it would do to Leah if she ever found out. She could never find out. "Is this all because you hate me and you don't want me with your daughter? You'd risk your whole life, your reputation, all to break me down?"

He kept his glare on me, his face stern as he took deep, calculated breaths.

"I knew she watched you," he said defiantly. "Years ago, my wife had taken pity on your family. Seems my daughter did the same once my wife passed away, and I knew. I'd seen her go to the places you were, hiding from sight and watching. She'd been to hell and back, losing her mum at such a young age, so I didn't make a fuss, I ignored it. It was a childish crush and she'd get over it. I knew that. She spent enough time at the church with me and in the youth group, it was only a matter a time before she'd get bored or have her head turned elsewhere. Only, she never did. I waited and it only got worse."

His gaze moved from me to the chapel we were now

enclosed within.

"How ironic." He smirked, and then his expression turned grave and angry. "I found my faith in this chapel. This is where I first spoke to my God, pledged my soul to follow him, speak his truth, and serve him. And now look at me. A faithless man riddled with hatred for a devil on earth who thinks he can bulldoze through my life, destroy everything I hold dear, and take the one thing that keeps me going. My reason for living. She is all I've got." His voice cracked as he spoke about Leah May. "I'll die before I ever let you take her."

I was about to fight back, tell him I loved her and I'd die before I ever gave her up, but he kept going, spouting his truths like he was righteous in his cause for bringing about my downfall. And all I could do was stand in front of him and listen. Take it all in and try to absorb an impossible lie.

"I'd have left you alone if you'd stayed away, but you couldn't, could you? That morning, when I walked across the gardens after morning service and saw you standing at my front door next to Jodie, your eyes on Leah," —he winced, distaste from the memory making his face contort—"I knew things would change. You came to my door, so I went to yours."

"My mum's," I said by way of explanation.

"Yes, your mum's. I stood on the corner of the road, and I gave her that salute Vincent always used to do. I did it a few times. You came to my house to cause trouble, so I did the same to you. An eye for an eye." The way he grinned back at me; I could tell he felt zero remorse.

"Doesn't the bible refute that? Turn the other cheek? Isn't that what it says?" I argued.

"I don't give a fuck. When it comes to my daughter, all bets

THE REAPER 309

are off."

I shook my head, still struggling to comprehend the situation.

"But how did you know? Were you one his friends? Did you hurt me?" Anger surged inside me. "Did you hurt Leah?"

I turned to grab a sword from the stand at the side of the wall, intent on using it if he told me he'd harmed a hair on her head.

"I'd never hurt my daughter," he spat. "I'm not a filthy animal like Vincent and his friends."

"But you knew what they did? You knew, and you did nothing to help me? Were you there, watching?" All my memories from back then were a little hazy, but I thought I knew everyone who'd been involved. I thought I'd taken them all out.

"I didn't see anything," he snarled. "And I did tell social services, on numerous occasions. They told me they'd put you on the at-risk register, even made home visits…" He trailed off, realisation that his feeble attempts to be pious had failed.

"Those visits were a fucking waste of time. They did nothing, and he beat me harder after each one. That still doesn't answer my question, though. How did you know? The darts? The sick games? Were you in on it?"

"No, I wasn't!" he shouted angrily, pulling at his restraints in protest. "I'm a good man."

"A good man who's been threatening me. Sending me letters and photos of me with my girl."

"She isn't yours," he hissed.

"Oh, she's mine, and right now, she's upstairs in my bed asleep." His eyes widened, a mixture of anger at what I'd said paired with the fear of her finding out reflected back at me.

"Don't worry," I told him. "The last thing I'd do is tell her you're here. I wouldn't want to rip her heart out. I'll leave that to you."

He scoffed, then speaking quietly he added, "The church isn't the only place that people come to repent their sins. And it's not the only place that I visit to listen to my flock. I'm a modern man, I know sometimes the church must come to the people. That's why I used to go and drink in the Red Lion pub from time to time. It's surprising what you hear when people have had a few drinks.

"Your stepfather was always in there with his friends, laughing and bragging about what he'd done to you. The more he drank, the louder he got. He didn't realise I was listening. I tried to talk to him a few times, tell him he needed help, you all did, but he always brushed me off. Said he didn't believe in God and pushed me aside. I told my wife, Claire, and she contacted child protection services too, but then she died, and everything fell on me.

"I did my best, but caring for Leah came first. Then the news started to trickle down the Brinton Manor grapevine that Vincent had gone missing. After that, it was friends of his disappearing. I knew you'd been thrown out of school, sent to a referral unit and joined some gang. You were a lost cause."

I was stunned into silence.

The reality that this man had lost his faith when he lost his wife was glaringly obvious, but I don't think he realised it. He was so intent on revenge and hatred towards the world, a hatred he seemed to have channelled into tormenting me, that he couldn't recognise that he needed help too. He was unhinged. A man on the edge.

"So the lost sheep got left in the cold, in your version of the parable?" I challenged him.

"You're not the sheep, you're the wolf, and I made sure I kept you from our door. That was until you forced your way in."

"I love your daughter."

"You're not good enough for her," he spat back.

"You don't get to have a fucking say in that!" I shouted. I was trying to keep a level head and not go full fucking psycho on him, but he wasn't making it easy for me.

"What now?" he asked, baring his teeth at me as if he was daring me, trying to push me over the edge.

"I should kill you for what you've done. If it were anyone else in front of me, I would."

He lifted his head, and grinning like a mad man he said, "Why don't you? You killed all the others. I know that, and I won't stop until everyone else does too. I'm going to fucking destroy you."

"And you think they'll believe the ramblings of a mad man? Not to mention, you're chained in my chapel—"

"Your chapel," he said, laughing sarcastically.

"Yes, my chapel. I might leave you down here to rot for eternity. That way, I don't have to live with the guilt that I killed her father. You'll waste away from natural causes. Starvation, dehydration, the possibilities are endless."

"No, you'd take the cowards way out."

He had hit a nerve with that one, and so I threw the sword that I held down onto the floor and stalked around the room, gathering my crossbow, a spear, and then I unhooked my katana sword from the stand it was encased in and carried them all over to a table nearby, placing them down and then picking up the crossbow to aim at him.

"*If* I was going to kill you tonight, and the emphasis is on the word if, because it's still not fully off the table, I'd show you how a proper warrior fights. A true warrior. One that doesn't hide behind a pen and paper, a photograph, or a weak-ass telephone call to the authorities. I'd show you how a samurai operates, the ultimate fighter."

I took a step closer to him with my crossbow pointed right at him, my finger hovering, tempting me to take a shot.

"The early samurai used to charge into battle with a bow and arrow first. The long-range weapon was used to disarm their enemy, take them out if they were lucky." I stepped to the side, moving around the room slowly to validate my point. "It doesn't matter where I am in this room, because with this crossbow, I could take you out. Fire it right through you heart, or better yet, a shot into the stomach you don't appear to have. Or is it a lack of guts to stand up for what's right? Should I aim there first?"

He sat still, stoic, his face daring me to make good on the promises I was giving him.

I shook my head and put the crossbow down, picking up the spear.

"Once they'd incapacitated their enemy, had them writhing on the floor in pain, the samurai would move to their next weapon, the spear." I brandished the spear, twirling and then jabbing it in the air. "It's got a longer range, but not quite as long as the arrows. I could do a lot of damage with this, but you know what? I don't think it'd give me as much pleasure as the third weapon the samurai used. You see, for me, it's all about hand-to-hand combat. Looking my enemy in the eye and seeing the fear. Sending them to hell with my face imprinted on their brain. Having the power at my fingertips to end it all, and I will.

THE REAPER

That's my job. I am the reaper, after all."

Nathan scoffed again.

"You think that name gives you power? Kudos? To me, it makes you sound ridiculous."

I ignored him. I knew he was goading me, and I didn't care. I put the spear down and picked up my katana, holding it in my hand and feeling that sense of pride that I always felt. No one touched the katana, only me.

"The katana sword could only be owned by the samurai, it was known to be a superior sword, unparalleled in its levels of strength and versatility. A bit like my fury right now," I added.

Nathan huffed, but I carried on.

"The art of making an authentic katana sword is a craftmanship that's dying a death, a bit like the honour of some men here in Brinton." I smirked to myself. "A decent sword can take up to six months to forge." I twisted the blade in front of me to marvel at it. "They use different heat treatments, you see, cooling it at different rates to create a stronger edge and a more flexible spine. That, along with the perfect composition of metals, the tamahagane steel—that's high carbon steel to you laymen—that's what makes it so great."

I swung the sword in front of me and took a step closer to him.

"The katana was said to represent the soul of its master. Kind of ironic, don't you think, for a taker of souls like me?"

"You have no soul," he bit back.

"Maybe not, but my sword does."

One more step and I was right in front of him. My sword pressed against his stomach, our eyes burning pure hatred towards each other. Breaths panting, waiting, ready to go into battle.

"There's different blade lengths, but the perfect length is about sixty to seventy centimetres. That makes it easier to wield when you're on the battlefield. Is that what we're doing here? Going to war? Because you know you can't win. I hold all the cards."

He didn't speak, and so I gave him my last fact.

"They used to test the blades of the katana swords on corpses to see how powerful they were. The more bodies it sliced through, the more valuable the sword was." I leaned closer to him. "I can tell you this one cost me a hell of a lot of money, so I'm betting it's seen a lot of corpses. A lot more than I've shown it."

"You don't scare me," he said, and from the still, steady way he was carrying himself, it was true.

"I don't need you to be scared to reach my objective."

He smiled, and I knew then that his end game had changed. He sent me the messages because he wanted me gone. He came onto our land to threaten me. But now that he was chained up and held at our will, the tables had turned. If I killed him, he still won, because eventually, she'd find out. I'd never be able to keep something like that from her. And when she did, she'd never forgive me. I was in a catch twenty-two situation here and he knew it. Furthermore, he didn't seem to care. He didn't care about himself. All he wanted was Leah away from me.

"I'll never leave her," I stated, and he gritted his teeth. Under his eye, I noticed a twitch, and I knew it was a tell-tale sign that I was getting to him. "She'll never leave me either. She loves me. She wants to be with me. If I brought her down here and told her everything you've said and done, and then I asked

THE REAPER

her to choose, we both know she'd choose me."

He grimaced; pain seared into his features as he digested the reality.

I was right.

"You wouldn't dare," he goaded again, but I knew he didn't mean it this time. He didn't want Leah down here any more than I did.

"Try me." I met his challenge with one of my own.

We stood staring at each other. Me, with my sword aimed right at his stomach, and him boring hatred into me with his glare. Each breath laboured as the fight in us turned to something else.

"When I came in here, I asked you a question. You still haven't answered it," I said, and Nathan frowned at me. "I asked you why?" I added.

"And I told you," he replied, but I shook my head.

"You gave me a load of bullshit about the history behind it. Told me all about your passive aggressive method of parenting that quite frankly is a crock of shit. You threw out a load of facts, but I want to know why you're so intent on destroying your daughter's life?"

It was at that moment that the curtain fell away, and the real Nathan Johnson came forward.

"I'm not doing this to hurt her. I'm doing it to protect her. She's everything to me." His voice broke and I saw emotion pour from him, his eyes welling as he stared at the ground. "When I lost my wife, I vowed I'd do everything in my power to give my little girl everything she needed. Keep her safe, love her, make sure the evils of this world couldn't taint her pure innocent heart." He looked up. "Evil like you."

"But she isn't a little girl anymore. And what you're doing isn't keeping her safe. It's bringing violence and revenge to her door." I glanced behind me. "Do you know I have four brothers right outside, ready to come in here and mutilate you like a pack of rabid dogs if I shout for them. Seconds, and they'll slit your throat without a care. Is that what you want? She lost a mother, and now you want to play God with your own life just to keep her away from me? Are you fucking crazy?"

His nostrils flared, but I carried on.

"I've been paranoid, looking over my shoulder, convinced I'm being haunted by ghosts of my past. Spending time chasing demons when I should've been with her. I'm not evil, *Nathan*, but I can be if someone threatens what I love. And her? I love her the most."

He squeezed his eyes shut and on a whisper, he said, "Everything I do is for her."

"Including destroying the man she loves?" He turned his head away from me, but I wouldn't let him side-step me. "Because she does love me. She has done for a long time. You can't stop it. You could kill me, but she'd spend the rest of her days feeling like she was living a half-life because she'd lost me. If you'd do anything for her, then you'll be the one to walk away. Let her live her life, and maybe, if you can learn acceptance, you'll get to spend time with the grandchildren we'll give you. Be a part of the family we make. Because I will marry her. I'll build my whole world around her."

A tear fell from his eyes, trickling down his cheek, but he stayed silent.

"She might be our little raven," I said, and he took a sharp breath in at my use of the word 'our'. "But you can't cage her anymore. She needs to be set free to make her own choices. Live the life she wants to live. Love the man she's chosen."

He started to sob silently as his head hung, guilt keeping him from looking me in the eyes.

"I won't breathe a word of this. On my honour, I will take what has happened here tonight to my grave. She doesn't even know about the letters and the photographs. This can all be buried. Not forgotten entirely, but you're her father, she loves you too, so we have to find a way to make this work. I won't steal her away, Nathan. She's mine now, but I still want her to spend time with you. You're her dad, nobody can ever change that."

He let out a cry, his heart breaking for what he thought he'd lost here today.

Her.

I took a step back, then turned and placed the katana back on the table. I wouldn't be using it tonight. I wouldn't be using any of my weapons. I fought for justice. I stood for what was right. I wouldn't attack a defenceless man whose actual crime was loving his daughter too much. He might have a fucked-up way of going about it, but he wasn't a monster.

I crouched down in front of him and started to untie the binds that pinned him to the chair.

"What are you doing?" he asked.

"I'm setting you free. You need to walk away. Leave this chapel and go home. Tomorrow, I'll bring her to see you. We'll spend time together. We will work this out. But now, you need to leave."

I unwound the last of the ropes and then, on the table, I saw the keys for the cuffs and I picked them up, walking over to the chair and unlocking him from the last of the restraints. He rubbed his wrists and then peered up at me.

"I don't have anything more to say to you," I said, and turning my back, I began to walk away.

I heard him stand, then I felt the rush of air behind me as he must've darted for the table. The sound of metal sliding across the wooden table as he grabbed the katana. My stomach dropped and I spun around shouting, "No!" Everything happened in a blur as I lunged forward. I was ready to die on that sword, but it wasn't me he was aiming for. He'd turned it on himself, and he was about to push the blade right into his stomach.

I threw myself forward, grabbing the sword handle to pull it out of his grip, get it away from him, and push him to safety. Hearing my cries, the door behind me slammed against the stone wall as it flew open. There was a flurry of action as I grappled on the floor, trying to restrain him. Instantly, I felt the arms of my brothers pinning him down too, holding him and taking the weight off me.

"He isn't hurting me," I shouted as I noticed from the corner of my eye Colton grabbing a blade from the collection on the wall, ready to defend me. "He was going to hurt himself." I gasped, breathless from the effort it'd taken to prise the sword away from him and hold him down.

We had Nathan pinned down on his front, his hands behind his back, but as I held him tight to stop him from moving, his body began to give up. Muscles gave up the fight, limbs became loose, and we fell silent as he cried right there on the floor.

"He needs help," I told them, each one of them staring back at me, not sure how to play this. "We need to get him to a hospital. He's a danger to himself. He's having a breakdown."

They didn't question me, just nodded and Adam asked, "What do you need us to do?"

Of all the brothers, I knew Adam and Tyler would be the best in this situation. Colton and Will would be more useful staying behind and making sure the girls were okay. It wasn't that I didn't trust them, but we didn't all need to go to the hospital, and the pair of them would be better at keeping cool in a crisis. Colton and Will would distract Liv and Leah May better than any of us.

"Adam, Tyler, can you drive us to the hospital? Colton, Will, if you stay here and let Liv know we're okay, but that we have business to attend to. Don't tell her who was down here and don't let either of them know where we are. Once things settle down, we'll call."

Colton and Will nodded their agreement and stood up. I did the same, pulling a broken, quivering Nathan up with me. He was trying to speak through his cries, but I couldn't understand him. I just put an arm under his as Adam did the same on the other side, and we walked him to the back door of the chapel that led to the car park.

Tyler went first, opening the door for us and then sprinting on ahead to get to the car.

I got into the back with Nathan and Adam jumped into the driving seat with Tyler sitting next to him.

"I can't... I don't..." Nathan stuttered as the engine fired up. "I want to die." He slumped forward, his body giving up the fight.

Sitting next to him, I could feel the power of anger and resilience rising up inside of me. He might be giving up, but I wasn't. I had enough fight in me for the both of us.

"No, you don't," I said through gritted teeth. "I won't fucking let you. You're not giving up, Nathan. Leah needs you."

CHAPTER THIRTY-FIVE
Devon

Nathan's body, even his brain, was shutting down. When the nurses showed us into a side room to see the doctor, I had to lead him, speak for him, tell them what had happened but in a vague, roundabout way. They didn't need to know about the letters, the chapel, or the threats. Instead, I painted a picture of a broken man. A man who'd tried to hurt himself because he couldn't see any other way out of the dark clouds that hung around him. A man that didn't want to live and one that desperately needed help.

I gave them as much history as possible from the limited facts I knew about Leah's family. But as I spoke, it was clear that he'd never gotten over his wife's death. He'd stowed away all the grief into a locked box in his head, channelling every ounce of energy he had into caring for his daughter and distracting himself with his work. But he couldn't hide from it forever and what we were witnessing tonight was evidence of that. The box in his head was full, bursting free, and like a leaked poison, it was affecting his brain.

He couldn't cope with the reality of his life. The fact that time was moving on. Leah wasn't the same girl, and in his eyes, he had nothing left to live for without her. Change for him had always been negative. He clung to the familiar memories of a life he'd lost, but his nails were broken, and his fingers bled from clinging too hard. Life had lost all control, and with it, he'd lost his way. Stuck down a well with no chance of escape.

I wanted him to see what the future looked like through my eyes. That things would change, that's how life goes, but they could change for the better. One day, he'd be a grandpa. He'd be loved again by a little boy or girl who would worship the ground he walked on. But I knew that wasn't something he could do right now. That was an image his brain couldn't comprehend. Not yet. We had to take this step by step, hour by hour, day by day. All he cared about was Leah. He needed to find a way to love himself as well. And he would. I'd make damn sure of it.

They did some initial assessments, admitted him to a ward, and then asked me if I would stay with him. He needed one-to-one care throughout the night to make sure he was safe, and with staff shortages, they hoped I'd step up. Adam offered to stay, but it had to be me. He didn't know Adam, and as much as he hated me right now, at least I was somewhat familiar. Tyler suggested ringing Leah and asking her to come down, but I didn't want her to see her dad like this. She was strong, but I didn't want her to be. I wanted to take this one.

So, I sent Leah a message, telling her that I'd had to go

to my mum because there was a family emergency and they needed me. I asked her to wait for me, letting her know I'd be back home as soon as possible. Then I messaged Liv, giving her a more watered-down version of the truth, but asking her to keep it to herself.

Once Nathan was settled on the ward, I made a list of things for Adam to fetch for Nathan from the rectory, and he left shortly after with Tyler. The nurses let me stay on a camp bed next to Nathan's, and eventually, after being sedated, he drifted off to sleep. But I stayed awake. My mind whirling from everything that'd happened.

An hour later, a nurse popped her head around the door and then came in, holding a bag filled with things Adam had dropped off.

"Your friends said they'd be back in the morning," she whispered and then left.

I had nothing better to do, so I got up and walked over to the bag, unzipping it to unpack what was inside. On top, I found Nathan's mobile phone, and when I picked it up, I saw one message on the main screen. A message from Leah.

I shouldn't have read it. It wasn't my business to look at her messages or his phone, but I did. There was no lock on the screen, and when I tapped into his texts, I saw what she'd sent.

Leah: Please don't be mad. I know you don't like me staying out, but I'm safe. I'm staying with Devon tonight. I might stay a few nights. Dad, he is the best thing to ever happen to me. I know you're a little cynical, but please trust me. He's

> so amazing, and I can't wait for you to
> get to know him properly. He treats
> me like I'm a princess. Better than that
> sometimes. I love him. I really hope you do
> too someday. I'll call you in the morning.
> Remind Hilda to fetch the flowers from the
> florist ready for Tuesday's service. I love
> you. L x

I should have left it there. I should have put the phone down, but I couldn't. Instead, I typed out a response and held my breath, hoping I was doing something that might put us on the right track. I checked through a few of his older messages, making sure I kept a similar tone, and I pressed send, trying not to overthink what I was doing.

> Dad: Sweetheart, it's not that I'm cynical, I
> just worry. I want the best for you. Thank
> you for messaging me. I can't say that
> I'm happy about you staying out, but
> knowing you love him makes it a little
> more bearable. As long as he always treats
> you like a princess, that's enough for me.
> Just know, I loved you first. You might be
> his princess, but to me, you're a queen.

I saw the three dots dancing, indicating that she was responding. It worried me that she was awake, but when I saw her response, it put my mind at ease.

Leah: Oh, Dad, you're always so soppy, but I love you for it. He might be my knight in shining armour, my prince, but you'll always be my king. I love you, Dad. Speak tomorrow. L x

I put the phone back into the bag and left it where it was. It was enough to know she was okay. I had to focus on getting us through this night, and then whatever we had to face the next day, we would. It wasn't going to be an easy road, but we were here, at the start, and we would take that journey, no matter how long or how torturous the steps.

***

I stayed overnight, watching Nathan as he slept. In the morning, the nurses came in and brought tea and toast. Nathan was still out of it, but they handed it to me and said they'd be back with more once he woke up. As they left, I heard one nurse turn to the other and say, "Now there's a son to be proud of. I don't think my Mark would sit up all night with his dad like that. He won't even make him a cup of tea, let alone watch over him."

They thought Nathan was my father, but I didn't like to correct them.

An hour or so later, Nathan began to stir, and when he opened his eyes, he stared at me, blinked, and then in a gravelly voice he said, "Where am I?"

"Sandland General. I brought you in last night."

"Does Leah know?"

"No." I decided to come clean. He'd find out eventually anyway. "I sent her a text from your phone. I pretended to be you and told her everything was okay. I didn't want her to worry."

"Thank you." He was quiet, a little disorientated, but he frowned and then asked, "Have you been here all night?"

"Yes. I wasn't about to leave you on your own, and even though they said they could assign a one-to-one nurse, I felt better doing it myself."

"You watched me?"

"I watched over you. It wasn't anything sinister, Nathan."

He nodded, but from the look on his face, he was confused.

"Believe it or not, I do care. I don't want anything to happen to you."

He didn't speak, just wrung his hands in his lap.

"I'll call the nurse, get them to bring you something to eat." I pressed the buzzer above the bed, and moments later the same nurse came bundling into the room.

"Morning," she said to Nathan, taking a thermometer from her pocket to take his temperature. Then she checked his blood pressure and glanced across at me. "You've got a real diamond there. There aren't many sons who would do what he did last night."

I expected Nathan to announce that I wasn't his son, to show disgust, but he didn't.

"I know," he said quietly. "I don't want to be a burden."

"Enough of that." The nurse scoffed. "No father is ever a burden."

My own father left when my mum was pregnant. I'd never met him. My stepfather degraded me, hurt me, beat me until I felt soulless, useless and unloved. My fathers weren't a burden,

THE REAPER

they were a gaping hole of disappointment. Two dark figures that tainted my past, but that's where they stayed, buried deep in memories that weren't worth a penny.

The man lying in bed next to me was so much more than that. Once upon a time, he'd been her everything. He'd raised her, given her values, hopes, dreams, and because of him, she'd become the beautiful woman she was today. For that alone, I had to give him the respect he deserved. Without him, there would have been no Leah.

The nurse stayed for a few more minutes, explaining what would happen next and who Nathan would be speaking to. Once she'd finished, she asked, "Is there anyone else I can call? Someone to take over so your son can have a break?"

He looked at me, and I could see he was thinking the same thing I was. Not Leah. He wasn't ready to tell her, and I didn't want to bring her here. She'd have to know eventually, but not yet.

"I've got a sister that lives in Merivale. Lizzie. I have her number saved on my phone," he said, and I stood up, going to Nathan's bag to take his mobile out and pass it to him. "I'll ring her myself if that's okay?" Nathan added, speaking to the nurse. "I don't want her to freak out when she hears it's the hospital calling."

The nurse smiled and left, and I did too, telling Nathan I'd give him some privacy on his call but that I'd be right outside the door.

Once I heard Nathan's muffled voice tail off at the end of the conversation, I went back in.

"I still can't believe you stayed here." He stared into his lap and sighed. "I don't know what to do."

"You don't have to do anything. Concentrate on getting yourself better. I need you to do that for me because she needs you. But more than that, you need to do it for yourself."

His eyes welled up as I spoke.

"I know we haven't started out on the best footing, but I know better than anyone about moving on and leaving the past behind. Everything you're bottling up inside, it has to come out eventually. You can't hold it in anymore. It's not healthy."

I wasn't an expert, and I was afraid of saying the wrong thing, triggering him and making him feel worse. At the moment, he was on a knife's edge, and I didn't want to be the one to tip him over. So, I did what I thought was best. I stayed quiet and just sat with him, waiting until his sister, Lizzie, arrived.

When a woman with frizzy blonde hair burst through the door, I knew it was his sister. They looked so alike.

"Nate, what on earth has happened?" She looked across at me then thrust her hand forward. "I'm so sorry, I'm Lizzie. And you are?"

I stood up to shake her hand, but Nathan interrupted me.

"This is Devon. He's Leah's boyfriend. He found me and brought me in."

Lizzie grinned, and still gripping my hand, she turned to Nathan.

"Boyfriend? You both kept that quiet."

"We'd like you to keep this quiet too, if you can. Leah doesn't know I'm here."

Lizzie sighed.

"You can't mollycoddle her forever, Nate. She's a grown woman."

"I know that, but I just need a few days. I'm not ready yet."

He turned to look at me. "Will you… I mean, I can—"

"I'll tell her," I stated, knowing exactly what he was getting at. "Just let me know when and I'll tell her whatever you want her to know. I'll bring her to you, when you're ready."

"Thank you," he replied, his voice full of emotion.

I left soon after that. I knew Nathan would be in good hands with Lizzie, and I wanted to get back to Leah and make sure she was okay. Things had become fractured, but we weren't broken. All of this was just a bump in the road. Life wasn't easy, not for anyone, but with her by my side, I felt ready to tackle anything. We'd get Nathan the help he needed. I'd do anything to make her happy. It wasn't going to be an overnight cure, I knew his recovery would be tough, and there'd be setbacks, but we'd get through this as a family.

My family.

Leah, me, her dad, my mum and Brooke. The soldiers would always be my brothers, the family I chose. But now, I had a family of my own to take care of.

Mine.

And I would do a damn sight better job than any of the male role models I'd had growing up, because I'd be there, loving, listening, giving it my fucking all. Leah May was it for me. The end goal. And I couldn't wait to start living my life with her.

My little raven.

My world.

My end game.

CHAPTER THIRTY-SIX
Devon

Four months later

It had been a rollercoaster of a ride, that was for sure. A few days after Nathan's breakdown, I told Leah what'd happened. I left out the letters and the incident with her dad in the chapel, but I told her I'd gotten a call in the night, and that I'd gone on my own to help Nathan. She wasn't happy that I'd kept it from her. We argued, and she froze me out for not waking her and taking her with me. She was equally as mad that I'd kept her in the dark in the days that had followed. She was right, of course. I should've told her, but the damage had already been done. It was a decision I'd made and all I could do was learn from it. Leah didn't like secrets, and neither did I. After a lot of heated discussions, we vowed never to do that again. That was a promise I was intent on keeping.

As for Nathan, he'd had a few relapses, spent some time in a unit that catered for mental breakdowns, and he was starting to improve. He still had bad days, but the good were starting to outweigh the bad. He was currently living back at the vicarage, and Lizzie was staying with him. I think he quite liked having her around, even though he complained about everything she did whenever we were there.

The church had appointed a temporary vicar to cover his work. He didn't like that either, but he was slowly coming round to the idea of accepting help. That was a big hurdle for him, that and acknowledging me as a permanent fixture in Leah's life.

Leah had been staying with me more and more, and since her dad seemed a little more settled at home, we'd decided it was time for her to move in with me permanently and become a fully-fledged soldier's wife, as Colton had joked. She would be my wife, but I wanted to take a little more time for us before we moved to that stage. Enjoy the little moments. Treasure them.

We both sat on the sofa together, opposite Nathan's armchair. I held Leah's hand as we chatted to her dad about our plans. Leah had a few more gigs booked. Her music was really starting to take off. I was so proud of her. Lizzie sat in the corner doing her crochet and giving the odd murmur of support. But what meant the most to Leah was how her father's face lit up whenever she talked about the new songs she'd written or the score she was working on. And when Leah turned to me and said, "Dad gave me the best gift any father could give his daughter, he always believed in me," I felt my heart burst, so it was no surprise that when I looked over at Nathan, he was wiping a tear from his eye.

"I always knew you'd make it as a song writer," Lizzie

piped up. "You've got a way with words, love."

She was right. Leah's words were like gold dust. Sometimes she was quirky, maybe a little crazy, but those were the times that I loved the most. Because that was her, unedited, unfiltered, honest and yet delicate in the way she dealt with others. She had empathy and a kindness that made you feel brighter, lighter for being around her. She was magnetic.

"Just like her mother," Nathan said, smiling. "The pair of them could charm the birds from the trees."

"Or the ravens," Leah added and then smirked to herself.

We stayed for a while longer, but as it began to grow dark outside, we said our goodbyes. Leah hugged her aunty, then went to her dad and held him for a moment longer, giving him a hug that said, 'I might be going, but I'll never leave. A piece of my heart will always be here with you.'

I walked to the door, and we headed out to the car, but as we strolled down the path, I took the keys out of my pocket and handed them to Leah.

"I left my wallet inside," I told her. "Jump in the car and I'll be with you in two minutes, okay?"

"Okay." She shrugged, walking on ahead.

I had left my wallet inside, but I'd done it on purpose. I wanted two minutes on my own with Nathan. Just two minutes to say what I had to say.

When I walked in, I could hear Countdown playing on the TV and Lizzie fussing in the kitchen. I stepped into the living room, and when he saw me, Nathan muted the TV and frowned.

"I left my wallet," I explained, bending down to retrieve it from the side of the sofa where I'd stuffed it earlier.

Nathan kept his head down, but I knew I had his full

THE REAPER 333

attention.

"She can love us both, you know. And she does. I'll never keep her from you." I smiled to myself. "Just think of this as me borrowing her for a while."

"If you borrow something, you intend to give it back." He lifted his head to look at me. "And as much as it pains me to say this, I don't want you to do that. It'd break her heart, and that would break mine."

"I have no intention of breaking her heart." I sighed and slid my wallet into my pocket. "We want what you had, you and Claire."

"You already do." His eyes shone with tears he didn't want to shed, not in front of me. "The way you look at each other, the fact you have to be touching each other all the time, holding hands, even the way you speak, joking and teasing, that's what we had. Watching you is like seeing Claire and I all those years ago."

I let that sink in for both of us and then I added, "One day, I hope you'll feel proud walking her down the aisle to me. Or better yet, being the one that marries us."

He took a few deep breaths, and I couldn't second guess how he'd react, but when he stood up and put his hand out for me to shake, I took it.

"I'd be honoured, son. That would be…" His voice broke, and he turned away, sitting back down and busying himself with the newspaper that was open at the crossword. Anything to distract himself from the emotions I'd just tapped into.

"I'll see you on Sunday," I said, walking towards the door.

"Yes, Sunday," he replied. "But don't sit at the back this time."

I smirked. Maybe for one week I could move from our favourite position at the back of the church.

CHAPTER THIRTY-SEVEN
Leah May

I couldn't believe what had happened over the last few months. Things hadn't been easy, but through it all, Devon had been my rock, my happy place. I couldn't wait to move into The Sanctuary and be with him forever.

We pulled into the car park and then took a few boxes from the back seat to carry up with us. There was other stuff in the boot and a few things we'd decided to collect later, but right now, all we wanted to do was get inside, close the door on the world and be in our little bubble, losing ourselves in each other.

When we reached the top floor, we heard Colton calling out to us from the living room. Devon rolled his eyes then said, "We may as well get it over with. If we don't go in, he'll only end up knocking on our door until we open it."

"I don't mind being with them all, Colton makes me laugh."

"That's why he keeps monopolising you whenever you're here, you're the only one who laughs at all his jokes."

I did laugh, but that's because I'd never been around someone like Colton before. He could see the funny side of any situation. I had my suspicions that he might be slightly psychotic, but after my father's diagnosis of a mental health disorder, I wasn't about to throw shade on anyone's state of mind.

We walked into the living room with the boxes still in our hands.

"Make it quick," Devon barked. "We're tired and want to be alone."

"You have the rest of your lives to be alone. Come and sit with us." Colton patted the sofa next to him, but Devon stayed standing, putting his arm on mine to stop me from sitting down too. "Okay then," Colton said in a sing-song voice, then reached to the side, picked something up from the floor, and stood up, hiding it behind his back. "I just wanted to say, on behalf of all my brothers"—he glanced at Liv and winked—"and sister here, that we are so glad you are now officially part of the family." He took his arm from behind his back and held out a little pink box tied up with a red ribbon.

"Oh, hell, no," Liv said. "Whatever he's put in that box, we weren't a part of it. We've all clubbed together to buy you a weekend away. Some time alone, away from Brinton. Whatever twisted gift Colton's got is all on him."

Devon went to put his box down and take it off him, but I sprang into action, dropping my box onto the table and grabbing the present.

"Thanks, Colton."

He bowed and then grinned up at me.

"You know, I admire you. You, and these two." He pointed his thumb at Adam and Liv. "But it'll be a cold day in hell before you ever see me settling down."

"It'll be a cold day in hell before any woman chooses to settle down with you," Tyler added. "No need to stock up on thermals quite yet."

Colton ignored him and stood proud as he announced, "The women out there are pining for a bit of the King. Colton King, love machine. Why tie myself to one girl when they all have their merits?" He shrugged, believing every word he said, and nobody in here wanted to argue with him.

Why argue?

It was pointless.

But we all knew that one day, some girl would come along and knock him off his feet. And we couldn't wait for that day to arrive. Watching Colton King fall in love was going to be something.

"What did he get?" Will asked, coming over to stand next to Colton.

I pulled the ribbon and it fell away. When I opened the box, I half expected something to jump out or to be drowned in exploding confetti, but there was delicate pink tissue paper lining the box, protecting whatever was inside.

I put the box on the table and knelt on the floor, moving the tissue paper aside, and then, when I saw what was in there, I gasped, pulling it out carefully and placing it on the table.

"I hear you singing in the shower most mornings. Hell, we all hear you sing all over the damn place. We love your voice. Please don't ever stop. So, when I saw this in the jewellers on the high street, I had to buy it. It plays that Carpenters song you sing a lot of the time, see?" He leaned down and started to twist the bottom of the snow globe that had silver hearts suspended inside. It really was the prettiest thing I'd ever seen. As he shook it, twisting and winding it up, the glitter snow swirled inside. Then he laid it back on the table and it tinkled the melody that my mum used to sing to my dad and me when I was little. I'd hear her sing it in the shower, when she was washing dishes, even outside doing gardening.

A Song for You.

I started to well up hearing the familiar tune, and I heard Liv say, "Colton, that's beautiful."

"Yeah," Devon replied. "That's really thoughtful. Thank you."

I stood up and went to Colton, hugging him my own thanks, and he hugged me back. "I'm glad you like it."

I picked it up in both hands, holding it tightly to my chest. "I love it. I'll cherish it. Thank you so, so much."

I left my own box on the table and walked out to our room, holding the snow globe. Devon followed me, and when he pushed the door open, I went to the chest of drawers and placed it on top. Twisting it so that it sat just right.

"Everyone has made me feel so welcome," I said, sighing and feeling contentment wash over me. "I'm going to love living here."

I spun around, smiling wide, and then from the corner of my eye, I noticed something.

My heart stopped. My body shivered.

There, sitting on the pillow on Devon's bed, was a black origami raven. Perched perfectly. Looking right at us.

"Did you do that?" I pointed at it, and then turned to see him staring in wonder.

"I have no idea how that got there. Do they know about the paper ravens?" he asked, referring to the others, but they didn't. I hadn't told anyone. The only people who knew about them were Devon, me, Jodie, my dad… and my mum.

"It can't be…" I put my hands over my face, and I started to cry. I could help it. "She's happy that I'm happy," I managed to say through my sobs.

Devon didn't doubt me. He didn't try to belittle what I was thinking or saying. He just took me in his arms and held me, rocking me and whispering that he loved me.

I blinked away my tears and held him tightly. No moment in my life had ever felt this perfect. Nothing had ever been so right until now. We had been down a rocky road to find each other, but I'd do it a million times over if it brought me back to him. He was my everything, and knowing that my mum was looking down on us, giving us her blessing, meant more than anything.

I could still hear the chime of the snow globe as we held onto each other, and so, when it got to my favourite part, I sang it to him, meaning every word that I said. My mum loved me in a place where there was no space or time, just like the song said, a place that I'd love Devon, when our time came to be parted. I'd always sing for him, be with him, love him, just like my mum had done for us. Remembering when we were together, keeping those memories locked away, memories more precious than anything.

He was my heart, my soul, my present, and my future. In this life and the next, I would always search for him.

He was home.

My Devon.

The boy with the darkness, and the man with the spark that lit a fire inside me.

He would forever be my everything.

The raven had found her reaper.

And she would never let go.

THE END.

But hold on…
There's someone who wants to have the last say…

COLTON

Hey, reader!

So, you've come to the end of Devon and Leah's story, and I'm guessing you're probably left wanting more. Let's face it, those two were made for an epic love story, and maybe there will be more of the reaper and his raven when you get to my book, because let's be honest, there's not going to be a romance for me.

What's that?

You disagree?

You think there's a woman out there that can tame the joker?

I love your optimism, but I must disagree. I wasn't made to love one woman. I'm not even sure I love myself at this point, but that's a whole other story, and... yeah, you'll probably find out why when you read my book. I love being the joker, but there's a reason I laugh in the face of adversity. How does the saying go... laugh and the world laughs with you, cry and you cry alone... or something along those lines.

I'll be sure to entertain you. Life is for living and I live mine to the full. But romance? That's a hard pass.

I always tell my brothers I'm too much for one woman to handle, but the truth is, I doubt there's a woman alive that would want to take on my baggage.

Love is for the lucky, and my luck ran out a long time ago.

Coming soon.
THE JOKER.
Colton's story.

AUTHOR ACKNOWLEDGEMENTS

I must start by saying the biggest thank you to my husband and two children for living with a soldier obsessed, slightly… okay, a lot more than slightly, crazy wife and mum. I've spent most of the time writing this in a daze, living in Brinton Manor in my head, and occasionally coming back down to earth to visit reality. These boys have taken over my life. They have become real people. So, thank you for listening to me ramble on, for supporting me, and for cleaning the guinea pigs and doing the housework so I wouldn't have to. You're the best. I love you. And I promise not to put you in any of my books.

To my best book buddy, my alpha reader, editor, and all-round awesome friend, Lindsey Powell. You've pulled me off the ledge more times than I care to mention. You're always there to listen, help and offer advice. I don't know what I'd do without you. Thank you so much for being you. I would be lost without you.

I would also like to thank the amazing people that created this stunning cover. Michelle Lancaster, who takes the most amazing photographs. Her images are the best. I love her work. Lori Jackson, who added the sparkle and brought the cover to life. Your designs are second to none. And last, but not least, Mick Maio, for being my Devon, my reaper. This image was made for this book. Thanks for the smouldering eyes. You killed it.

To Lou J Stock, for taking a word document and creating magic. Your formatting always blows me away. Thank you so much for making my book the best that it can be. Also, Caroline

Stainburn, for neatening my words and making The Reaper shine. You're awesome.

To Shauna Casey, and everyone at Wildfire Marketing Solutions. Thank you for organising the cover reveal, release day, and all the promotions for this book. You have made my life a million times easier, and I will be recommending you. You're amazing. Thank you!

To all the bloggers, bookstagrammers, booktokers, and everyone who takes the time to read, review, and make such brilliant edits on social media. I appreciate each and every one of you, from the bottom of my heart. I wish I could list you all, but my book might end up being a trilogy because there are so many of you.

And finally, to you the reader. Thank you for taking a chance on my book. Thank you for reading Devon and Leah May's story. You make it all worthwhile. Please stay tuned, because Colton is up next, and you will not want to miss it. He's going to take us on a crazy ride.

Until next time,
Lots of love
Nikki x

Printed in Great Britain
by Amazon